The love Susannah Hanford felt for her husband was transformed by the alchemy of despair into fury . . . .

"Everywhere I look I see nothing but moth, and dust, and cobweb—it may suit you to live like this, but it does not suit me! Laceby is my house now, and I don't intend to sit and watch it crumble to gravel because you're too proud to lift a hand to it!"

She'd gone too far.

"Oh, but I did do something about Laceby," he said with deadly courtesy. "I married you, Susannah."

THE ILL-BRED BRIDE

Rosemary Edghill

FAWCETT CREST • NEW YORK

To James Henry Wenk (1925–1989), without whose diligent dedication to the acquisition of research sources neither this book nor any of my others could have been written

—R.E.E.

Author's Note

In the Regency period a footman's wage was five pounds a year, while a formal gown, destined to be worn only once, could cost three hundred pounds. To give some idea of the coins in circulation in the period of *The Ill-Bred Bride*, I have compiled the following list of relative values.

12 pennies (or two sixpence) to a shilling
5 shillings to a crown (also called a "coachwheel")
4 crowns to a pound
2 pounds, 18 shillings to a sovereign
The guinea, also known as a "yellow-boy," was a gold coin sometimes equal in value to the paper or silver pound and sometimes more valuable.

Coinage and its relative values were in fluctuation during the Regency period. My source for the amounts was James Mackay's *A History of Modern English Coinage*. All the mistakes are, of course, my own.

—R.E.E.

Prologue

IN THE YEAR of Our Lord 1084, Adeluin Honeforth took seizin of Leyseby-town and the lands that surrounded it. The new baron was the younger son of a Devon family, granted a Warwickshire barony by Conqueror William for services upon the field of war. He added a "de" to his style in homage to his Norman overlord, and a castle to the highest hill in his dominion, and proceeded to render every duty to his king that policy and courtesy required while keeping everything else he could grab for himself.

This pleasant idyll of the de Honeforth family was brought to a halt a century later, when the wars of King Stephen and the Empress Maud laid waste to the countryside, and even an astute political observer was hard-pressed to know where best to tender his allegiance. The family lost most of its lands, a number of its sons, and Leyseby Castle.

During the reign of Henry the Second and his notorious queen Alinor, the de Honeforths remained in eclipse and prudently refrained from expressing any opinion at all. Unfortunately Alinor remembered this when the power of the English throne came into her hands, and the de Honeforths did not prosper at Richard Lionheart's court.

The seventh Baron de Honeforth re-entered the

world of statecraft by taking the field against Alinor's youngest son John in the matter of the Great Charter of England. Against all expectation, the gamble paid off handsomely, and the resulting improvement in the family fortunes led to the building of Laceby Place, named for the town near which it stood.

For the next few centuries the de Honeforths prospered, until another king's Great Matter troubled all of Europe. By now the de Honeforths had become the Hanfords, and the Catholic Hanfords were not welcome at the court of Great Harry and his (some said) adulterous queen Nan Bullen.

The nineteenth Baron Hanford's repudiation of his ancestral faith came too late to repair the family fortunes, and his grandson's exile from England in the Stuart train finished the family's political hopes. During the civil war that followed Laceby was used as a munitions dump by the Cavalier forces; the untimely detonation of that cache by a Roundhead troop finished the family seat as well.

When the Glorious Restoration came at last, and Charles the Second mounted the throne of England and a number of mistresses, the twenty-fourth Baron Hanford set a standard for degenerate profligacy that a number of his descendants tried in vain to equal. Averil Hanford spent every silver penny he could squeeze from his restored estates on his pleasure and his king's amusement, and cemented an attachment to the Stuart line that was to prove disastrous ninety years later, when his grandson Christian was executed on Tower Hill for his part in the Glorious '45.

Denzil Hanford was instrumental in his father's capture, but he did not long enjoy his parricidal inheritance. The twenty-seventh Baron Hanford survived by barely a year the coronation of Farmer

George in 1760, and left behind him two infant sons.

Jocelyn Fitzwilliam Arthur Earnshill Hanford came to his title too young to remember either sire or grandsire, or any of the gaudy pagan glories of an England ruled by English kings. Such Hanford lands as remained for him to inherit were placed in the care of stewards just as he and his younger brother Brabazon were, and both were placed in the indirect care of George the Third. It was hardly surprising that when the management of the estate passed into his hands twenty years later Lord Hanford saw his lands as nothing more than a source of revenue.

The demands Jocelyn made on his inheritance were enough to put a swift end to any hope of financial recovery, but though the family was impoverished, the name was of the oldest. It was perhaps this patina of ancient history and heroic deeds that caused Sir Philip Masham to bestow his daughter Clementina upon Lord Hanford when he came to ask for her. She took her husband well in hand, and between the gaming tables and the moneylenders, Jocelyn contrived to keep her in the style she told him his consequence demanded.

And then, of course, he died, which is where a proper tragedy would end. But this is not a tragedy, except perhaps a most improper one, and so here, at the end, is where our story begins.

PART I

The Bartered Baron

Chapter I

JULY 1817

THE BRILLIANT JULY sun streamed in through the windows of the gracious country house, turning everything it touched to gold. Beyond the library's oriel windows lay the green of extensive parkland that had not been subject to the whims of recent fashion, surrounding the magnificence of Laceby Place as a setting for its proper jewel.

But closer inspection would reveal that fashion was not the only thing to pass the sprawling Stuart manor by. The bramble-rose and ivy ran wild over the untended walls, and everything the eye could see wore an expression of apologetic neglect.

On this particular July day, Denzil Alban Christian Brabazon Fitzwilliam Averil Hanford, twenty-ninth Baron Hanford and master of Laceby, had been the sole support and refuge of his mother, two brothers, sister, and young cousin for a little over six years. His father's body had long since gone to dust, and his soul to the appropriate paradise, but there was a part of Jocelyn Hanford that, it appeared, would endure for as long as moneylenders could enscribe their duns.

The household accounts that were his ostensible purpose for being inside in such glorious weather lay unregarded on the scuffed and stained leather

of the library desktop. Hanford chewed meditatively on the end of his pen, his mind far away.

*If music and sweet mystery's airs your soul
delight/Then spurn the golden palanquin of
changeling day/And be thou borne upon the wings
of ravished night—*

The sonnet he envisioned was doomed to incom-
pletion, for Lady Hanford chose that moment to enter the room.

"Oh, my darling!" Lady Hanford sang on a little
trill of rapture. "Pray tell me I am not intruding! I
only wished to speak to you—for the merest moment, I assure you!"

Her son set down his quill and thrust the sheaf
of papers under the desk blotter. His expression was
wary as he regarded her.

At forty-two—an age known to none but her
dresser—Lady Hanford still retained the classic
beauty that had captivated her husband. She resembled a not-so-very-much older edition of her
daughter Orinda, and in her lace widow's caps she
worked very hard to create the air of a child dressing up in her mother's clothes. It would take an
astute observer indeed to mark the pettish lines of
temper about the mouth more usually drawn into
a becoming pout. She bore a basket full of roses on
her arm, and as she spoke she began to arrange
them in the blue-and-white bowl of Chinese porcelain that stood on Hanford's desk.

"Oh, it is nothing. I knew you were settling up
the accounts, and only wished to be sure you would
write to Mr. Soberton and tell him a house must
without fail be rented for the Season next year. And
tell him upon no account to procure one without a
ballroom! If I am to present your sister you must
give a ball, and it would hardly do to hold it in
rented rooms. And tell him it will be wanted from
the first of March—oh, I know it is shockingly early

to go to Town, but I would not dream of having a robe cut in the country, and Orinda will need—oh, ballgowns and riding dresses . . . We will need new carriage horses as well—you know, my love, that I would never dream of saying a word against anything you chose to do, but I must admit that I cannot see the economy of selling one's stable when one only has it to purchase again! Greys, of course—your father was always partial to grey horses, and they do make such a pretty turn out with a blue carriage and livery—"

Lady Hanford rattled on, her hands in their lace mitts busy with the roses. The light shining through the windows behind her haloed her chestnut hair and her gown of pale-green jaconet muslin, and struck warm gilt-and-oxblood tones from the backs of the few books remaining on the library shelves. The bulk of the library had been sold at auction the year before, and the bill for Lady Hanford's dress was one of those on Hanford's desk. Her fringed shawl and ivory-handled parasol, both of silk and shatteringly expensive, were less than a year old. Hanford regarded the pretty picture his parent made and saw instead the cost of creating it. Part of him despised himself for thinking like an account-clerk while another part wondered how the newest expense Mother was so heedlessly proposing could be met.

"Hanford! My love, you are not attending!" Lady Hanford cried chidingly.

Dutifully he regarded his mother and forced a smile. Of course she did not know how things stood: how could she? Ever since Soberton had let him know the condition of the estate, he had worked desperately to continue the illusion of ease his father had created. But every year it was harder.

"I am sorry, Mother. I was just thinking what a pretty picture you make: quite countrified. Shall we rent this old pile and go live in a cottage some-where? I am persuaded it would be the very thing; everyone would take you for an Arcadian shepherd-ess," he said teasingly.

The raillery had its intended effect. Lady Han-ford's pouting expression softened, and she seated herself in a chair by his side. Though her eldest son was still the moon and sun of her idolatry, Lady Hanford did have to admit, if only to herself, that her beloved Hanford had grown very strange in the last six years. Perhaps grief at the loss of her dear Jocelyn had shattered him much as it had her, but more and more these days Lady Hanford looked in vain for sign of her sensitive, sweet-faced boy in this grim stranger who seemed to be able to speak of nothing but penury. Penury! How could they be reduced to that, when it was well known that when Jocelyn was alive they had never lacked for any-thing, never?

"My little rogue—what a flatterer you are!" Lady Hanford said caressingly. "And when I am per-suaded your poor head must ache so! All these dusty bills, when you know that when your dear father was alive he never paid the least attention to duns and everything was managed in the most delightful fashion!"

"Yes, Mother, but I was thinking about Orinda."

His sister's come-out. And a dowry to be found for her, somehow, that it would not shame him to bestow.

Lady Hanford beamed. "I can already see it—you know, my love, you have let me get very backward of recent years, but now that my darlings are grown we must contrive to send them off in style! Peveril, too, you know, must be creditably established—and who knows but that Orinda might make a brilliant match that will delight us all, though only if she is presented to the *ton* in the first style of elegance!"

Money and more money—and even if Orinda were to marry "Golden Ball" Hughes (an occurrence unlikely in the extreme), it would not bring enough. The amount of money it would take to bring Laceby and the family about was more than could be covered by a loan between even blood relations.

Lady Hanford gave a little trill of laughter and resumed the thread of her argument. "You cannot expect a Hanford to make her bow to society at a country assembly, now can you? Why, I remember my own Season—it was at the very height of the Terror, though we didn't mind that! I vow I never wore the same dress twice, and Papa gave me a necklace of sapphires to match my eyes—and your papa, darling, told me that at first he had taken them for trumpery glass, so eclipsed were they by my beauty!" Lady Hanford sighed meltingly, overcome by the reminiscence.

"Yes. That is—very well, Mother, but Orinda is very young. Perhaps a ball would be too grand, do you think? A smaller party—"

"My dear! Your sister is rising eighteen—though I own, it seems only yesterday that I first held her to my bosom. Next you will be saying she should be married quietly from the schoolroom—and though her constitution is as delicate as my own, still she is as prepared as I to immolate herself upon the altar of family duty!"

"Mother—" Hanford began, prepared at last to try to give his mother some idea of how things actually stood.

But she forestalled him neatly, rising to her feet with another musical little laugh. "But there! I promised I would only take a moment of your time, and I will hold to my resolve! You will write to Soberton today, won't you, dearest? I know he has been with us for ever so, but sometimes it seems to me that he is becoming the least bit forgetful—age,

11

you know! You will write?" The Dowager Lady Hanford turned a steely gaze upon her eldest, and Hanford, who knew that Soberton's derelictions were entirely at his command, sighed and acquiesced.

"Yes, Mother, I will write." His mother was, after all, only correct. The Honorable Miss Orinda Lovelady Hanford of Laceby Place couldn't be brought out at a country ball. Orinda must go to London for her debut, or the Hanfords might as well retire from Society on the spot—and then the careful illusion of solvency would shatter forever. The loans and extensions of credit would cease, mortgages would come due. And Laceby would—inevitably—be lost.

And then what would become of any of them?

"And remind him: a large house, with a ballroom—and a good address. Oh, I know you will chide me, since when one rents it is not as if it is one's own address, but I think it is a false economy to save a few shillings by not taking a place practically in the center of the City, since then one is obliged to have the carriage out constantly, which I am persuaded is a far greater charge upon one's resources."

"Of course, Mother." Hanford forced another smile, and Lady Hanford blew him a parting kiss upon a flutter of fingertips. She floated gently from the room, leaving stillness and the scent of roses in her wake.

The year his youngest brother was born and his father died, the soon-to-be Baron Hanford was seventeen and at King's College, Oxford, intent on prolonging his University career past the point when more ardent spirits left in search of a wider stage for their ambitions. His interests lay with music and poetry, but the two things the Honorable Denzil Hanford primarily wished for from the world were peace and quiet and his own way, and Oxford was as far away from his parents as he could get.

It was not that Hanford did not love his parents, although he did not know them well. Since his birth the family had grown by the addition of a younger brother, Peveril, and a sister, Orinda; the children were exiled by custom, convenience, and economy, to the rambling country estate their city-bred parents disdained to visit. It was to Laceby that Hanford and Peveril returned on their school vacations, and it was during these long holidays that Hanford came to love Laceby as his father had never learned to. The servants spoiled him and stuffed his ears with tales of how Laceby had been in his grandsire's day, and the tenants welcomed their future landlord with a warmth Hanford was still too young to understand. Lulled by the eternal golden afternoon of the English countryside, Hanford never noticed the moment when the certainty that Laceby would be there for him always drew the pain from his parents' constant absence. When he was grown, he would have Laceby. Hanford could imagine no other life, and was content.

Then he was summoned to London by his parents.

It was the year that he was fifteen. He was nearly grown; his father wished to see his heir, and his mother wanted her darling to see firsthand the glittering playground of Society and the *haut ton* in which he would soon take his place. So Hanford left Laceby and his brother and sister, and went to visit his parents and their world.

When he came home to live permanently, when he came home. . . . It was all his mother could speak of. Home, he was told, was London, not "that moldering pile in Warwick." Home was London, the Big Smoke, the center of all the world. He would come home to London when his University days were through.

His mother would give parties, and they would all be shocking squeezes and horridly uncomfortable. He would, of course, marry immediately. She would personally select her new daughter-in-law, and young ladies would vie with mad duplicity to become the new Hanford bride. Lady Hanford would introduce him to all of Society. He would learn the people who mattered and the people who did not, and the people whose only interest in him was that he was a Hanford of Laceby.

Hanford realized with a sinking heart that nothing in the Warwickshire countryside he had come to love had prepared him for this, and that this was his all-too-certain future. There could be no thought of escape. He must do as Hanfords had always done, and Hanfords had always taken their place in the world.

But not just now. For a while longer he could pretend that his future was Laceby—its mellow walls and gracious rooms, and the gentle acres his family had husbanded for over seven hundred years. But when the news came to Oxford—of his father's death amid the celebration of the birth of yet another brother—Hanford felt as much relief as guilt.

Guilt, because no dutiful son would rejoice in the death of his father. Relief, because now the waiting was over. He could give up this secret rebellion and be what his mother wanted and his father had intended: Lord Hanford of Laceby.

Relief and guilt were both short-lived. Within twenty-four hours of his arrival home Hanford realized that the only thing he had ever counted on—Laceby and the Hanford estates—was built on a foundation of shifting sand. Jocelyn Hanford had seen his lands only as a source of revenue. During his London sojourn Hanford had become familiar with the sight of tradesmen and moneylenders waiting in the antechamber for his father to attend them, but he had given the matter no thought. Everyone had debts. One must live, after all, he said, echoing the watchword by which his entire class was putting an end to itself with gaudy efficiency.

Now Hanford sat in stunned silence day after day with his father's man of business—now his—as the toll of bills and mortgages that had supported that belief was accurately told up at last.

Bills that had run for years had come due at the death of his father, and for every one they could find, Mr. Soberton told the new Lord Hanford gently, he must expect two or three more when they searched the London house. In the end, the only thing found to be untouched in the financial ruin of the Hanford family was Lady Hanford's jointure. Even Mr. Soberton could only shake his head and say distracted things about how charming his late lordship had been.

Hanford looked for help in this crisis and found none. His uncle Brabazon Hanford had made a career of the Army, and becoming his nephew's trustee did not alter his life appreciably. He brought his foreign wife Genevieve and his delicate daughter Ancilla to live at Laceby Place in token of his guardianship, assured Hanford that he would support any decision the new Baron cared to make, and dashed off to Portugal again. Clementina Hanford took prematurely to the style of Dowager Baroness, which she was still young enough to think dashing, and embraced the study of genealogy and Brussels lace caps with equal facility. She took up her niece Ancilla to spite her sister-in-law, and assured her eldest son that she was certain he would manage beautifully.

Captain Brabazon Hanford did not live out the year, and Brabazon's wife remarried with almost indecent haste. Genevieve Rogier then commended her daughter's care to her dear sister Lady Hanford and departed.

The new Baron was too busy either to notice that he was now in sole control of his estates or to mourn the uncle he had never really known. Night after night he sat up late—not over brandy, but account books. The lives and futures of his family were in his hands, and more—the household servants and the tenants of his lands depended on him to keep them and care for them and see that the disaster that had struck never touched them. All the ancient feudal responsibility for lands and dependants came crashing down upon his shoulders until Hanford thought the weight would crush him. It was a weight he had never been trained to bear and a responsibility he should never have had to assume at all, let alone at the age of seventeen. Many young men in his situation would have given up—scattered the family among relatives willing to take them in and let the house and lands be sold for debt. No one would have blamed him had he done so. He would have been the object of universal pity, for as long as he was remembered. But he was Lord Hanford of Laceby, and a Hanford did not surrender, so Hanford did his best.

The interest on the Laceby mortgages was paid. But the racing stable was sold, then the yacht, then the carriages and the riding stable. The London town house was sold, over Lady Hanford's bitter protests. For a while the Seasons were spent in smaller rented quarters, far less fashionable, until finally that too was halted. But they managed.

Hanford alone had known that the time when they could no longer manage was coming, but he had not expected it to come so soon. Something would turn up; some unexpected inheritance that would let them re-enter the glittering world of privilege his mother spoke of. But nothing had come, and now after six years he knew that nothing would.

He must give Orinda her Season nevertheless. His father would have managed it (how, he could not imagine), and if Orinda was not brought out, how could she make the marriage that Hanford owed it to her to provide? If she married, he thought dismally, it would at least provide a home for her and Mother and his newest brother Athelstane.

Squaring his shoulders against a phantom burden, the twenty-ninth Baron Hanford gathered up his stillborn sonnet and slipped it into a drawer of the desk.

Ancilla did not trouble to knock on the study door. If Hanford was writing she could simply go away again, and would disturb him far less than if she had knocked. She had been on easy terms with her three-years-older cousin since the day she had first been introduced into the household as a vastly unpromising brat of fourteen, and had by degrees become Hanford's closest friend and confidant.

But Hanford was not writing, though he was still sitting at his desk. He had been pulling the petals from the roses in a blue-and-white bowl one by one, until the desk was mantled in a drift of sunset-colored snow. He looked up when Ancilla entered, and his eyes lit with a smile when he saw her.

"Come in, Cilla, and scold me for wasting my time." He brushed the flower petals from his hands as he stood and led her to the sopha set beneath the library window.

"I shan't do that," she said, smiling. "But I collect, from certain subtle signs, that Aunt Clementina has been with you, and therefore that Orinda's come-out is much on your mind." She drew the cashmere shawl she wore more snugly about her thin shoulders and favored Hanford with an amused grey-eyed gaze.

"Oh, aye." Hanford stared down at his fingertips. "Orinda must be brought out—so a house must needs be procured. In a fashionable part of town, and not neglecting a ballroom. Further, it is wanted from the beginning of March, so there will be time for a suitable Town wardrobe to be purchased." He did not need to add that Lady Hanford might as well have asked for roses in December.

"Oh, but you are not considering the advantages in such a plan! Perhaps Orinda will attach a Royal Duke, or a German Prince, or perhaps even an Italian Count of sinister mien and volatile temperament! Of course, he will have to straightaway expire after the wedding leaving her in sole command of his entire fortune," Ancilla suggested consideringly.

"Wretch!" said Hanford, laughing. He took her hand and drew it to his lips in a light salute. "What would I do without my Cilla to make me laugh?"

"Oh, I daresay you would contrive somehow, my lord Hanford," Ancilla said gravely. She withdrew her hand, and the spots of hectic color that burned in her pale cheeks were lost for a moment in a rosy blush. "But what you must contrive now is to bring Orinda out, for Lady Hanford is right about that at least, even if she does not perfectly understand how things are. I think she knows more than you believe, you know, and you are mistaken not to tell her the whole. But that is none of my bread-and-butter, as you have frequently told me! Perhaps Lady Hanford can be brought to see that it would be far more delightful for one of her brothers to give Orinda's ball. Then the Mashams can all shine in reflected glory and . . ."

"And I might as well invite the bailiffs in and be done!" said Hanford savagely. He leapt to his feet and roamed about the room. "I am sorry, Cilla—but you know that the Mashams will never be brought to do any such thing. If Orinda is to make her debut at all, Mother and I must contrive it. And she is right: the thing must be done in the first fashion, or not at all."

He returned to the sopha and sat down. "But I will not tease you—it cannot be easy to be asked to plan another girl's Season when you have not had one of your own."

Ancilla snorted derisively and then began to cough. Hanford slipped an arm around her shoulders with the ease of long custom and held her close.

Each year her cough persisted longer into the summer, and the cordial prescribed by the village doctor—and paid for, unknown to Ancilla, in bottles of wine from his late lordship's cellar—grew less effectual. Ancilla should have had the best London practitioners to attend her and spent her winters in the life-giving warmth of Italy or Greece. Instead she made her home at Laceby, and though Hanford loved his home far better than most of his relatives, there was no denying it was damp.

"A Season!" Ancilla gasped mockingly, setting off another round of spasms. "Oh! Hanford! I pray you will not make me laugh!"

When the coughing fit had passed she sat holding her handkerchief to her lips. Hanford went to pour her a glass of brandy. When he returned with it he reached for the handkerchief, but she deftly whisked it back into her pocket.

"Nothing at all to do with you, sir!" she told him crisply. "And bother my delicate feelings into the bargain. What, pray, do you suppose I would do with a Season if one was dropped in my lap?" She took the glass from Hanford and sipped at the brandy.

"And bother my stupid cough, too—you know it does not signify!" she added fiercely. "You will manage a Season for Orinda somehow, and I will help you!"

"Brave Ancilla! If you were Lord Hanford instead of I, I am persuaded you would have brought us all about years ago. Laceby would be a showplace, the Hanford Thoroughbreds would win the Derby every year, and you yourself would be Prime Minister!"

"And what would I do with such rubbishy commonplaces, when there aren't enough hours in the day as it is for me to do all I wish? But enough of your airs and graces, my lord. I know you were doing the accounts today—how do things stand?"

Hanford took a deep breath. "I will rent Laceby if I can. It is the only way."

"Good God, is it as bad as that?" Ancilla demanded. Hanford nodded, and she thought a moment. "I have Mama's address in Paris. Perhaps if I wrote to her she could be persuaded to make me an allowance—I could offer to come live with her, you see, and . . ."

"No! Cilla, you will not be reduced to that—unless you very much wish it?" Hanford said doubtfully.

"Idiot! Mama would wish me to live with her as much as I wish it—which is not at all! And that being so, she will do all that she might to keep me here. She is married again now, you know, and I daresay the descent upon her household of a daughter quite twenty years of age would be only the keenest source of embarrassment!" Ancilla chuckled breathlessly and stifled another cough. "I will write to her at once."

"You will do no such thing," Hanford said firmly. "Nothing would be likelier than Aunt Genevieve taking the notion that she should come and see how you did, and you know that she and Mother never did get on."

"Don't I just! With Mama saying that thus-and-so was not how it had been under the *ancien régime,* and Aunt Clementina burning to give her a set-down, since I am sure Mama knew as much about the *ancien régime* as I do myself, and that is nothing at all!"

"And Mother dared not, as certainly then Aunt Genevieve would recollect that Mother's Uncle Masham had emigrated to the West Indies to become a farmer and—"

"An Overlord of Black Slaves!" they finished in chorus. Ancilla took his hand in hers and squeezed it.

"But for myself I cannot see that being a gentleman farmer is so very bad—and I beg your pardon, but surely it is worse that Lady Hanford has forbidden that his name should ever be mentioned beneath her roof," she resumed.

"Mother's sensibilities are easily overset," Hanford said gently, "and I fancy the first rift occurred on Great-uncle Robert's side. He did not approve of Grandfather Masham marrying his daughter to a man whose grandfather had been executed for treason, and was not backward about saying so."

Ancilla was quite familiar with the career of Christian Hanford, executed in the 'fifties for his loyalty to the Stuart cause, and needed no clarification of this remark. "Well, at least the estate came to your grandfather intact—though do you know, Hanford, if it had been attainted at that time neither you nor I should know or care? How peculiar Life is—the simplest difficulty can have roots stretching back centuries."

"Hardly centuries: the Rising was, oh, only eighty years ago or so. And in eighty years more I am sure I will not know or care what becomes of Laceby—but I care now. I am the head of the family, Cilla. It is my business to make provision for everyone else. That means school for Athelstane, and something for Peveril, and a Season for Orinda. The thing must be done." He lapsed into silence, staring off into space. He did not mention the most urgent need because she would only laugh and make a joke, but somehow, somewhere, money must be found to send Ancilla to Italy.

"I do not think that it will answer to rent Laceby," Ancilla said slowly, squeezing his hand. "It is only too likely that your tenants would wish you to make improvements. For the roof leaks, you know—"

"And the chimneys don't."

"And the floors slant."

"And the ceilings too."

"And the west wing is very dark."

"Which is only to be expected since the shutters have been rusted shut these sixty years."

"And there is no ornamental ruin."

"Unless you account the entire house." The cousins smiled at each other in perfect amity, and Hanford turned Ancilla toward him and dropped a gentle kiss upon her brow. "Still, I am fond of it, Lord alone knows why. Don't worry, Cilla, I am sure we will manage."

"Liar," said Ancilla. "You are sure of no such thing, though it is plain you will manage. You always have."

"With your help," Hanford replied. "It was you who first said that we might very well sell any number of historic family treasures without causing ourselves the least inconvenience."

"And it didn't did it?" said Ancilla with mendacious cheerfulness. "At least, it was not inconve-

22

nient once they were got into crates, though I own I am sorry about poor Peveril."

"I am sorrier—it was not enough that he should try to move the Diana out of the garden by himself, but after it fell on him and broke his arm he insisted on saying he had been brought low by the chaste huntress of the night—to Mother!—and—"

"And Aunt Clementina was sure he had broken his skull and was raving in the brain-fever—and then she found the statue was gone from the garden! And it turned out she had known what we were doing all along—and she said it was very wise of you, Hanford, to dispose of those pagan idols, which could only have a lowering effect on the moral character of the servants!"

Hanford smiled at the memory, but the smile was fleeting. "Very well, Cilla. If I cannot rent this vast historic pile, I must sell something else to raise the wind. It has always worked before. But what," said the twenty-ninth Baron Hanford, "can there possibly be left at Laceby that anyone would want to buy?"

Chapter II

JULY 1817

ON LOWER CHAPMAN Street, east of New Road and comfortably north of Ratcliffe Highway and the London Docks, stood a luxurious residence quite out of the common way. It was barely three miles from the center of London, and considerable pains, in the way of marble facings and sconces of gilded bronze, had been taken to give it a serene and spacious elegance quite superior to that of its neighbors. The elder daughter of the house, Miss Susannah Elizabeth Potter, was equally elegant, though far from serene.

Her father had sent for her to attend him in his study at ten o'clock this morning, and the purpose could only be to decide her future. Since she was quite old enough to be considered thoroughly educated, and marriage was the only future to which a gently reared young lady of Susannah's class and expectations could aspire, on this July day in 1817 her father would talk to her of marriage.

She had no doubt of her ability to captivate the as-yet-unmet paragon who would become Jacob Potter's son-in-law: at Miss Farthingale's Female Seminary in Bath, Adelaide Featherton had once bestowed the ultimate encomium upon her person by telling her that she thought blue eyes and black curls the most despiteful thing in Nature (Miss Featherton's eyes, it must be mentioned, were grey, and her hair was straight and brown). And, personal charms aside, Susannah would have quite a large dowry.

She was instantly caught up in pleasant dreams of her future, when, with keys at her waist, she would oversee the mysteries of kitchen and pantry and preside over a nursery full of rosy-faced smiling grandchildren for Papa. Never again would she have to listen to sneers that Stepney wasn't anywhere, or hear cries of disbelief that she lived in London year-round. She had left all that behind her forever when she left Miss Farthingale's.

A little before the hour Susannah knocked upon the ornate mahogany door to her father's study, then turned the knob and thrust it open without waiting to hear an answer.

"Sit down, Sukey. It's time we studied what's to become of you." Jacob Potter beamed fondly upon his daughter. It was known in the City that Mr. Jacob Potter was a knowing 'un and a warm man indeed, who could have a handle to his name nearly for the asking, but though a man of nice discrimination and high standards, Mr. Potter had no interest in ennobling himself. His tastes were homely, his ambitions far from social, and his patience limited when it came to the feckless and dazzling members of the Upper Ten Thousand.

In the matter of his daughters, however, he was of quite another mind. In 1799 Mr. Jacob Potter of Brooks & Potter, Mercers & Drapers of the City of London, had married the Honorable Miss Amelia Clarendon of Crown Clarendon in Derby. This would not, in gentler times, have been even remotely possible, for Amelia Clarendon was the daughter of one of the oldest families in England,

and Mr. Potter was a City man—or, in the fashionable new slang of the noble families of England, a Cit.

However, Amelia and her elder sister had lost their four brothers and both parents to the earliest of Bonaparte's forays, and each of their surviving relatives was more impecunious than the next. The marriage was made, and against all expectation the new Mrs. Potter loved the earnest City man who insisted she was as far above him as the stars in the sky.

Miss Susannah Potter arrived the same year, but Amelia Potter was gentle and lovely, not strong. When Susannah's sister Dinah followed less than two years later, Mrs. Potter did not survive this second confinement. Left with two motherless infant daughters to provide for, Jacob Potter turned his hand to business with a will, and never forgot what was due their mother's blood.

"You see, Sukey," her father said, "I've been thinking, and now you're home it's high time we settled your future."

"Yes, Papa," Susannah said obediently. A faint dimple appeared by her mouth as she waited for him to tell her that this young man or that was a fine likely chap who would be coming to dinner tomorrow night.

"And after all, it's not as though you've forever to blow this way and that! Best to get matters well in hand as soon as possible, then, if waiting's wanted, there's time for delay."

From long experience Susannah recognized that it was not her own objections being dealt with, but her Uncle Abner's, though she could not imagine why Uncle Abner could possibly object to her meeting eligible young men.

"Now, you'll say I haven't thought matters out," her father continued, "and that it's a bad bargain

26

I'm making—but don't you say a man's struck a bad bargain until you find out what it is he intends to buy!"

"Indeed, Papa," Susannah said again. She felt a sudden pang of nervousness. A bargain—did Papa mean that he had already accepted an offer for someone she'd never met? She wished desperately that he would get to the point.

"Now you know that I've always tried to do right by you and your sister, Sukey, and there's never a groat I've grudged on the keeping of you to turn you out in high style with everything of the best. But there's things I can't give you—things you should have. You've a right to 'em, just as my Melia had, God rest her, and I won't rest either until you've got them, for yourself and Dinah, too. Now, what if I was to tell you, Sukey, that there was a fine young gentleman just a-waiting to make me an offer for you—a Viscount, look you. Family as old as the hills; Lady Susannah, you'd be, with horses and jewels and all. What would you say to that?" Her father beamed, confident of her approval.

It was thought, by the teachers at Miss Farthingale's, that Susannah Potter had beautiful manners and a pleasing reserve. What was more nearly the case was that Susannah Potter had a conscientious control over a temper every bit the equal of her father's. Unfortunately, all she was conscious of at the moment was a strong sense of betrayal.

"I should ask you, Papa, how much he cost."

"Now see here, my girl—"

"Who is he—this so-obliging Viscount? Never mind; you need not tell me. I fancy I already know him well enough. You sent me away to school to learn, you know, and so I have. I know precisely how such things are arranged in families of quality. This bridegroom—whoever he may be—is punting upon the River Tick, as it is fashionable to call

27

gross indebtedness. With a very great many bills and—and no money. Just a title. And a name. And when one has a title, and a name, and a very great need of money, one sometimes will do things one would not otherwise do—like marry a Cit's daughter."

"Susannah!" her father roared, astonished.

"But he shall have to find some other young person to marry," Susannah went on inexorably, "because I shan't have him."

It is fair to say that Mr. Potter could not have been more stunned if one of his own shop-clerks had turned on him and read him a resounding scold.

"Are you telling me, Sukey-girl, that when your father tells you he's found someone to make you a fine lady just like your mother was you won't have him? You'll marry who your father tells you to marry, my girl, and we'll have no more talk about it! Now I haven't met this fellow, but Mr. Coltharp says—"

"Mr. Coltharp!" Susannah interrupted furiously. "I don't doubt Mr. Coltharp approves. Depend upon it, Mr. Coltharp is this Viscount's banker as well as your own, and could think nothing finer than to see your money allied with his client's debts!" She heard her own words and was appalled. "Oh, Papa, I am so sorry!" Susannah gasped. "But don't you see—"

"That's enough! No, I don't see—and I won't see—but I own I never thought I would see my own daughter coming the archwife in this house, much less raising her voice to her own father! Are these the fine Society manners you learned at that high-toned school of yours? Never mind that—you go to your room, Miss, and think about doing as you're told—and be glad I don't take a strap to you!"

Mr. Potter had never raised a hand to either of his daughters in their lives, a fact that did nothing to interfere with Susannah's flight from the room in tears. Her father, infuriated by the baffling and unfilial reception of his grand plan, slammed out of the house not five minutes later, leaving the servants in a froth of curiosity.

The sun was just setting over the housetops, and Susannah, who had been watching for him from her window for hours, had nearly given up hope of seeing him when Mr. Potter returned home.

Without giving herself time to think she ran for the door. She must go to Papa and apologize—but how could she apologize when she would say the same thing again, given the chance? Well, perhaps, she allowed, she would express herself more politically. Perhaps. But everything she'd said was true. Why couldn't he understand that?

She met Mr. Potter in the hallway and saw him recollect, with an effort, that he was angry with his eldest daughter. With a flourish worthy of Drury Lane, he gestured for her to precede him into his study.

"Well, Miss?" Jacob Potter said.

"I will not marry a man who must be bought, Papa," Susannah said steadily.

"Then you'll defy me, Susannah?"

"Yes, Papa," she whispered.

The explosion she expected and felt she deserved didn't come. Instead her father walked over to the sopha and sat down heavily on it. He patted a space beside him and she joined him.

"Sukey-girl, don't you want to be a Viscountess? You're just as good as any of them; never doubt it. You'd have a grand house, and servants, and go to parties, just as your mother would have wished. Isn't that what you want?" Her father's voice was bewildered more than angry, and his dutiful, sensible daughter buried her face in her hands.

"I . . . No, Papa."

"Is it love you're waiting for, Sukey? That comes rare. You can't depend on it." There was an odd sad note in his voice she couldn't remember hearing before.

Susannah raised her head and looked at him. She wished she could throw herself into his arms as she had done as a child and have him tell her that problems were no more than a bag of moonshine, but she felt far too old for that.

Mr. Potter sighed deeply. "Well, I won't make you do what you don't want, daughter, as you know full well—but I wish I knew what you did want."

"I want . . . I want a husband who wants me, Papa," Susannah said slowly. "There should be more to a marriage than the wedding of a title and a dowry. It is not love I look for, Papa, although I should hope to be fond of my husband. But marriage should be . . . I should like it to be an equal match."

"Abner said that was how it would be, but I wouldn't believe him. Very well, I shall tell Coltharp my daughter hasn't any mind to fripperies like titles and honors, and we'll say no more about it. You're just a child yet, Sukey. Happens you might change your mind about being a Viscountess—"

"Oh, no, Papa!" Susannah assured him, light-headed with relief. "And—and you're not angry with me? I didn't mean to say those things about Mr. Coltharp, indeed I did not—"

"Indeed you did, baggage!" her father assured her fondly. "Mind me of my Melia, you do—she never did hold with calling a thing out of its name. Let it bide, Sukey-love, and come and help me eat my dinner. We'll find someone you like, never fear."

There was no more talk of marriage, into the *ton* or out of it. Jacob was determined that his daughter should be happy—perhaps too determined, thought the fathers of boys scornfully dismissed by Jacob Potter as unsuitable suitors for his daughter's hand. Seventeen was much too young, he said to all inquiries. Next year, perhaps. Or when the proper time came.

But the proper time never came for Jacob Potter. On a raw February day in 1818 a rope, slippery with ice and rotted with salt, broke on the London Dock, and the hundredweight bale of American cotton it was unloading to be spun to calico in English mills fell and struck Jacob Potter.

It was not so very serious an injury—a broken leg, some cracked ribs—but the pneumonia that inexorably followed upon it in the winter damp was serious. For all the mustard plasters and laudanum, expert nursing and rooms kept blistering hot, once the hacking cough had deepened to rales the outcome was never in doubt. He fought valiantly for weeks, but in the raw early spring of 1818 the mortal clay of Jacob Potter was committed to a fine white tomb of Italian marble to lie beside his wife in the burying ground of St. George's In The East on Ratcliffe Highway.

Chapter III

SEPTEMBER 1818

THE AWFUL DAYS after the funeral passed in a blur. Susannah hardly attended as her Uncle Abner and Mr. Gamaliel Coltharp of Drummond's Bank explained that she and Dinah were now very great heiresses, and that Mr. Potter and Mr. Coltharp would take care of their fortune for them until such time as they chose to marry. She did rouse herself long enough to suggest to Uncle Abner that it would be best if Dinah remained at school in Bath until "things were more settled," and to her relief this suggestion was accepted. But Susannah's own situation was more difficult to resolve. She could not take up residence in her uncle's bachelor establishment, nor could she live, either alone or with Dinah, in the house on Lower Chapman Street. There was really only one solution to the dilemma, and after some negotiation, Susannah was escorted to the small row house at 19 Coram Place, where her only other surviving relative resided.

Mariah Potter had been the youngest of the three Potter siblings, and the good fortune of the Potter dynasty had largely passed her by. When she was barely Susannah's age (as she liked to explain), she met and married Mr. William Doolittle, a clerk in chambers at Temple Bar. She had (as she would further explain) been carried off by the rigors of romance, and then she would heave an ill-used sigh and say nothing further.

At first nothing could have been kinder or more particular than the attentions of Aunt Doolittle to her cruelly orphaned niece. But Susannah had been patronized all her life because of her father's inferior social position, and she was not slow to realize that she was now being patronized because of her mother's superior birth. She soon found that her aunt's fascination with her late sister-in-law stemmed from a dislike well-rooted in envy, and Amelia Potter's name was always linked to small improving homilies on the nature of "each cobbler to his own last" until Susannah quite dreaded the introduction of any discussion of genealogy into an evening's talk.

It was a little after that that she realized where such discussions were leading.

On a day in early September six months after her father's death, Susannah was occupied with stitching together a shirt from the pile of pieces that lay atop her workbasket. It had taken her a considerable amount of effort to convince Aunt Doolittle to allow her to help with the work of the house, and more before Susannah could convince her abigail, Ruby, that she too was expected to help, but Jacob Potter had never encouraged his daughters to sit idle and she could not bear to do so now that he was gone.

Until these last few weeks Susannah had been too grief-stricken to be anything but thankful for her aunt's insistence that it was not at all proper for her to go out of the house, or for the Doolittles to have even the quietest callers, but now she began to hope for company to shake her out of her blue-devils. In a moment her unspoken wish was gratified in a fashion she might not have wished, as her cousin Ethan entered the room.

The only child of William and Mariah Doolittle was twenty-six years of age, and all his mother's frustrated hopes reposed in him. He was a well-enough young man if you discounted his complexion, which was spotty, his mouth, which was weak, and his person, which was ornamented in far too high a style. He always treated Susannah in a fashion that made her suspect the company of gently bred young females was foreign to him; and it was young Mr. Doolittle's presence as much as the oppressive domestic atmosphere that had made her encourage Dinah to spend her summer elsewhere.

On this bright September afternoon Ethan Doolittle chose to display himself in an outfit consisting of a too-tight coat of an ominously lurid green, an embroidered peacock waistcoat festooned with fobs and seals, a shirt consisting of starch and ruffles in equal measure, and bright yellow trousers with three pearl buttons at each ankle that led the eye irrevocably to narrow pointed slippers of glazed burgundy kid. A wide black armband of some shiny fabric, in token of family mourning, did little to dim the splendor of such a turn out.

In defense of Mr. Doolittle, he was very much what his mother had made him. Susannah always did her best to remember that, although sometimes it was very hard.

"Hallo there, Sukey!" Mr. Doolittle, as was his wont, hailed Susannah as if she were a hackney carriage.

"Hello, Mr. Doolittle," Susannah said, continuing to stitch in what she hoped was a discouraging fashion.

Mr. Doolittle took this recognition as permission to make himself at home and bestrode a chair, folding his hands upon the back. "Well, now, how's my girl today?"

Susannah regarded Mr. Doolittle with well-schooled blankness. As she had feared and expected, he did not take the hint.

"What? In the mopes again? That won't answer; devil it will. What you want is some distraction—" Mr. Doolittle then proceeded to disclose several plans for her entertainment, enabling Susannah to gently remind him that she was still in mourning for her father, and so could not be expected to take an interest in the things of the world until next spring at the very earliest.

"Oh? Ah?" Mr. Doolittle was only momentarily discomfited. "Well, then. Spring, eh? Well, that's convenient. Do the thing then. Tell you what: you can finish off this mourning business and then we'll get ourselves spliced. Put off these weeds and step into something with a bit of color. Have to say it, Sukey. Damned attractive girl, but it'd take a regular knowing one to tell under all that black!"

"Pray forgive me, but I have not the least understanding of what you may mean," responded Susannah in arctic tones.

"Well, it only stands to reason, don't it? Fine-looking young female such as yourself—"

"Mr. Doolittle! I beg you—earnestly—do not continue on that head!"

"Not your line of country, eh? Not surprised. All that schooling'd take the starch out of anyone's frillies. Couldn't stand it myself. Which reminds me: don't you have any fear you'll find Ethan Doolittle a dull dog! Why, once I've stepped into parson's mousetrap I'll undertake to show you the best time you've ever had—and I'll be the chap with the blunt to do it!" he said gaily.

It was obvious what source Mr. Doolittle looked to for his enrichment. "Wedding," said Susannah, staring at him blankly.

Her cousin remained oblivious. "As to that, I

daresay I should have made a show of asking you, only Mama said you were far too levelheaded to want all that trumpery nonsense, and for my part I hold it a great relief to deal with a sensible female for a change. You'll want someone to look after you and the business; here I am, ready to hand, as it were. No need for moonlight there, is it? All in the family. Of course there won't be any plans made until you're out of mourning. Mama says you wouldn't want anyone to think there was anything irregular about the match. But once we're running in double harness, then you'll see a bit of fun! P'raps we'll honeymoon in Paris, just like quality. So you see, if you're hipped now, you can remember it's only for a little while."

Susannah was at a loss for words. The confidence with which her cousin assumed their wedding was a certainty, and the equal confidence with which Aunt Doolittle must have assured him of it, left her literally speechless. She could only cling to the thought that she must do nothing to make Mr. Doolittle offer further proof of how well they would deal together.

"You know," she began, and swallowed hard. "You are aware of course that my marriage is entirely in the hands of my trustees." Until this very moment Susannah had never considered what a delightful fact that was.

"Course I do. What of it? Uncle Abner's hardly going to kick up the dust over you marrying your own cousin—'specially if you put in a good word for me, which I daresay you're bound to do! But no point in talking about that out-of-hours! What I really came to see is if you'd lend me a fiver out of your pin-money, there's a good girl! I don't know where mine goes, devil I don't, but you're always swimming in lard."

Susannah thought that that sounded extremely unpleasant, but not nearly as unpleasant as another minute spent in her cousin's company. She rang for Ruby to bring her her purse.

Mr. Doolittle took the purse from her abigail's hands and helped himself liberally, saying jovially that a yellow-boy was as good as a pound to him as he pocketed the coins. Susannah was too grateful to gain his absence to raise the slightest objection.

The interview that followed Mariah Doolittle's return home was painful in the extreme. Aunt Doolittle could not be brought to see anything amiss in her son's behavior, and when Susannah said, quite honestly, that she had never thought of marrying her cousin Ethan, she was told that in that case she should think about it now. Susannah, taking the last of her courage in her hands, said quite firmly that she could not possibly marry Ethan Doolittle.

"And why not? I suppose you think he's beneath you! Well, let me tell you, my fine lady, he's your own blood and bone, and nothing could be more suitable! I won't have you make the mistake poor Jacob did when he married that spiritless snirp of a nob; Ethan's your own kind, and your cousin. You owe it to him to help him make his way in the world, and who else do you think you can marry? Answer me that!"

"I—I'm not sure, Aunt. Papa—"

"Your papa, God rest him, has been called to glory this half year, and he hasn't anything more to say in the matter! Now he gave you into my charge, Susannah," her aunt said inaccurately. "You just make up your mind to do what you're told, and everything will be for the best."

"I beg your pardon, Aunt," Susannah said miserably, "but Uncle Abner and Mr. Coltharp are my trustees, and they must give their consent before I am married." She could not muster any other arguments to match against her aunt's conviction, and certainly she had no bridegroom to offer up in place of Cousin Ethan.

Her aunt drew breath for another stirring rejoinder, then, amazingly, smiled. "Well, Susannah—is that all the trouble is? Just leave Abner Potter to me and don't you worry; we'll have you in church this time next year and you won't have to lift your hand to a thing."

That evening Susannah lay on her bed and brooded. She wished Dinah were here to leaven the situation with an application of her shattering common sense, but each time she thought of Dinah and Ethan beneath the same roof she was just as glad her reckless younger sister was far away.

Had she been right to say she would not marry Ethan? It was plain that Aunt Doolittle saw the matter as settled and had told her only child as much. Was Susannah so sure she knew better than her aunt? She could, in all fairness, see her aunt's view of things. A cousin and a member of the family—what could be more respectable? It was only what Papa had tried to do for her, but as much difference as time lay between Jacob Potter's fantastic scheme for her ennoblement and Mariah Doolittle's pragmatic plan. The same inner voice of warning that had prompted her to draw back when her father had proposed her marriage into the *ton* the year before sounded now.

Was Ethan Doolittle any more suitable a match than that unknown Viscount? If he had not been family, Susannah would not have hesitated to call him shiftless, and Papa had never liked him.

And then there was Dinah. Certainly, when Susannah married, her sister would make her home with her, and she could not like the picture conjured in her mind of Dinah and Ethan together.

But if she did not marry Cousin Ethan, who

would she marry? To marry and make a home for her husband, to have children and see them in turn marry and have children of their own, was as much her profession as clothselling had been her papa's. All her life Susannah had never considered if she would marry, but when.

But it was not likely that suitors would dangle after her while Aunt Doolittle told the world she was engaged to her cousin, and where else could she meet eligible young men except as guests in her aunt's home? Perhaps, Susannah told herself hopefully, her misgivings were groundless.

And if they were not, Uncle Abner would tell her so.

It was not much after ten of the clock when the hackney pulled up in Fenchurch Street. A young lady alighted, dressed all in black from her deep poke-bonnet to her sturdy elastic-sided boots. Her abigail hovered close behind.

Susannah's Uncle Doolittle had gone to his office and her aunt was at the market. It was not that she was sneaking, Susannah temporized carefully, merely that no one had asked where she was going.

"Oh, Miss, are you sure it's wise?"

"Of course, Ruby; I have lived here all my life—or near here, anyway. Do you expect me to shrink now because Aunt Doolittle thinks it not quite genteel?"

As there was no answer to this that did not defame either Miss Potter or Mrs. Doolittle, Ruby relapsed into silence. Her mistress led the way into the stately stone building with its handsome ornamented pediment depicting Ariadne and Penelope, the patron, if pagan, saints of spinning and weaving.

Abner Potter, the surviving partner of the firm of Brooks & Potter, Mercers & Drapers of the City of London, rose from behind his massive oak desk, a look of surprise on his features.

"Oh, Uncle Abner!" Susannah cried, flinging

herself into his arms. He thumped her heartily on the back, then held her at arm's length.

"Here now, Sukey-girl. What's the meaning of this, eh? You're a long way from home."

"I—I particularly wished to talk to you, Uncle," Susannah said. She darted a look of constraint toward her abigail, who was regarding her mistress with long-suffering curiosity.

Abner Potter followed her look, and his expression darkened to a frown. He said nothing, merely ordering the abigail to a bench outside the office, after which Susannah settled herself as decorously as possible on her stool and prepared to divulge all.

But it was more difficult than she had thought. The conversation meandered through details of life at Coram Place, and Dinah's progress at school, until Abner Potter demanded she come to the point.

"For while it's plain to see you're that far from being all to flinders as Mariah would have you, I've never heard such roundaboutation from you in my life or yours! What the devil is ailing you, Susannah?"

But Susannah still could not bring herself to speak plainly. What she had tried to view as a humorous incident in her aunt's house took on more and more unpleasantness seen in the clear light of her uncle's office.

"Uncle Abner, it is true that you are one of my trustees, is it not?" she said at last.

"Aye, as you'll remember, Jacob tied it up between Coltharp and myself."

"I wonder," said Susannah, "why he did not think to choose Uncle Doolittle instead of Mr. Coltharp?"

The effect of this artless question on Abner Potter was immediate. His face turned a very fine shade of Turkey Red, such as dyers at Birmingham paid ten and six the hundredweight for.

"You never wondered such a thing in all your life, Sukey, and I've known you since you were born. What has that old—" He broke off with an effort that left him breathing heavily. "What makes you wonder now?"

Susannah studied her fingertips. "Because Aunt says I am to marry Cousin Ethan. Do you— Ought I—"

This time it took several seconds for Uncle Abner to regain his composure.

"Marry that gormless park-saunterer, that over-dressed maw-worm, that—You'll do no such thing, my girl—you can set your mind at rest on that head! You're not marrying anyone at all without my permission, which I'm not giving for you to marry that young lily-hands, and that settles the matter!"

"Thank you, Uncle!" said Susannah with a deep sigh of relief. "I had not thought you would approve—and I am so glad you don't!"

"Approve of—!" Abner's color deepened until Susannah became quite alarmed. "That nevvy of mine is bad blood, Susannah, and his character isn't what. . . . Well, there's no use telling you things you'll just have to forget, though I always have wondered. . . . But that's neither here nor there. Your aunt is a fine woman—for a stubborn, opinionated old antidote—and as for you, missy, I'll see you leading apes in hell before you marry Ethan Doolittle. You keep yourself to yourself, and nothing to do with him."

"I—I try, Uncle Abner," Susannah said. It did not take long for her to put her uncle in possession of the rest of the facts, including the moneylending of the day before, and her comparison of Cousin Ethan to the notorious and long-lost Viscount.

"I've always thought Jacob did wrong by you there, Sukey, but you were the apple of his eye and he didn't want to lose you."

"Did wrong by me? How?"

"You ought to've had him. Viscount St. Herriot, I mean. Put you where you belonged. I'll admit, it was my idea to begin, and I think if it'd been left to me ... Well, you see now there's worse to be had."

Susannah digested this alarming intelligence in silence. "Do you mean then that I ought to have married ... an empty title who would have a Cit's daughter on account of his duns?"

"You never knew your mother, did you?" said Abner inconsequently. Despite herself, Susannah smiled.

"No—how could I? She died when I was a baby. Aunt Doolittle is forever going on about how unsuitable the match was, and how it is far better to marry one's own kind than to go among strangers, but I think Mama and Papa must have been very happy. And since we were discussing my marriage, not Papa's, I collect this has to do with it."

"Oh, it does that. It has to do with your being more than a Cit's daughter. You're a Clarendon too, and it's a thousand pities your mother's sister went to America: I'd've sent you to her a million times sooner than to Mariah. You're more like your mother than you know, and you could do worse than to marry a young man who could bring you into her world, Susannah."

"And spend my money for empty trumpery!"

"But Ethan will do that—and a lot more you can't even imagine."

"Uncle Abner!" gasped Susannah, as much amused as shocked.

"Don't you 'Uncle Abner' me, saucebox. You haven't any idea what I'm talking about, and God willing, you never will. Now, I'll have a word with Mariah. I daresay that will be the end of Cousin Ethan. You just leave everything to me."

Susannah returned home without incident, and as nobody asked her where she had been, she was not obliged to tell them. Life proceeded smoothly, and a week later Abner Potter came to dine in Coram Place.

Susannah was never made privy to what Abner Potter said to his younger sister. She only knew that in the days that followed, Mariah Doolittle's conversation turned entirely on the sin of willfulness in young girls. True, she was never again alone in young Mr. Doolittle's company, and certainly he never again mentioned matrimony to her, but in the weeks that followed an idea began to take strong possession of Susannah's mind, until she could no longer dismiss it as a product of her own fancy.

Cousin Ethan Doolittle intended to elope with her.

A chance remark of Aunt Doolittle's told Susannah her aunt had decided the objection of the marriage lay entirely with Abner Potter (under a sentence of banishment from Coram Place since that last ill-starred dinner), and the hints dropped by Aunt Doolittle on the simple solution to this obstacle soon made matters pellucidly clear. A Special License, a flight to Gretna—even more gothic possibilities beckoned if Ethan were to try to marry her with the connivance of his mother.

Susannah tried to dismiss these new fears as airdreaming and hysterical sensibility of the worst sort, but nothing in Ethan Doolittle's character inspired her to believe he would dislike an elopement, and nothing in his mother's made Susannah expect that Aunt Doolittle could be brought to see how unsuitable it was. She confided her fears to paper in a letter to Uncle Abner, but suspected, from Ruby's dark remarks, that it had not been sent. She was nerving herself to make a second attempt when a summons arrived for the Doolittles and their niece to dine with Mr. Abner Potter in Lower Chapman Street on Thursday next.

Chapter IV

SEPTEMBER 1818

MISS ORINDA HANFORD did not make her bow to Society in the spring of 1818.

Throughout the previous fall Mr. Soberton had dutifully presented listings—first for houses Lady Hanford considered suitable, then for houses considered possible, then for any London house at all. Hanford had rejected them every one. The Dowager complained delicately, then wept inconsolably, and then Hanford succumbed at last to Ancilla's advice to let Lady Hanford know exactly how financial matters stood. He had managed to simplify matters until even her ladyship understood them, and at the conclusion of his explanation the Dowager Lady Hanford took to her bed. Unfortunately, Ancilla removed the distinction from that particular diversion by collapsing unconscious on the stairs.

The doctor called it advanced pernicious consumption and told Hanford a number of things he already knew. Her ladyship dipped open-handedly into her own money to pay for the doctor and the apothecary and the coal fires kept burning every minute of the winter and spring in Ancilla's room—but Lady Hanford's jointure was encumbered so many quarter-days in advance as to stretch well into the next decade, and even this generous gesture could be only a temporary relief.

The Dowager spoke hopefully of the virtues to be found in presenting Orinda on a smaller stage, such as Bath. Hanford agreed politely, but he was not listening. Orinda could live without her Season, but another winter at Laceby would kill Ancilla. After his mother was gone he went up to the small corner bedroom where his cousin still spent most of her time and sat for half an hour with her.

Then Hanford went to Town to see if the entail on Laceby could be broken.

It took him the better part of a hideous and memorable day to make his way to London by public coach. The following morning he appeared in Mr. Soberton's chambers and received news that made the discomfort of the journey pale into irrelevancy.

"As you know, my lord, entailed property is not, legally speaking, your own property, but a matter of property held in trust by the present holder of the title for all future possible holders of the title. To break the entail, my lord, would require you to obtain the consent of all interested parties—that is to say, the person who might be expected to inherit if you died without issue—"

"Peveril's my heir."

"And the person who would inherit in the event Master Peveril deceased—I believe the young man's name is Athelstane?" Mr. Soberton looked rather as if he disbelieved it, but it was so entered in his documents nonetheless. "And so on until the extinction of the title. Then, these permissions having been obtained, the matter would have to be brought to law. Admittedly this is only a minor formality—"

"Get to the point," Hanford said. His head still ached from the jolting journey of the day before, and Soberton too was telling him nothing now that he had not known years ago.

"Very well. To break the entail, my lord, would take more time and money than you have, and re- alize you nothing."

"What? But you said—"

Soberton coughed delicately. "It is true that some years ago I suggested that entering upon the pro- cedure to break the entail might be a useful course of action. At that time your lordship gave me to understand that nothing could ever induce you to undertake such an infamous course."

"Some years ago, Soberton, I was an idiot. I won- der that you did not wash your hands of me the moment you saw how things stood. I see now that you were right. I'm ready to do what must be done."

"Unfortunately, my lord, due to the passage of time and the increase of debt on Laceby, dissolving the entail is no longer a course of action your lord- ship may profitably undertake. It would take years."

"And long before that Laceby would already have been sold—for debt! My grandfather ought to have died a richer man, Soberton, or—" With a great ef- fort Hanford closed his mouth firmly and said no more. "It was the last thing I could think of to do, you know," he said quietly. "And that too late."

"If your lordship will permit me to make a sug- gestion . . . ?"

Hanford laughed without humor. "By all means. I am entirely at your disposal—not to mention your mercy."

Mr. Soberton permitted himself a small smile at his lordship's jest. "Your lordship's situation is un- fortunately not unique. Yet, if I may venture to say so, other men in similar circumstance have re- paired their fortunes by advantageous marriage."

Soberton meant an heiress, of course, whose vast

dowry could meet all Hanford's financial entanglements. But no young lady of fashion, fortune, and family would be allowed to throw herself away on an impoverished mere Baron with a needy family.

No young lady of family. . . .

"A Cit." It was not a question.

Mr. Soberton winced. "My lord. As you are aware, I have had the felicity of conferring with your lordship's bankers in the small matter of some trifling consolidation measures . . ."

"There's no need to be tactful. Drummond's owns Laceby down to the last china dish—and that! for your entail," Hanford said, snapping his fingers.

"As your lordship says." Mr. Soberton accepted the rebuke in the spirit it was tendered and continued. "Mr. Coltharp says that the girl is acceptable in every particular. She has been gently brought up, respectably educated; I believe in fact she is somehow a distant relation of yours. Her mother was a Clarendon; the family stands in some relation to her ladyship, I fancy."

"Yes; one of Mother's great-aunts was a Clarendon, and—What girl?"

Mr. Soberton could not quite conceal the sensation that victory at last was near. "Miss Susannah Potter, my lord. The heiress. And, if I may say so, my lord, the answer to all your troubles."

Chapter V

NOVEMBER 1818

A SAINTLIER MAN than Abner would have seen that sudden unearned wealth would not be the making of Ethan's character. Abner Potter was not saintly, and only saw that marriage to her heedless cousin Ethan would purchase for Susannah an existence of shocking misery. And, as Susannah had already guessed, so long as Mariah Doolittle thought it was right for Susannah and Ethan to wed, Susannah would not have very much opportunity to do otherwise.

Abner was glad now that he had left the house on Lower Chapman Street partly staffed against the possibility of renting it. It had been a relatively simple matter to open it for this dinner party—the only thing simple about the entire affair. Now all was prepared, and hung upon two people—the stubborn, hot-tempered girl he had known all her life and the quiet young man he had met six days ago.

"Don't you fret yourself, my lord," Abner Potter said to his guest. "They'll be here soon enough, and you'll set eyes on that niece of mine."

Hanford kept his features schooled to an emotionless mask of courtesy and murmured some polite commonplace forgotten even as it was uttered. He had come here at Mr. Potter's invitation, and now there was no turning back. Lord Hanford of Laceby, sold like a black slave—as his mother would surely say, when she knew. And—as Peveril would say—if his ancestors were alive to see this day, they would be spinning in their graves.

Mr. Potter was more aware of his guest's mood than Hanford guessed, but indicated nothing of it in his manner. "After dinner I'll make some shift to let the two of you have a few words—not that that'll be easy, with—ah! here they are!"

Hanford rose to his feet as his host did, and a moment later he got the first sight of his future wife.

Susannah had left veil, bonnet, and black pelisse in the front hall. Entering behind the rest of her family, she did not realize for a moment that there was a stranger in the room.

He had blond hair, paler than straw, and was dressed in the height of *ton*nish fashion, from his deep-blue coat to his charcoal-colored knee-breeches. A seal-ring carved of some translucent red stone adorned his right hand, and a small gold pin steadied the folds of his immaculate cravat. Beyond that he wore no jewelry, and his face was as grave and composed as that of a man facing surgery. As she stared, some emotion seemed momentarily to transform the set of his mouth, and then he looked away again as Abner Potter began the round of introductions.

When he had agreed with Soberton to seek a marriage to the unknown Susannah Potter, Hanford had known the process would not be pleasant. He had not expected to enjoy, as he did not, the interview with Miss Potter's uncle wherein the extent of his liabilities was laid bare and the extent of the girl's expectations made known to him. In the end Hanford had known everything about her but what she looked like, and hadn't thought that could be important. He would marry her no matter what she looked like, after all. It wasn't as if he had a choice.

But even in her mourning black Abner Potter's niece had a delicacy and poise that spoke of pride and breeding, and when she swept her shy, startled gaze to his face he saw her eyes were as blue as the violets that bloomed at Laceby in the spring.

No vulgar tuft-hunter this, he thought, and, at the same moment: How could she want him? Why under heaven did a beautiful young heiress wish to buy a husband for a title that even Hanford knew was valueless? Consumed with sudden lively curiosity, Hanford bent over her hand.

"And this, Susannah, is Lord Hanford. Lord Hanford, Miss Susannah Potter."

"I am charmed to make your acquaintance, Miss Potter," Lord Hanford told her. His voice was soft, but with an edge that robbed it of hesitancy. This close she could see that his eyes were grey; they gazed down at her with a compassion that was unnerving and a puzzlement that matched her own. She could not keep from contrasting the faint light scent of his cologne with the stifling odor of her cousin's pomade.

"Lord Hanford and I are in a way of being in business together," Abner explained, "and I thought you wouldn't mind, Mariah, if I asked him to eat his dinner with us."

Mariah Doolittle was not a stupid woman, but neither was she used to subtlety in others. It was Susannah, suspicious by nature, who turned upon Lord Hanford a stricken gaze of intuition. He caught her eye and, to her astonishment, bowed ever-so-slightly in mocking acknowledgment.

Armed with her secret knowledge, dinner became an exciting meal for Susannah. She signified this by keeping her eyes fixed on her plate and responding to all conversation directed her way in monosyllables.

Her cousin Ethan was not so made.

"Oh, I dessay, my lord, that this is all very tame to you, dining with the Prince of Wales and all every night. More o' the same, eh? Well, if—" Ethan's face was flushed with wine and his neckcloth was unbecomingly askew. He regarded Lord Hanford with owl-eyed pugnaciousness.

"Ethan!" interrupted his mother. She waved the butler away from her son's wineglass, but that worthy took his orders from a higher authority, and filled it again. Ethan drained the contents at a draught and prepared to air his further opinions on the nobility.

"William, I'm sure that Abner would like to hear your views on the situation in Europe—I'm afraid I have no head for politics," she said in an apologetic aside to Abner's guest, "and make a terrible audience, but William is very clever. It is where Ethan inherits it, I believe."

"Likely you're right, Mariah," said her brother agreeably, and refused to participate further in his sister's rescue.

"Well, what I think is that they should have had that Napoleon fellow's head off and then he wouldn't be coming back from anywhere! If I'd been with Wellington, now . . ." Ethan said fiercely.

"Are you interested in a military career, Mr. Doolittle?" Hanford asked with a certain ruthless politeness.

"Now where's the use of that? There's nobody to fight—not the froggies, not the yanks—and it takes money to be a Sir Do-Nothing parading around barracks all day in a suit of gold lace! Though you—"

"Lord Hanford isn't interested in your opinions, young Ethan," William Doolittle said with ponderous decisiveness. He made it sound like a serious moral flaw in Hanford's character, and Susannah glanced up to see what effect the pronouncement had.

Lord Hanford was looking at her again, and the thoughtful expression in those wide grey eyes made her flush and return her attention to her plate.

"Now, Willie, you did always know how to stop a conversation flat," said Abner Potter cheerfully. "It might be that Lord Hanford has the keenest sort of interest in Ethan's opinions."

Every eye at the table turned expectantly toward their guest.

"I should not like to express an opinion such as to foment strife within the bosom of a family," said Hanford gently. "May I confess instead that I had hoped to induce you, Mr. Potter, to tell me what news you may have of India? With your, ah, mercantile resources, your news is undoubtedly fresher than any the Home Office is able to provide."

There had always been unrest in India, as the French fought the English behind a screen of Moghul princes, and the recent defeat of Napoleon had dimmed neither nation's empire-building ardor. Though the Indian Army, composed of English and Irish regiments seconded to its service, was universally despised as an inferior and ragtag force, no less a commander than Wellington had conducted his first campaigns under its auspices. Hanford skillfully drew his host on the exotic difficulties of doing business with so alien a culture, though as Susannah quickly realized, he could have no possible interest in the information imparted.

Finally the meal was over.

"I hope the gentlemen will not keep us too long, Aunt," Susannah said meaningfully, fixing her aunt with a brilliant and determined gaze. After a moment Mariah Doolittle's brow cleared.

"Come along then, Susannah, and leave the gentlemen to their wine—and mind you, William, that you don't tip back too deep."

Aunt Doolittle settled herself comfortably on the slick surface of a sopha upholstered in a heavy green-and-coquillot striped satin. The drawing room had also been opened for the evening, and everything swept and polished, but it was sadly bare of ornament, and Susannah knew that the other first-floor rooms would still be shrouded in dust and Holland covers.

"Really, Susannah, how you fidget!"

"I'm sorry, Aunt Doolittle." Susannah seated herself on a slender Queen Anne chair and tried to relax.

"Not that I fault you, dear. I've said for years that Abner is becoming quite odd—to introduce a business associate of his into a family party, and you not yet out of mourning.... Well, I shall have William speak to him about it! Not that you could ask for anything more pretty-behaved than this Lord Hanford, but you know, Susannah ..." Aunt Doolittle then launched into a lengthy homily about how unhappy was the marriage of every woman who ever married into the peerage—or away from it. Susannah kept her face smooth and her eyes downcast, and hoped that her aunt did not suspect that her mind was several rooms away. Business associate! Yes, she dared swear—and she the business, no doubt! With a suffocating mixture of wild hope and dread she knew that before the evening

53

was out the stranger she had met at dinner would make her an offer of marriage.

The automatic outrage she expected to feel did not come. Her circumstances were very different now from what they had been a year ago. Now she knew that there was no safety for an heiress outside of marriage; and with her father's benevolent protection gone, her choice of husband was sharply limited.

Whoever he was, Lord Hanford must be a more desirable husband than Ethan Doolittle—but how desirable was that? She was pondering the question with a far from disinterested curiosity when Abner Potter joined them.

"There you are, Sukey! It's only me; I've got a little matter of trusts and all that needs talking over, and I thought this was as good a time as any, with the wine still going around."

Aunt Doolittle stirred herself to rise, but Abner forestalled her. "No use your being bored by it, Mariah—and what would Willie do if he came in here and found both of you gone? Come along, Sukey."

Susannah, heart pounding, followed her uncle out of the room. They stopped before the closed library door and Abner turned to her.

"Now you know I don't hold with deceiving Mariah, but there's nothing settled yet and I don't see any need to rile her until we have to. This Lord Hanford's a baron with an estate somewhere up Birmingham-way; he'll marry you if you'll have him. I told Jacob I'd take care of you the best I knew how, and this is what he'd want for you himself. I've spoken to Lord Hanford—and his bankers, look you, niece—and I think you could fare farther and find worse, but it's not me as has to marry him. He's waiting in the library, but if you don't want to go in I'll take you back to your aunt and that'll be the end of it."

Susannah took a deep breath and nodded. "Thank you, Uncle Abner," she said, in what she hoped was a steady voice. She put her hand on the door.

"There's my girl, Sukey," he said. He clapped her on the back in awkward affection, and Susannah opened the door.

She closed the door quietly behind her, unable to be aware of anything save the pounding of her heart. So this is what it feels like to sell oneself, she thought numbly. It isn't so very bad. Many people's marriages are arranged for them. This is no different. And Dinah ... A little surge of realization uplifted her, and suddenly everything was better, if not all right. *Dinah shall be able to do just as she pleases!*

Susannah looked around, preparing to confront her fate. But her fate, perversely, was nowhere in sight. The library furniture was still ghostly in Holland covers, but the flames of the wall-sconces glittered brightly in their glass chimneys. A heavy silver candelabrum stood incongruously in the middle of her father's desk, the tapers only a little consumed.

"Hello?" Susannah said self-consciously. The books on the shelves behind the desk, purchased job-lot by the decorator to fill the shelves, glowed red and blue and buff and gilt against the wood.

And they should not have. Someone had been removing the veils of fine white Holland that kept them from dust and moth.

"This," came a decisive voice out of nowhere, "is an extremely fine Aretino, and why it isn't locked up is beyond me."

Susannah gave a small squeak of startlement and whirled around. The long bays at the end of the room behind her still wore their coverings, and as she watched, one of them billowed magnificently and Lord Hanford appeared.

He held a tall book bound in scarlet leather in his hands, and when he looked up his expression made it clear that he had expected to see her uncle, not her. He closed the book carefully and slipped it into the shelf.

"If I were Mr. Potter, I certainly should have done so," he added. "Think of its effect on the morals of English womanhood. Miss Potter, what brings you here? Is this my cue to say it is a pleasure unlooked-for? Or shall I simply apologize for making myself at home in your library? It is a fine collection; I see by the bookplates that some of the volumes come from the Duke of Owlsthorne's library, and he was a notable collector. It is a pity his library was broken up to be sold. But you will not have come to talk of books," said Hanford, changing the subject abruptly. "Tell me, Miss Potter. What has your uncle said to you?"

"He said—He said you were from Warwickshire." She could feel herself blushing and was powerless to stop it. She turned her back to him and stared into the unwinking flames of the candles.

There was a rustle behind her as Hanford removed the cover from the sopha. "My," he said non-committally, at the multicolor brocade thus revealed. It had been imported from China to fill a special order, but the customer had refused delivery after seeing it in all its more-than-oriental splendor; the thrifty Jacob Potter had ordered the library sophas recovered in it.

Susannah turned around. "I am very fond of that particular pattern," she said argumentatively, but Lord Hanford was not drawn to that lure.

"Then, Miss Potter, you will have no objection to disposing yourself on it. It is obvious we are intended to converse."

She had expected him to sit beside her, but instead he unveiled one of the side chairs and drew it forward as Susannah spread her black skirts against the gaudy embroidered pattern of dragons and phoenixes.

"It is very awkward being thrown together in such a situation, but we must do our best to keep it from being too difficult," Hanford went on smoothly. "Your uncle has told me a little about you. You are nineteen, are you not?"

"Yes. Today." Until that moment Susannah had forgotten it was her birthday. She looked back at Hanford in surprise and chagrin.

"And I am to be your present—if you care to unwrap me. How charming." He saw the expression on her face and stopped, and when he spoke again it was in a different tone.

"I beg your pardon. I know it is unreasonable to expect you to repose your confidence in a stranger, Miss Potter, but let me assure you ... If you are being in any way coerced into this transaction— There have been no promises exchanged as yet. It would be a simple matter for me to withdraw."

"Oh, no," said Susannah, too quickly. Hanford looked at her quizzically. "I mean ... You do not wish to withdraw, do you?" she added.

Hanford smiled without warmth and leaned forward. "I am for sale," he said. "Along with my family name, my title, and a moldering family seat of exquisite antiquity—mortgaged, of course."

"Oh, I know that. I am not entirely ignorant of the customs of the nobility," Susannah interrupted with a twinge of malice.

"Then nothing more need be said on that head," Hanford finished firmly, "except that I will make no offer of my person and my title to an unwilling female. You have beauty enough and dowry to marry as you choose. Why should you wish this particular match?"

The gallantry and pride that made him present himself in the worst possible light to a woman he needed desperately to marry was lost on Susannah, but she did see that if he spoke so glibly of these things it would not be so very wrong for her to be honest too.

"I don't wish it. What I mean is, I must marry someone, and my uncle thinks it should be you—or someone like you. It hardly matters—my mother was a Clarendon, you see, and—"

The garbled explanation that followed would have made no sense even to a member of her own family, much less to a stranger, but Lord Hanford had guessed from meeting the Doolittles, as Abner had meant him to, that he was to serve as a rival to Ethan Doolittle for Susannah's hand in marriage.

"And so you must marry. Very well. But why purchase a husband?"

"For the title, of course," said Susannah bitterly. "The *ton* doesn't marry Cit's daughters, and everyone says I must have horses, and carriages, and parties, and all the elegancies of life! Just as Mama would have wished—but she wouldn't!"

"Then perhaps—" began Hanford, but Susannah was too overwrought to listen.

"Oh, you don't understand! How could you—you have always had and done everything you ever wanted. How can you possibly imagine what it is to be forced to do something you don't want to, just because you can't see anything else to do? I have a sister and I must take care of her somehow, and—"

She turned away, glaring fiercely at the opposite wall to keep from dissolving into tears.

"Susannah." She had not made him free of her name; his use of it made her turn back to him. His mouth was sharply drawn, but when he spoke, his voice was level. "It is terrible to be forced to something out of desperation. Listen to me. If you need a husband, and want a title, have your uncle procure you a chaperone who knows how these things are done. It is not difficult. My mother, I believe, will know the names of some ladies who oblige. You

58

can have a Season, and undoubtedly you can do far better for yourself than a mere baron. Money is a great leveler; you might even become a duchess—it has been done."

Susannah thought of what Aunt Doolittle would say if she suggested that she should make her debut to the *haut ton*. And to what purpose? No one she met in Society would think of her—they would speak of love and think of her dowry. At least Lord Hanford was honest about what he wanted from her.

"And what about you?" Susannah asked, her tears forgotten.

"Undoubtedly I shall contrive something."

What it was to be, he could not imagine. Far easier to have gone through with the thing in cold blood, but the chit had made that impossible. Damn her for blue eyes and black curls and a vulnerable beseeching softness about her pretty mouth. And damn him for caring about such things when his own family were counting on him to save them.

"Are you very badly dipped?" Susannah said suddenly.

"Dipped?" Hanford regarded his nails. "Yes, quite badly, I'm afraid. But that hardly concerns you, now. Leave the matter to me; I shall tell your uncle that you were everything acquiescent but that we will not suit." He smiled a little crookedly and held out his handkerchief. "Here. Dry your eyes. Mr. Potter will not like to see that I have made you cry."

"You haven't," Susannah said gruffly, but she took the white lawn square and scrubbed at her eyes. Lord Hanford's barbed kindness comforted her as nothing had done in the long months since her father's death. "You don't understand," she said finally. "About the Season, I mean. There isn't any point to it, Lord Hanford. It wouldn't do me any good."

"Then should I continue to parade my advantages with loverlike ardor? Your uncle should not have left you to this, you know; it is cruel." He settled himself on the side chair as if preparing to make a greater effort than heretofore. "You do not know me, Miss Potter, so my character can be no inducement—and am I correct to understand that you do not care for my kind, or for velvet robes and ermine, jewels, champagne, and a court presentation—all of which, as my wife, you would have?"

Susannah shook her head.

"That is unfortunate." Hanford took her hand and held it firmly. "Then I will say this. Your uncle has selected me as an eligible suitor for you. Marry me and give yourself into my care, and your sister, at least, shall be free to marry as she wishes."

The words were so close to what she had comforted herself with that she stared at him for an agonized moment as if she suspected him of sorcery.

Hanford's face was politely expressionless as he waited for her answer. Susannah swallowed hard several times and when she spoke at last it was in a voice she hardly recognized as her own.

"Since you are in need of money, I imagine you will wish the wedding to be soon."

A light she had not known was there until it vanished died out of Hanford's eyes. "Quite soon, yes. You are still in mourning, so I am afraid it will cause a bit of a scandal; but we will contrive. Am I to understand, Miss Potter, that you are doing me the immeasurable honor of accepting my proposal?"

"Oh, yes," said Susannah bleakly. "I shall marry you, Lord Hanford."

PART II

And the Ill-Bred Bride

Chapter VI

FEBRUARY 1819

FRAMED BY THE chinchilla lining of her blue velvet traveling hood, his new bride's face possessed a childlike gravity. Hanford watched her sleep, lulled by the rocking motion of the excellent suspension of the most vulgar traveling coach he had ever seen. He had had, however, some time to get used to it. He had been married six weeks today.

The wedding arrangements had gone off smoothly—his mother had wept throughout the ceremony, then returned to Laceby to make things ready for his return. From there she would convey Ancilla to Italy, to reside in a warm villa by a sunlit sea . . . paid for, lock and stock, by Hanford's wife's money.

Hanford, in turn, had taken his wife not to Bath, or any of the other fashionable winter resorts of the *ton*, but to a borrowed hunting box near Kettering. If Susannah found her cloistered honeymoon disagreeable, she did not say so, and gradually Hanford's unease at the mésalliance he had made faded. Susannah was beautiful, and charming, and pretty-behaved, and as his confidence that she would not disgrace the consequence of the Barons Hanford grew, so did his desire to see her in her proper setting.

The coach pulled to a stop, and Susannah's eyelids fluttered. "Are we there yet?" she asked, straightening on the bench seat.

"We are somewhere, at any rate. I wonder where?" Hanford answered. He lowered the shade and looked out the coach window, but enlightenment was not forthcoming. Between the early darkness of a grey winter afternoon and the snow that had been blowing fitfully all day, nothing in particular could be seen through the misty isinglass panes.

At that moment the view was further obscured by the coachman, dismounting from the box to tap at his master's door.

"The lodge gates are locked, sir," he said with a patent air of revelation.

"Well, get them open!" Hanford said sharply, and closed the window again. He was eager to show off Laceby to Susannah and did not waste time wondering about minor mysteries.

"We are at the lodge gates. It will not be so very long now."

Susannah Elizabeth Potter Hanford, Lady Hanford, dug her hands deeper into her capacious chinchilla muff.

"I am sure Willoughby will be glad to get before a warm fire," she said, looking out at the scudding snow, "and so will I!"

Scraps of shouts wafted to the coach's occupants through the snow, and then the booming sound of the gate being flung open. After a further short delay, the coach lurched out of its frozen muddy rut and began to move forward again.

"Tired, my dear?" asked Hanford, tucking the coachrug more securely about her. Even with rugs and warming bricks, the interior of the coach could not by any stretch of the imagination be called warm.

"Oh, a little," Susannah said hesitantly. She glanced up at her husband from beneath demurely-lowered lashes. How strange a thing marriage was;

that in less than two months the anonymous titled dragon of her dreading imagination had been revealed as a quiet man—rather shy, perhaps, but unfailingly courteous—and not an arrogant spendthrift monster at all. He had spoken very little of Laceby, but when he had it was in such a way as she hoped he would someday speak of her. In her mind's eye she had already seen Hanford's home: the high painted ceilings; the glowing paneled walls; the furniture bright with beeswax and lemon; the warmth of the fire leaping importunately on the hearth, throwing bright shadows on the rich Turkey carpets and the kickshaws of silver and porcelain. A beautiful and dignified house.

After another half hour the coach pulled to a stop again. There was a pause, during which Hanford's expression went from carefully blank to thunderous. With an oath no less vehement for its silence, he snatched up his new beaver hat and flung open the carriage door.

"What is it now?" he shouted against the wind.

"Begging your pardon, sir, but—" Susannah heard before the coach door slammed behind him.

Susannah thrust the door open again. Managing her skirts and pelisse carefully, she negotiated the long step to the ground and looked around.

The coach was in the courtyard of a great house. The wan glare of the coachlamps did little to illuminate the scene, but ahead she could see a dark blur that was her husband's greatcape, and as she approached, Hanford turned around.

"Susannah! Well—never mind," he said to the coachman. He waved the man off—hesitantly, Susannah thought—and put his arm around her shoulders. "Come along, my dear—we shall soon be inside."

"Here?" Susannah said before she could stop herself. The walls of dark and lightless windows that reared up before her held nothing of welcome—or, indeed, of habitation. Hanford's arm tightened around her shoulders.

There was no butler waiting to open the door, and Hanford hammered with the knocker until Susannah could hear its echoes even above the wail of the wind. Just as she was certain her nose had frozen quite off, the door began to ease inward. Hanford, without ceremony, thrust her inside.

"But my lord— We had no word—" An elderly woman in the severe grey bombazine of an upper servant held a lamp high above her head and peered anxiously at him.

"That's not surprising; I didn't send any. But look here, Danvers, Mama must have—"

Susannah lost interest in the conversation in the face of her first opportunity to see Laceby. She took a few steps more into the house.

Instead of lemon oil and dried roses she smelled the suspicious sweetness of damp-rot and mildew. The paneling in the hallway was dim and dull with neglect, and she would be willing to swear that the tessellated marble beneath her feet had not been scrubbed in her lifetime. Nowhere was there any sign of light, or life, or welcome.

This was Lord Hanford's beloved Laceby? This ruin?

"Do you tell me," Hanford went on to the housekeeper behind her, "that Mama—"

"Lord Hanford," Susannah said, turning around, "are you sure this is the right house?"

She'd meant it for a joke, but one look at his face told her it had fallen dismally flat.

"This is Laceby," he said in deadly even tones. "Welcome home, Lady Hanford."

In moments Susannah was basking before a fire in one of the small front parlors. Branches of candles illuminated the room, and a cheering pot of tea stood steaming on a table. Her wet pelisse had been taken away, and Mrs. Danvers, the housekeeper, was even now scurrying about airing sheets, lighting fires, and attempting to bring some semblance of order to a homecoming that currently bore all the hallmarks of a particularly disorganized brand of chaos. Lord Hanford was nowhere to be seen.

Susannah held her hands out to the fire, squirming inwardly. Once more her tongue had run away with her common sense, and look what had come of it. It was only that she'd been so surprised to—

To see Laceby as it was? But Lord Hanford had told her before he married her that there was no money. Susannah shook her head, dissatisfied. Money or none, the house might at least have been ready for them. She flexed stiff fingers, glad of the returning warmth.

"Oh, hoity-toity miss," the sudden remembrance of her father's words made her smile, then look thoughtful. Since when did she, Miss Susannah Potter of Lower Chapman Street, expect to be waited on hand and foot? Obviously the house was not ready, but did that mean she had to sit lapped in velvet until it was? Lord Hanford was her husband, after all. She should be taking care of him, not the reverse.

It took her quite some time to find the kitchen. She had never been in a country house before, and wandered forlornly through parlors and galleries and withdrawing rooms before at last she stumbled upon it.

Here, at least, there was warmth. Tallow dips smoked and sputtered in glass chimneys, and the banked coals of the looming iron stove shone like red eyes in the shadows.

Then one of the shadows moved. Susannah squeaked, and the chamberstick in her hand jerked violently.

"Miss! Are you all right? Begging your pardon, your la'ship, but I didn't have a mind to scare you—" The shadows resolved themselves into the form of Willoughby the coachman.

"I beg your pardon, I'm sure, Willoughby; but Lord Hanford will be wanting his dinner. Is Cook here?"

"Gone," said Willoughby with elemental simplicity.

"Gone? In this weather? Gone where?"

"To the village, your la'ship. Lady Hanford—which is to say, ma'am, the other Lady Hanford—"

"The Dowager Lady Hanford; yes. Go on," said Susannah with mounting worry.

"—said that she might be off, and welcome to her—at least so Buckthorn said; he's the groom of the stables. She's been gone these two months, he said."

"But—" said Susannah, gesturing helplessly around the kitchen. "Surely someone has been here? Who has been cooking for the servants?"

"Mrs. Danvers, she's been in the way of obliging with a bit of the cooking, seeing as it's only Danvers, who's by way of being the gardener, and then Buckthorn, he that lives over the stables . . ." Willoughby's recitation faded into silence.

"Three servants? For a house this size?"

"Well, ma'am, it was Buckthorn as said as the other Lady Hanford—she took Mr. Peacock and the rest."

Mr. Peacock, Susannah decided tentatively, would be the butler. Surely the Dowager Lady Hanford could not have taken all the servants? She pulled herself together with the realization that that hardly mattered now, and set her mind to the present task.

* * *

Having installed his wife in a parlor and left the housekeeper to her own devices, Lord Hanford of Laceby had gone off to his library.

Here things were just as he had left them upon going up to town. Laceby had not been closed; there were no Holland covers over anything. It was just as if Laceby had been . . . abandoned.

He lit the candles and then lit the fire laid ready in the grate. It caught quickly, spreading warmth and offering companionship of a sort. Hanford poured himself a stiff dose of brandy from the decanter on the sideboard and tried to blot out the memory of his wife's face. But he could not be ashamed of Laceby, and that left him only one alternative.

Hanford flung his glass into the flames.

The bright sound shocked and shamed him. He thought of his great-grandfather, Christian, going laughing to the noose on Tower Hill: silk, it was, for gentlemen—and for traitors. *He* had made his choice and not sniveled when it had turned hard. Hanford too had made a bargain: he had married a Cit for her money. And having done so, it was ill done to mock her for being what she was. Susannah was his wife, and he owed her his duty. He had done his duty all his life; he would not stop now.

It seemed then that the library at Laceby was filled with ghosts: Averil and Christian; Roger and William; Adeluin and Ranalf and Makepeace; cavaliers, pirates, courtiers, and traitors—Hanfords back to England's dawn who had fought for and died for and gambled the land on which Laceby stood, knowing that there were always sons to carry the name forward. There would always be Hanfords, just as there would always be Laceby and an England to hold it.

The vision gave him strength, just as it always had: the infinite chain of Lords Hanford in which he was only a link. His father came before him and his son would follow him, and one day he would hold his grandson in his arms. And in that hour, could he but reach it, all his present pain would be no more real than the cockled silks in the paintings that hung on Laceby's walls.

But when Hanford went to find his wife and reassure her, and give dutiful attention to her comfort, he could not find her. The parlor was cozy and warm—and empty.

He wrenched a single taper from its sconce and went searching. In the bedroom he had occupied for nearly ten years he found Mrs. Danvers and Susannah's maid Ruby, setting everything to rights. A steaming can of water hung over the fire on its hook—the house was very old, and had certain conveniences—and Hanford thought lovingly of a hot bath.

Mrs. Danvers looked up guiltily as he entered. He knew instantly that something was wrong, and could not imagine why she had not come to him with it.

"Lady Hanford is not in the Blue Parlor. Do you know where she is?"

Mrs. Danvers smoothed her hands over her apron before she answered, and it struck him that she was not so much guilty as embarrassed. He looked and saw the identical expression on Ruby's face.

"Run along, girl, and unpack her ladyship's things," said Mrs. Danvers firmly. "My lord, Mr. Rakestraw had your things laid out, if you'd care to have a bit of a wash and change for dinner."

Had Susannah run off? Had she abused his servants? Broken something? He could not begin to imagine what she had done to account for his housekeeper's unease—and, irrationally, he blamed her for it.

"Mrs. Danvers," he said, and took a deep breath. "Where is Lady Hanford?"

"In the kitchen, my lord," said the housekeeper miserably. "Cooking."

* * *

The twenty-ninth Baron Hanford of Laceby would no more have dreamed of entering his own kitchen than he would have of shoeing his own horses. It was not quite true that he had to be shown where it was—he had been home from Eton the day the new stove had been delivered and had taken the keenest delight in overseeing its installation. But from that day to this he had not set foot inside the room that housed it. Whatever good effect on his temper the savory smells of baking and roasting that filled the air might have had were entirely negated by the sight of his wife—Lady Hanford—standing in the middle of it, peeling apples. Her sleeves were pushed back and there was a smut of flour on her nose.

"What do you think you're doing?" he demanded. Mrs. Danvers' presence behind him reminded him that everything they did here now would be known to every servant in the house in hours and every person in the village in days.

"I trust you are fond of chicken, Hanford," Susannah said carefully, "and will be satisfied with a simple meal, but I think we can contrive to be quite comfortable. I hope you will forgive my ordering your valet about, but I sent him down to the cellar, and—"

Hanford desperately reminded himself again of Mrs. Danvers' watching presence. "I think you have done quite enough. Come along, Susannah, and let us leave Mrs. Danvers to her duties."

"But I was doing that very thing, my lord. Mrs. Danvers, as you will recall, is your housekeeper and has more than enough to do without finding dinner for us. Since your cook has been sent back to Lewesby, I—"

"I do not care to have my wife slaving like a common scullion!" snapped Hanford, losing his inward battle.

"I suppose you would rather starve?" asked his wife. She reached for the carving knife at her hand and began determinedly to mince.

It was not, Susannah told herself, that she expected him to be delighted at finding her cooking in the kitchen, but to stare at her as if she had spontaneously reverted to some lower form of life was more than she felt she deserved.

"Mrs. Danvers, please be so good as to do what you can here. Lady Hanford is tired."

"Yes, my lord," said Mrs. Danvers, dropping a palliative curtsey. Hanford walked quickly over to his wife and took the knife from her hand. Before she could voice a coherent protest, he had gripped her firmly by the arm and swept her from the kitchen.

The door closed behind Lord and Lady Hanford. Mrs. Danvers, her mouth folded into a tight line of compressed pity, picked up the knife and began to slice the apples Susannah had peeled.

"Understand this," said Lord Hanford, his face very close to hers. "You will not flaunt your lowborn origins in this house. Do you hear me? You will not make mock of our servants. You will comport yourself with dignity—"

All the powerless anger he had felt through the last three months boiled over. He had made the ultimate sacrifice and was not to be allowed even the illusion of graciousness.

"Hanford, you are hurting me!" Susannah struggled in her husband's bruising grip. This icy fury was something utterly outside her experience; it terrified her even as she seethed with the injustice of it.

"I beg your pardon, Lady Hanford. I hope you

will forgive me, and I trust that in future you will be so good as to leave the servants' tasks to the servants. You will only confuse them otherwise."

But perhaps the self-control that allowed him to turn to her a face from which any vestige of strong emotion had been disciplined frightened her more. Something here had gone more horribly wrong than a roast chicken and apple tart could account for. Some battle Susannah had not known she must fight was being lost, and she didn't know what to do.

"Hanford, please! Let me explain—there was no one else to do it, you see—and I am sure that whatever Mrs. Danvers was doing was at least as important. I can cook, a little—Papa always said that one cannot manage servants if one does not know their tasks—your servants are gone, Willoughby told me—Mrs. Danvers could not do everything—and I thought . . ." The words died in her throat. She was babbling, and her husband was watching her with the polite disinterest he might accord an exotic zoological specimen.

"It has been a long day, Susannah, and you are tired. Ruby will have your things laid out so that you may change. Come upstairs."

Lord Hanford of Laceby looked at his beautiful unsuitable wife and did not know that she shared his frightening feeling of loss. But he did know that whatever there was of unhappiness in this house was his responsibility, and his alone.

"Come, Susannah," he said more gently. "It is warmer upstairs."

Between rising from bed the next morning and rising from breakfast Susannah was presented with a number of interesting pieces of information. She found that the reason Laceby was so cold was that there was no coal to heat it, that it was mysteriously unlikely she could engage servants in the nearby village of Lewesby, and that Lord Hanford had gone riding. She also discovered that in the cold clear light of day Laceby looked even more dreadfully shabby than it had seemed by candle-light. She rallied her spirits with the thought of what Adelaide Featherton from Miss Farthingale's Female Seminary would have done in this same situation (had Spasms), and congratulated herself that the management of even a household in such extremity was something she could handle.

She then spent an unpleasant morning with Mrs. Danvers. Neither woman alluded to the events of the evening before, but it was forcibly brought home to Susannah that she could have done nothing better calculated to undermine her position at Laceby than enter the kitchen and take on duties so far beneath her present exalted position. That members of her own class would have been equally outraged to find the daughter of a respectable London clothmerchant up to her elbows in peelings was something she doubted Mrs. Danvers knew or cared about.

"If you will just give me the keys, Mrs. Danvers, and find me the household accounts, I shall go over them this evening. Tomorrow I will see to the silver in the morning, and then you and I will go over the linens and towels in the afternoon." Susannah outlined her plans briskly, steeling herself against the housekeeper's outrage. Hanford had said nothing about his mother removing to the Dower House when she returned from Italy; if it was in any state similar to Laceby Susannah could see why she would not wish to. But it did mean that Susannah must not allow the servants to cow or bully her while she was sole mistress here—it would be bad enough when their former mistress returned.

"You must let me know what is needed for Laceby, Mrs. Danvers, and I shall do my best to get it for you. Certainly none of the servants the Dowager Lady Hanford"—she got past the unfamiliar jaw-breaking title of Lord Hanford's mother without a bobble—"has taken with her will be turned out of his place, but you must have help now to set Laceby to rights."

"As you say, Lady Hanford."

Susannah set her jaw and forced a determined smile, foreseeing nothing but a drawn-out campaign of petty grinding fights. She thought longingly of her own Mrs. Chatley and Lower Chapman Street, but turning the Laceby servants out into the snow was no way to endear herself to them.

"Now, if you would, please send Mr. Danvers to the stable to ask Buckthorn if there is a gig of some sort. I intend to drive into Lewesby and see if Mrs. Collins can be persuaded to return to us."

"Lady Hanford always used to take the carriage, when she paid calls."

Susannah smiled until her teeth hurt. "And perhaps I shall also, when I am paying calls. But today I would prefer to drive. It is so much more relaxing." Not only that, but with only Ruby accompanying her, there would be that much less opportunity for gossip.

Apparently there was a gig in the stables, as no one came to tell her there was not. She dressed in her warmest clothes and told Ruby to do likewise, and tucked her purse firmly into her muff, and went downstairs.

Rakestraw was waiting in the hall to open the door for her, an expression of ill-done-by-ness on his face.

Of course Lord Hanford's valet should not be opening the door. That was for the butler, or the upper footman—or the housekeeper, providing she wasn't in the kitchen getting lunch. But nothing at all at Laceby was as it ought to be.

Yet.

Rakestraw opened the door, and she saw a man who could be none other than Buckthorn, the groom, standing at the head of a most peculiar animal.

"Oh, Miss," wailed Ruby in town-bred accents, "whatever in the world is that?"

It was a horse. It had to be a horse, Susannah told herself wildly, because it was hitched to a gig. No one in his right mind would hitch a bull to a gig.

The animal standing between the shafts, head hanging disconsolately, was actually more of a pony than a horse. It was black, with a thick shaggy winter coat. Its mane and tail, luxuriant and unpulled, hung down; the one obscuring its eyes, the other trailing on the flags. It was nearly as broad as it was high, and that, combined with its color, made it resemble nothing so much as a Black Angus bull.

"Afternoon, your la'ship." Buckthorn doffed his cap in a spasm of civility. "This 'ere's Jupiter, as used to be Master Peveril's pony. He'll do for to draw a trap, and Danvers, he said as you were wishful to drive."

"Miss!" said Ruby more urgently.

"Oh, do be quiet, Ruby," Susannah said firmly. She advanced on the pony. "Surely you have seen a horse before."

"Ee's quite gentle, your la'ship."

"Yes, I'm sure he is. Nice Jupiter," Susannah said hopefully, tousling one muscular ear. There was no reaction. Except for the furry sides heaving in and out and his breath smoking on the air, the pony might have been dead.

"Come along, Ruby," said Susannah with more

assurance than she felt, "I don't want to be out after dark."

The pony trap was just big enough to hold her and Ruby, with a space behind the seat for parcels, or Susannah might have quailed at the last moment and asked for Willoughby to drive her. But after her morning's interview with Mrs. Danvers, she had no intention of allowing anyone at Laceby the slightest opportunity to say that Susannah Potter could not make up her mind.

She seated herself carefully in the trap, waited for Ruby to perch nervously beside her, and picked up the reins.

As soon as he felt the tug on the bit, Jupiter underwent a startling transformation. The shaggy, stolid head came up, the furry ears came forward, and the pony started off at a brisk purposeful trot. The trap bounced on the bare patches and ruts of the drive, and Susannah made a mental note to see about the delivery of a load of gravel some time in April. As they swept past the posts at the end of the drive she was just congratulating herself on her excellent driving, all things considered, when Jupiter took the left fork in the road instead of the right.

Susannah dragged back on the reins until her shoulders ached, but she might have been pulling at the mouth of a wooden hobbyhorse for all the impression she made. Jupiter would neither stop nor turn, and headed farther from Lewesby with every purposeful stride.

"Oh, dear," muttered Susannah under her breath. Perhaps this was Buckthorn's idea of a joke. In which case, he would undoubtedly ride after them eventually to lead Jupiter home, and it would be very poor tact on her part to offer him a show of hysterics when he arrived. Until then, she supposed, she must enjoy the drive, although it was not the sort of day she would have chosen to drive for pleasure.

The time had passed that the joke could be considered even remotely funny, and Buckthorn had not appeared. It was fortunate indeed, Susannah thought to herself, that Ruby had no idea where Lewesby was, and could not know that it did not seem to be their destination.

After a while the churchyard, then the church, then the vicarage appeared. A Mr. Matthew Goodchild had the living here, Susannah remembered. She thought of calling out for help, but before she could, Jupiter swerved into the driveway, pulled up before the vicarage door, and stopped. The door opened, and a grey-headed, bespectacled face appeared.

"Ah! I thought I recognized Jupiter," said Mr. Goodchild with satisfaction. He peered closer. "For a moment I thought you might be Miss Ancilla, but now I perceive that I am honored with a visit from the new Lady Hanford."

Susannah scrambled quickly down from her seat, less concerned with her dignity than with the thought that Jupiter might take it into his head to move again.

"Yes. I mean," Susannah said, gesturing toward the pony. "I did not intend to come here, at least not today, but—"

"But our Jupiter has been playing off his tricks again," Mr. Goodchild finished for her. "I hope he has not inconvenienced you too much, Lady Hanford—but what a zany you will think me, keeping you standing out in the cold! Do come in—is that your abigail with you?—and Mrs. Goodchild shall give you a nice hot cup of tea."

* * *

"Occasionally, you see, Lady Hanford, Jupiter will take a notion, and then there is no holding him. I would not call it bolting, precisely, and he always goes somewhere particular. We have had good reason to be thankful for his notions; once when young Master Peveril was even younger he took a notion to be riding out with the Meet—of course, this was after the old Lord Hanford's time, and they do not keep a pack at Laceby now, so young Peveril—" Mr. Goodchild brought the story to its expected close— that Jupiter, not wishing to rise in the middle of the night and travel to Market Arden, had deposited the twelve-year-old Peveril Hanford at the vicarage instead.

Susannah sipped at her tea and looked about the room. Religion was not notorious as a well-paid profession, and like all happy marriages, that of the Goodchilds was blessed with a profusion of offspring. Still, though their circumstances must be direly strait, the parlor in which Susannah sat drinking tea before an appreciative audience had a warmth to it that the equally impoverished Laceby lacked.

"But I daresay I am boring you with old family stories that can be of no interest to you. Do tell me, dear Lady Hanford, where it was you intended to go when you set out. I imagine Jupiter will be willing to take you there now."

"Thank you, Mr. Goodchild. I was hoping to reach Lewesby; but perhaps Jupiter was right in bringing me here first." She chose her next words with care; it would not do for the Goodchilds to think she was complaining of her new mother-in-law. "There was some silly cross-up in the mails that I do not precisely understand"—that was vague, and safe enough—"but they were not expecting us at Laceby until much later." Perhaps never, Susannah thought darkly. "So everything is at sixes and sev-

79

ens—Peacock has gone with the rest of the family, of course, and Mrs. Danvers tells me that Mrs. Collins was let go—"

"Let Jenny go!" exclaimed Mrs. Goodchild. "Whatever for?"

"I thought that Mrs. Danvers might be mistaken," lied Susannah, "And as I'm certain that the Dowager intended to be back from Italy in time to open Laceby for us"—Susannah took an encouraging breath and let her flight of fancy swoop for the finishing post—"I should like to have everything in train just as she would have when she returns."

"Let Jenny go!" repeated Mrs. Goodchild, loath to abandon this point of interest. "Why, she could not have meant to, Lady Hanford—why, Jenny Collins has been at Laceby since she was a girl. She has the most heavenly hand—you will excuse me for saying so, Mr. Goodchild, I am sure—with cakes and suchlike, and her macaroons . . ."

"I hope, then, that you will come to dinner at Laceby as soon as she is back," said Susannah decisively. "And now, if you will give me her direction in the village, I shall be on my way."

"I can do better than that, Lady Hanford," said Mrs. Goodchild. "If you like, David can take Jupiter and your maid back to Laceby, and you and I shall go into the village to bring Jenny back."

"—we were so glad to hear that Lady Hanford—I beg your pardon, Lady Hanford; we must all learn to call her the Dowager now, I'm sure—had finally taken Miss Ancilla abroad. I vow, after that turn she had last—was it November? I'm certain Mr. Goodchild would know; it is a pity we cannot ask him—and Dr. Oglevy sent for all the way from Deeping, none of us thought she would survive the winter."

Susannah untwisted the meaning of Mrs. Goodchild's speech from her numerous interpolations with only a little difficulty.

"Ancilla?" she said. "But I understood that Lord Hanford's sister was named Orinda—no one told me she had been ill."

"Bless you, child—oh, I do beg your pardon, your ladyship, I'm sure—but Miss Orinda is sound as a drum and always has been. Miss Ancilla is the present Lord Hanford's cousin; his uncle's daughter. Lord Hanford used to bring her with him when he called upon Mr. Goodchild, which is how we came to know her. He was so fond of her! But she has always been frail, poor thing."

Susannah took a moment to be thankful that David Goodchild had experienced no difficulty in turning Jupiter's head toward home and that his brother Jonathan now drove Susannah and his mother in the direction of Lewesby in the Goodchild trap. If she had been driving she would undoubtedly have put the gig in the ditch.

"I did not know Lord Hanford had a cousin," she said carefully. "He has never mentioned her—and I did not see her at our wedding."

But old Mrs. Goodchild was far too shrewd to be drawn to such a lure. "I daresay that he would have spoken of her in time. Poor chick! It is not likely Miss Ancilla will be returning to Laceby in her lifetime."

The conversation then turned upon the wonders of Lewesby-town, but in Susannah's heart the damage had already been done. Ancilla! The very name conjured up a vision of all that Susannah would like to be and wasn't: tall and stately and blonde. Did Hanford love her? Would he have married her if he had not needed to marry instead for money?

Had he in fact made such a hurried marriage precisely because his cousin had needed the medical attentions that only a great deal of money could buy? She recalled her own voice as from another lifetime, coolly supposing Hanford would wish their wedding to be soon, and his agreement. Why—if not for Ancilla's sake?

"Ah, here we are. Jonathan! Pull up at the Collinses!"

Jane Collins had been born and bred up in the village of Lewesby. At fourteen she had gone to Laceby as a kitchen maid, and when, some years later, the Hanfords' very superior man-cook departed in a flurry of vitriolic French (with most of the teaspoons in lieu of unpaid wages), she had become cook to the family.

Now she sat, stolid and rosy-faced, in her daughter-in-law's parlor while Susannah sat secretly wringing her hands within her muff and Mrs. Collins' son waxed as voluble as that long-ago Frenchman.

"Well, it's by way of being this way, your ladyship," said Mr. Collins for the uncounted time, "when a person has rights, and is by way of deserving a certain consideration, when a person's rights aren't looked to, then that person's got to look to them, is what I say."

And so he had said, several times, and it made no more sense to Susannah this time than it had the last.

"Hiram Collins!" said Mrs. Goodchild. "You aren't going to stand there and tell me that Jenny won't go back?"

"Turned me off, her did." Mrs. Collins spoke on her own behalf for the first time. "Said things'd be after changing up on the hill and she had no more need o' my 'country messes'—her called them!"

The hill, Susannah knew by now, was what the locals called Laceby, though as far as she could tell the land there was no hillier than anywhere else.

82

"Promised Mam a bit o' paper, her said," Mr. Collins began again. "A good character, her said. And what I says to that is, what's a bit o' paper, when a person has rights, and is by way of deserving a certain consideration—"

"But surely, Mrs. Collins, the Dowager Lady Hanford meant only that she would not need you at Lewesby while it was closed?" Susannah said.

Mother and son regarded her with an identical expression of peasant shrewdness, and Susannah knew with a sinking heart that not only was this not the case, it was going to take more guile than she thought she possessed to soothe Mrs. Collins' feelings and win her back.

"What her said—"

"But, Jenny, whyever didn't you come to me at once? You must have misunderstood the Dowager," said Mrs. Goodchild firmly. She darted Susannah a baffled glance, but Susannah would not have enlightened her if she could.

"What her said was—" Mrs. Collins began again.

"And what I say is," interrupted Susannah briskly, "is that I wish you to come back to Laceby as cook, Mrs. Collins. Plain country cooking will suit us admirably, and I have heard wonderful praise of your baking. If you will come, perhaps you will also know of some village girls who wish to go into service. There is a good deal of work to be done at Laceby."

There was a short pause. "Be'nt no Hanford," said Mr. Collins sardonically, and was frowned to silence by his mother.

"My father was Mr. Jacob Potter, of Brooks and Potter of the City of London. I am Lord Hanford's wife, and so it is my responsibility to manage Laceby as comfortably and efficiently as I can. If you do not wish to return to Laceby I shall quite understand, but I would like to have your answer at once." Many times the child Susannah had listened to her father engaged in the business of trade, but there was no one here to tell her how much she sounded like him at this moment.

"Ea! Molly!" Mr. Collins shouted into the other room, and a small cheerful woman entered from the kitchen, wiping her floury hands on her apron.

"Weren't it Rubin's eldest boy Jem as went up Birmingham-way to work in the mills? Here's her new ladyship, and own daughter to Jacob Potter as owns them!"

"No!" said Molly Collins, vastly impressed and only belatedly remembering her curtsey. "Lady Hanford, now, imagine! Do put by your things and set—can I get you some tea? And there's new scones, hot as hot out of the oven." She regarded their guest hopefully.

"Thank you; that would be very kind."

"Rich as might be, Mr. Jacob Potter were," Mr. Collins said lovingly. "And Jem said 'sound as a dollar, an' paid his bills cash on the nailhead, did Mr. Potter.'" A look passed between mother and son that Susannah could not interpret—and did not think she wanted to.

"That's no business of yours, Hiram, nor will be. And if her wants to pay what her old ladyship is after owing me and ask me back to the hill, then there's no business of your'n either."

Light dawned, and Susannah suddenly understood all the talk of rights and consideration.

"Of course I shall pay you any wages you are owed, Mrs. Collins. I am sure that is what the Dowager meant me to do."

Which, Susannah reflected grimly, was not as far from the truth as she might like.

Lord Hanford rose quite early that morning. The sun had not yet cleared the trees of the Park and the hoarfrost still glistened on the hummocks of un-scythed grass. The house was silent, having too few servants to make it bustle even when they were about their duties. He lingered for a while in his library, but today his retreat held no power to be-guile him. After half an hour's indecision he changed his clothes for riding.

Except for the coach horses he and Susannah had brought with them the stable was nearly empty, inhabited only by Jupiter, Peveril's rawboned knock-down, Hanford's own ancient hack, and his mother's dainty but elderly pleasure horse—except for the last, horses he would be ashamed to see his tenants riding, let alone ride himself.

His boots echoed on the rough planks of the sta-ble floor. But that would change now. Now he could afford to fill the stable properly, as Hanfords had always filled it, and keep it as it had been in his father's time. He could send agents to the spring sales and buy grey coach horses and hacks; a pony so Athelstane could try to break his neck; a pretty little mare so Orinda could break the hearts of county swains; hunters for Peveril—who would break his collarbone, naturally—and for Susan-nah. . . .

But Susannah, so she'd told him, couldn't ride; and the money he intended to spend on these fan-tastic steeds had been hers to begin with. Hanford raised his voice and shouted for Buckthorn.

A brisk gallop did nothing to settle his mind— only to clear it. It presented him with orderly ranks of problems that he wished to avoid.

Why had Laceby been in the condition it had when they arrived? True, he had not sent word of his arrival, but his mother should have returned straight here from London to put things in order before leaving with Ancilla and the rest of the family for Italy. Putting things in order did not mean making off with the butler, the cook, and half the other servants.

Undoubtedly some letter of explanation had gone astray. He would write to Mr. Soberton and see if the lawyer had his mother's direction. At least then he'd have some idea of when she was coming back. He must write to Ancilla too.

His mouth tightened and his horse, obedient to the signal of the reins, pulled to a stop. Hanford sighed and urged him onward. Ancilla would have known how to find the humor in all this mess of cold beds, no servants, and his wife slaving in the kitchen to save the servants inconvenience. But Ancilla was not here, and Susannah was.

He must apologize to her; no wife deserved to hear such things said of her by her own husband. But he must make Susannah understand that she was no longer in Upper Lower Wherever-it-was among her own kind. The *ton* might be lax about its morals, following the lead of the First Gentleman of Europe, but it was stringent about its manners. He would not allow his wife's behavior to shut his mother out of the world she loved, or keep Orinda from marrying as she chose. Those things were what he'd married for, after all, not for love of his wife.

His wife, Susannah Potter of Lower Chapman Street in London-town. A City-child; his father would have liked her for that. But no proper mate for the ancient blood of the Hanfords, only a very ordinary woman—with hair that was like drowning in a perfumed garden of black roses and eyes of a blue that made the sky more brilliant than the sun.

And an intemperate temper.

With no peace in sight, Hanford urged his horse into a brief gallop again, and when he finally returned to Laceby to apologize to his wife, Susannah was not there.

The early winter twilight made the long shadows point toward Laceby as the Goodchild trap drove through its gates. Susannah, chilled and shivering, thought longingly of the warm fires at her Aunt Doolittle's house and wondered if it were her fate always to freeze.

Unwarily she let her thoughts turn toward the one thought she had been avoiding all day. Cousin Ancilla. Ancilla and Hanford.

Oh, why had she been blind, stupid, headstrong enough not to consider that she was not the beginning of her husband's life—but the end? He had not wanted to marry a Cit heiress—just as she had not wanted to marry an impoverished aristocrat. They had each done it for reasons having nothing to do with love—but for Susannah Potter there had been no previous loves to forsake. What had Hanford had to renounce to get the money that he needed?

Susannah took a deep breath and felt Mrs. Goodchild look at her curiously. "It will be good to get back to Laceby!" she said brightly. "I do hope you will stay for tea."

The door was opened grudgingly by Mrs. Danvers—who did everything grudgingly, Susannah was beginning to think.

"I have brought Mrs. Collins back from Lewesby, Mrs. Danvers; please let me know if she needs anything. Now Mrs. Goodchild and I would like tea— in the Blue Parlor, I think." She hoped a fire was burning there, and doubted that it was.

"Lord Hanford has been asking for you, my lady."

"Please let him know that Mrs. Goodchild is here; I know he will wish to see her."

Mrs. Danvers bobbed and went away with their

outer garments. Susannah turned back to her guest to find Mrs. Goodchild regarding the hall with sad eyes. Mrs. Goodchild caught her glance and smiled. "But it was beautiful in its day, Lady Hanford. Many was the time, after Matthew got the living here, that we'd hear of Lord Hanford—the old Lord Hanford, you are to understand—riding down from London with a pleasure party like an erl-king out of the hollow hills; he'd set Lewesby on its ear for a fortnight and then be off again, but the county would gossip for months! And then, of course, he died."

Susannah wished desperately to confide in someone, but the dread of appearing ludicrous kept her from it. Mrs. Goodchild had known Ancilla—she too must have anticipated a marriage between Lord Hanford and his cousin.

"I believe the Blue Parlor is this way, Mrs. Goodchild," she said.

The massive silver tray that Ruby carried in threatened to overwhelm both the abigail and the small gilt table it was placed on. Susannah was just settling the lovely Sevrès teapot to her satisfaction and wondering why Mrs. Danvers had not sent up any teacakes when Hanford walked in.

His fair hair was swept severely back, and as usual the only jewelry he wore was his carnelian seal-ring. Susannah's heart leapt and thundered with her new knowledge, but Hanford seemed to suspect nothing. His watchful grey eyes lit with pleasure as he bowed to Mrs. Goodchild.

"How good to see you again. I trust Mr. Goodchild is well? Did he get the books I sent from London?"

"Yes, my lord; and he may thank you but I do not!" said Mrs. Goodchild in mock reproof. "Ever since they came we have had Latin for breakfast and dinner and Greek for nuncheon and tea!"

"Hanford," said Susannah all in a rush, "I went out driving with Jupiter this afternoon—"

"And Mrs. Goodchild brought you home once you had arrived at the vicarage. Buckthorn should have brought the carriage round for you if you wished to go out." He raised his eyebrows toward the tea table and Susannah, mindful of her manners, poured him out a cup. She noticed that Ruby was still hovering, alert for scandal.

"Ruby, go to the kitchen and see if there are any macaroons. Mrs. Danvers will know." Susannah turned back to her husband. "I asked Buckthorn to hitch up the gig; I wanted to go down into the village and I thought the carriage would be too much trouble."

Hanford's expression politely informed her that his wife had run mad. "Certainly, if you wish to go into the village you may," he said, sounding entirely uncertain of how to finish the sentence.

"Indeed, Lord Hanford, it was fortunate that Jupiter did bring Lady Hanford to us," offered Mrs. Goodchild. "Jenny had some idea that she'd been turned out of her place; I told her it was part of the muddle of the lost directions and we soon put her right. I vow, I never saw anything as comical as Hiram Collins' face when Lady Hanford started putting gold sovereigns on the table to pay up Jenny's back wages—he turned just the shade of my crabapple conserve!"

"And has Mrs. Collins returned to us?" asked Hanford smoothly. Any answer was forestalled by the return of Ruby, bearing a sliced and buttered country loaf. Hanford handed the dish around and Susannah effaced herself, nibbling at a crustless slice of bread while Mrs. Goodchild retailed the county news. Though Mrs. Goodchild tried hard to include her, Susannah knew none of the names and personalities discussed, and had the lowering reflection that she could have turned into a pillar of salt without affecting the flow of the conversation in the least.

"I trust, my lord, that we shall see you and Lady Hanford this Sunday?" Mrs. Goodchild said at last, setting her teacup down decisively. She rose to her feet, and Hanford did likewise.

"Of course; and you and your family must come to dinner afterward. How is Letitia? She must be nearly ready to make her come-out." Ruby, summoned by Lord Hanford, entered and left again with orders for trap and pelisse.

"You are sadly out-of-date, my lord; we brought Lettie out over Christmas—she is quite seventeen, you know—" Mrs. Goodchild stopped abruptly and made an abortive gesture as though she had said something in the worst of taste.

"—and of an age to be making her bow and thinking of marriage; you are quite right," finished Hanford with ruthless politeness. Then Ruby returned, and conversation was at an end in the business of leave-taking.

"I imagine I owe you an apology, Susannah." Hanford turned to Susannah as soon as Mrs. Goodchild was gone.

Susannah fretting over a collection of worries in which Cousin Ancilla, Mrs. Collins, and the silver vied for consideration with the Dowager Baroness's inexplicable behavior, was slow to understand.

"I had meant to render it earlier," he went on, "but you have been so exceedingly busy today that it has been quite impossible."

Susannah's bruised sensibilities flamed under the implied insult. He wished he'd never brought her into his house, that much was clear to her. "Naturally you would prefer I did nothing; but as your wife—"

"Quite," Hanford snapped. The combatants stared at each other in puzzled silence for a moment. "You are my wife," he said, as if that were an explanation.

"What did you wish to apologize for?" asked Susannah quickly, before the conversation could take another bizarre turn.

"Perhaps for that," said Hanford quietly. As Susannah was trying to think of a response, he turned and left.

The evening meal was a marked improvement on that which had gone before it, at least in terms of what was set upon the table. Hanford seemed to have forgotten his baffling mood of the afternoon and was all that was amiable, and the glow of the candlelight on old oak did much to make the room look as it must once have done.

But in the long months since her father's death Susannah had learned to mistrust surface impressions, and one day spent at Laceby had confirmed her mistrust. There were too many unanswered questions. Why had Laceby been in the state it had? Why had the Dowager turned Mrs. Collins out without her wages?

She wished she had paid more attention when Uncle Abner had tried to talk to her about mortgages and settlements, but she had been in a giddy blur, thinking Lord Hanford was charming and gracious and everything was going to end happily like one of the romances she was so fond of. But Lord Hanford had married for the money to save his family, and she was fortunate to have discovered it before she made any declarations of her feelings. Now she must put away her childish dreams and think only of money as well, just as Hanford had.

There was money settled on her that Hanford could not touch, and money settled on Dinah, of course, but the bulk of the Potter fortune had passed to her husband the moment the marriage lines were signed. She thought Uncle Abner had stipulated that some mortgages be paid, but he certainly would not have concerned himself with tradesman's bills and servants' wages. If the Dowager had left Mrs. Collins unpaid, how many other unsettled bills were there?

The worry kept her silent through dinner, until at last Hanford stopped trying to amuse her. Susannah excused herself immediately after dinner on the pretext of letters to write, and when Hanford knocked at her door later, she pretended she did not hear.

Susannah woke early, to the unaccustomed sound of the rising wind. Hanford could have told her that it meant nothing and was in fact almost a certain guarantee of afternoon sun. But Hanford was not there.

For a moment she was tempted to throw on her wrapper and run down the hall to him; burrow in beside her husband in the lovely warm and let him tell her that everything was just as he wished at Laceby; that he was proud and happy to have her for his wife.

But he wouldn't. Susannah sat up in her lonely bed and shivered. He didn't want her here, and he didn't want her for his wife. There was no reason for him to seek her out. Next year would be time enough to think about an heir to the Hanford title.

Susannah bit her lip hard and resolutely turned her mind from those thoughts, just as she had always done when things she could do nothing about tormented her. There was more than enough here that she could do something about. She must begin to put Laceby in order. She had been trained to hold house, not run a country estate; for every task she understood, there must be a hundred she didn't even suspect the existence of. But at least she would be doing something.

What had she meant to do today? Oh, yes—inventory the silver in the morning with Mrs. Danvers; linens and towels in the afternoon. And she must get her hands on the account books, too, and discover the full extent of her husband's indebtedness.

Most of the silver in the inventory was gone, but oddly enough, no modern accounting had been drawn up. Susannah was in the midst of trying to reconcile the *"one silber sallet—pair"* written in her inventory in spidery Elizabethan script with the unspeakably tarnished set of cruets Mrs. Danvers was showing her when Ruby appeared, a messenger from the upper world of light and air.

"If you please, my lady, there's a person to see your ladyship," said Ruby.

After a preliminary reconnoiter of the silver closet Susannah had gone to her room to don the oldest gown she owned; as a result she was wearing last season's somber black, fortunately included among her trousseau by her literal-minded abigail. And a "person," she translated from Ruby's newly-acquired vocabulary of snobbery, would be someone somewhere between a member of the local gentry and a servant.

"Did he give his name?"

"No'm. He said as your ladyship had best see him." Ruby looked affronted.

More than ever before Susannah understood the wisdom of having a good stout manservant between you and whomever came to your door. She wished the absent Mr. Peacock at Jericho before wondering if the Laceby butler was indeed with the Dowager in Italy—and if not, where?

"He asked for me? Not Lord Hanford?"

"Oh yes, your ladyship." Ruby brooded on her wrongs. "He asked for Mr. Potter's daughter."

Mr. Andrew Gammadge of the village of Lewesby was a well-rounded man. He was so particularly well-rounded that his roundness strained at his waistcoat-buttons, and the numerous fobs and seals decking the gold chain that swagged his belly stood out stiff, like bullion fringe. He was a prosperous dealer in coal and tallow, and that very morning an order for both these commodities—plus an order for wax candles in astounding numbers!—had been conveyed to his shop from the new mistress on the hill.

The order—written on heavy cream paper that smelt of violets and conveyed by Danvers, the Laceby gardener—had arrived almost as the shutters were being thrown back, but it had not arrived before the gossip that had started the night before in Hiram Collins' parlor. There was a new lady on the hill, open-handed and generous—and not one of those who were forever buying and buying and then looking down their nose at you when you asked for a bit on account. She'd paid all Jenny Collins' wages for last year and this—and in good sound gold, too, none of this paper money that might be anything at all.

Andrew Gammadge had looked at his account books, weighing the latest order in his hand and thinking of shining yellow-boys gleaming on the green baize tables of his counting room. Then he put on his hat and his Sunday best and headed for the hill.

He was admitted to the house by an uppish maid-servant with a London swagger, but Mr. Gammadge was firm. He would see her new ladyship that had been Jacob Potter's daughter and no one else. He seated himself on the best chair the Blue Parlor had to offer and prepared to not be moved.

He was not prepared, however, to confront a slender dark girl in a plain black dress, who slipped into the room without so much as a by-your-leave and stood staring down at him with grave blue eyes.

"Here now!" said Mr. Gammadge, incensed. "Where's your mistress, now? I warn you, I shan't be put off by any of your rigs nor rows, so look sharp!"

"Oh, I shall," said the dark girl, a martial amusement in her eyes. "You see, I am Lady Hanford, and you wished to see me, Mr. Gammadge."

It was, as she'd expected, bills. The amount written out on the flimsy yellow sheet made her blink: she mentally compared it with similar charges in Lower Chapman Street, doubled her figure because Laceby was so much bigger, and concluded that the accounts had been running for years.

"Naturally we shall pay for today's order in cash, Mr. Gammadge, but as for this—surely you see that it is impossible for me to settle this bill?"

A foxy dissatisfied light came into Mr. Gammadge's gaze. "And how might that be, your ladyship? We've been more than generous to your husband's family in the past—"

"And of course Lord Hanford intends to settle with you at his earliest opportunity. But you can hardly expect him to pay without a bill of particulars showing the date and amount of each purchase." Susannah smiled sweetly.

Mr. Gammadge looked taken aback. He had heard that her new ladyship was open-handed. He had not expected this genial shrewdness.

"Now, your ladyship, you being a stranger to these parts might not know, but anyone in the county will tell you there's no one more honest nor fair than Andrew Gammadge, and have my word questioned I will not. Now there's a true account of what his lordship owes, and I want it paid before I send one candle or coal to this house!"

Susannah opened her eyes very wide and cudgeled her brain for every scrap of business gossip she had ever heard her uncle and her father exchange. "Why, Mr. Gammadge, surely you were not—" She broke off and cast her eyes down, willing the color to rise in her cheeks. Since she was thoroughly ashamed of her performance, this was not difficult. She raised her gaze to his face, the picture of pretty confusion. "Oh, I did not mean to imply that you were not trustworthy, but"—she lowered her voice conspiratorially—"one's clerks, you know, are inclined to miss things." She sat back and looked sympathetically at Mr. Gammadge, who was at that moment recollecting that his nephew had been known to occasionally transpose a line in the company's books.

"Naturally Lord Hanford's concern is that you do not cheat yourself—since once he has settled your bill in whatever amount he will consider it payment in full for all past charges on his account."

"Er. Well. Yes. Very wise of my lord, I'm sure, your ladyship. Now, ah—"

"And while Lord Hanford is waiting for you to present a proper bill of accounts, the current order . . . ?"

"Cash, you said, Lady Hanford?"

"Yes, Mr. Gammadge. My family always pays cash." Susannah rang for Ruby and her pocketbook. "I trust you have the bill for that order ready in proper form?"

* * *

The bill was in proper form, each item itemized (and overpriced, Susannah was sure). She paid out the amount required, reducing the contents of her purse to nearly nothing, and then Ruby drove Mr. Gammadge doorward before her.

Alone in the empty room, Susannah's cheeks burned with rage. The indulged daughter of a wealthy merchant, she had never before been forced to endure the insolence that comes with indebtedness. She did not hear the door open again behind her.

Hanford entered and stood beside her.

"Susannah, Mrs. Danvers told me a tradesman had called. You do not need to see them, you know; it will only distress you. I'm sure you are trying to do too much all at once, and you cannot be used to it. Mother always left the servants to their own devices, and the rest you may leave to me."

"I think that Laceby has been left quite long enough, thank you, Hanford." She took two quick steps away from him, head up and breathing hard. "I saw Mr. Gammadge because he asked for me. And he asked for me"—she went on inexorably—"because he did not believe he could be paid any other way! Hanford, the bill for coals has been running for years! How could you let it get so behindhand—it will never be straightened out!"

"I never told you I was a rich man, Susannah."

She turned at the sound of his voice. There were spots of high color in Hanford's normally pale cheeks, and the love Susannah Hanford felt for her husband was transformed by the alchemy of despair into fury.

"Even if there is no money, is that any reason to live the way you have? I never heard that it took money to polish silver! Everywhere I look I see nothing but moth, and dust, and cobweb—it may suit you to live like this, but it does not suit me! Laceby is my house now, and I don't intend to sit and watch it crumble to gravel because you're too proud to lift a hand to it!"

She'd gone too far. She knew that by the sinking feeling in her stomach the instant before Hanford spoke.

"Oh, but I did do something about Laceby," he said with deadly courtesy. "I married you, Susannah."

She gasped as if she'd been physically struck. Blinded by the sudden sparkle of tears, she did not see him come forward.

"Susannah." His hands were warm on her arms through the cloth of her dress as he tugged her gently toward him. "Forgive me. I have no right to speak to you like that. But I did not marry you to subject you to . . . people . . . like Amos Gammadge."

"Andrew," said Susannah against the clean linen of her husband's shirt.

"Very well, then, Andrew. But Andrew or Amos or Ahiloam, you have done nothing to deserve the presence of him or his ilk. Leave Laceby to me. No one expects you to understand the running of a country estate. It's nothing to do with you."

In the seductive comfort of her husband's embrace, Susannah nearly agreed. Then the sense of Hanford's words reached her and she pulled back.

" 'Nothing to do with me'? Hanford, Laceby is my home."

"Of course it is," he said, puzzled. "But I don't make the mistake of assuming it's what you're used to. Laceby isn't some smart London town house on a new-built square. It's a part of the land, and the county. People here aren't used to London manners; you'll only confuse them."

"I didn't notice Mr. Gammadge being in the least confused when I offered to pay him what he was owed!" Susannah snapped.

Hanford released her as if he'd been burned. Susannah rushed on, trying to make him understand about the debts—he could not know their extent, or he would have paid them already. "Perhaps some London manners might not come amiss in Warwickshire. There's so much that needs to be done at Laceby; and the accounts must be settled first. Hasn't it occurred to you, Hanford, that—"

"It has occurred to me that I am tired of talking of people and being answered back in pounds-shillings-pence! I will not have my financial arrangements thrown up to me morning and night beneath my own roof—if it is my own roof yet! Susannah, I chose a bride, not an estates-manager."

"Well, perhaps you had better hire an estates-manager, my lord, if you want to keep *your* roof over *my* head."

She had meant, truly, only to point out that the roof was falling in and wanted mending. It was only after she spoke that she realized it sounded more like a threat to leave him.

"Hanford, I—" she began.

"If that is what—"

They both stopped as the door opened.

Ruby tested the atmosphere and bobbed a nervous curtsey.

"My lady, if you please, Mrs. Collins wishes to know if she should send up nuncheon now, and what is she to do about the butcher's boy?"

Chapter VII

MARCH 1819

AFTER THAT, THINGS went quietly and inevitably from bad to worse. It was easier to lie to her husband about her thoughts than to risk another of those agonizing and bewildering clashes, so she did. It was easier not to think about Hanford if she kept busy, so she did that too. At the head of a covey of village maidens, Susannah turned Laceby inside out from tower to cellar. Ice-cold March winds howled through rooms that had not been opened in years. Rugs were beaten soundly, furniture polished until it gleamed, and through it all Susannah made notes of all the things she would have to buy to make Laceby live again. She ferreted out and settled all the accounts in Lewesby, and thrust away the unwelcome knowledge that every shilling she paid out made the locals glorify her and damn her husband.

Even the Sabbath was not exempt from toil. On those Sundays when the Goodchilds did not dine with them, Susannah sat barricaded among her pattern books, estimating how many yards of silk and brocade and velvet she must order and wondering whom she could find in Lewesby to make drapes and cover chairs and walls and pillows.

Linen and lace; coal and gravel and candles and

flour. Inventories of silver and towels and paintings and chairs. These became the compass of her world. She hardly noticed that none of the local families had left cards at Laceby, nor that she had not driven out to make the round of calls that custom demanded of the new Lady Hanford.

But she did notice when Hanford began avoiding her.

It began simply enough. He was up early, she was up late. They had not shared a bedroom since the first night they had spent at Laceby—such was the way the Quality conducted its marriages, and Susannah was determined Hanford should have nothing to reproach her with.

He was out before breakfast. She breakfasted while dressing, letters from contractors piled on her tray. No use to take to Hanford the things that puzzled her so; he would only advise her not to do them at all. She wrote long letters asking her Uncle Abner his advice; she wrote long letters to Dinah saying how happy she was. She and Hanford dined together most evenings; she had nothing to say to him—how could she, when she had sworn to herself not to utter one word about the tasks that occupied her days? He spoke when addressed, briefly, kindly, then dawdled over his wine while she occupied the grand salon in solitary splendor. He did not talk of Laceby.

And one evening Susannah rose from the table and went to the salon, and found new music arranged on the pianoforte. She tried out a few bars with hesitant fingers and found it tricky, and thought that Hanford must show her the way of it. And then she realized that he would not be in for more than three-quarters of an hour, and then only to bid her good-night on the way to his rooms.

No time to play over the pretty Mozart cantata. No time, in fact, for anything done together.

She wondered how it had happened, and saw years before her stretching grey and cool, alone in this house with no one for company but the servants—and, if she were lucky, her children.

And then, because she was practical and dutiful, she sat down at the delicate ebonywood desk to answer Dinah's latest letter and tell her sister again how happy she was.

The candles stood tall and slender, clustered like young trees and rising out of gleaming silver candelabrum, and Hanford knew to the penny what each had cost. The room smelt strongly of honey and lemon and turpentine—from the candles; from the ferociously-polished sideboard, still hulking but several shades lighter; from the table and floor and chairs—all administered by an ever-increasing army of servants. He did not know their names, but he knew what each was paid. The table was swathed in Susannah's snowy white bridal linens, and on it stood a decanter of brandy and a decanter of port—replenishments to the Laceby cellars recently purchased and paid for, cash in advance. Hanford refilled his glass with brandy and gazed moodily into the spirits' coppery gleam.

If music and sweet mystery delight . . .

But there was no music, and no delight—and no mystery.

He withdrew the heavy packet of letters from his jacket. Waves of chypre wafted upward, overpowering the honey-scent from the wood.

All his life he'd listened, half-indifferent, half-disbelieving, to the mockery of his schoolmates, classmates, fellows, peers, for those they considered beneath them. Birth, not fortune, was the delimiter. The mobile could topple kings and titles could be bought, but never could there be any true inter-mingling between cash and class. Blood would always tell.

And to expect a shopkeeper's daughter, however wealthy, to behave like anything but a shopkeeper's daughter was to engage in the sort of air-dreaming he had put behind him when he was seventeen. Reality was harsh and unforgiving. To accept that was to insulate oneself forever from rude surprises.

He turned the heavy vellum of the letter over in his hands. His family was coming home.

Mother had written from Florence. All was chaos, and—something, he could not make out quite what—was simply shocking. Orinda would have been a great success, had she only been Out; despite this she had—Hanford skipped several paragraphs.

He must do something about Peveril (his mother wrote). His younger brother had fallen in with bad companions—half-pay officers and wild young sky-larks on Tour. Rumors had reached her ears that she scarcely dared credit and would blush to repeat. . . . Then several paragraphs about the people who had insisted on telling them to her in the first place, segueing inexorably into shopping and the purchases ("—just the merest trifles, my love, as you know I have a horror of extravagance—") his mother had made. Hanford skipped more lines.

Ancilla was well, Ancilla was happy, Ancilla was staying at the villa of Lady—no, that couldn't be right. Dragonsbane? Ridiculous.—Hanford would remember her as an old family friend and distant relation.

Hanford remembered no such thing, and skimmed the rest. It was taken up with the travel arrangements Peacock, the Laceby butler, had made for the family. If they were not all killed by bandits or otherwise waylaid, which she was certain would happen, would he meet them at Dover, as his Mama was perishing for a sight of her darling boy, and Peveril was far too young to be reliable, and ... He made a note of the date and ignored the rest.

The enclosure to the Dowager's letter he read more carefully. The paper was pale blue, and if it had ever had any scent of its own it had since been overpowered by the chypre that had enclosed it.

My Dear Cousin:

We have all arrived safe and sound, and you may, if you wish, direct your letters to me care of Lady Daggonnet at the Hotel della Spheria. [Hanford was relieved: it was not Lady Dragonsbane after all.] There is a Doctor Elphenstone here who scowls a great deal so as to look older than he is, and as he has an unfortunate habit of speaking the truth, he is not-at-all to Aunt Clementina's taste. Can you imagine—he told her that she was not the least delicate and ought to marry again and provide Athelstane with some younger brothers and sisters! You may imagine Aunt's response to such plain speaking—but as I am so improved under Dr. Elphenstone's care, she could hardly give him the right-about.

We have not spoken since you chose to marry—if it had been only my welfare at stake I would have counseled against the match, but as you are the Head of the House you must do what seems best for all. Be assured that through your kindness and that of your bride I am quite set up in my own esteem and lack for nothing, and I hope you may find contentment in your marriage. I wished to write to Susannah to welcome her to the family, but that must wait for the next courier, alas, or I will not make the post. I may send it with Aunt Clementina when she leaves. I will close now and add this to Aunt's letter, hoping it finds you well and happy and in other such states as are usually expected of bridegrooms.

Your loving cousin,
Ancilla

Hanford folded the letter carefully and placed it in a different pocket than that of his mother's letter.

Well? Happy? He had done what he thought was best for all—but was it best for Susannah? Or him?

"I shall have to go away for a few weeks, Susannah."

Hanford had entered upon Susannah's morning dressing. She was wary, fearing a scold, then hopeful that he might be coming out of his sulks and willing to see reason. Then disappointed, unreasonably so, when he revealed the reason for his visit.

"Oh?" she said with what she hoped was proper wifely disinterest. Circumspectly she spread the sleeve of her dressing-gown to cover the mass of letters and bills that had been sent up with her coffee. She had already depleted the housekeeping money, overspent an exceedingly lavish allowance, and borrowed so heavily against next quarter's money that she knew she would have to ask Hanford for assistance. He would ask to see her accounts, of course, and then he would be furious.

"Mama and the others are coming home from Italy. She wants me to meet her, of course, and then—" He stopped.

"Yes, Hanford?" Susannah said brightly.

"They will be coming here, you see, and . . . Susannah, I do not wish you to think that I am unaware of what you have done, but you may not realize how it might seem to others," Hanford said with laborious tact.

What she realized was that her husband was no different than the schoolmates who had despised her for daring to enter their charmed circle of privilege. And as she had learned to, Susannah struck first.

"You mean," she said dulcetly, "that they might think they've come to the wrong house? Because it is clean, and there are no bailiffs in the parlor?"

Hanford drew back. "If you like. They will see, of course, that my wife has made extensive renovations to Laceby and paid out lavishly to refurbish it. And while you are at it you may as well let me see those bills—your pin money was never meant to cover the releading of the roof."

Susannah flushed, defeated, and handed him the bills. He leafed through them in silence until he came to the last.

"Stonemasons? What do you want a stonemason for?"

"The fountain in the courtyard doesn't run, so I thought—"

"Susannah, that fountain hasn't run since my great-grandfather's time," Hanford protested.

"I suppose that's a justification for leaving it as it is? If you're going to have a fountain at all, why not have one that works?"

"If you will kindly confine your eradication of my family's presence in Warwickshire to the inside of Laceby and leave the outside alone, I will—"

"You'll what, my lord?"

"I shall be very surprised."

The unexpected rejoinder startled her into a laugh, and Hanford smiled too.

"You cannot clean, polish, and reupholster every shrub and cottage in the county, Susannah." His tone was only lightly chiding.

"I suppose not," she said grudgingly. "But there's so much to do!"

"Is there really? Must everything at Laceby be changed from what it was?"

"No; just the parts that don't work, or are inefficient, or outdated—or fall apart when you try to clean them!"

"Ah, yes." His gaze lifted from hers, to the mullion-paned window that looked out over the garden. "And soon enough everything is tidy and efficient and functional, and we are all cut adrift from our heritage to bob like corks on the ocean." He drew her to her feet and turned her to look where he was looking. "You lose so much by doing that. Look, Susannah. You will say that this window is drafty, and rattles, and the glass is so bubbled that you cannot see out. But when Charles the Second took the throne my several-times-great-grandfather chose those panes from the cargo of a Holland merchantman and shipped them here to make this window. The best glass came from Holland then, you see, and it was frightfully expensive, but Averil Hanford was rebuilding Laceby so that the new house would stand as long as the old had, and he wanted only the best. And when he was done, his wife looked out this window knowing that her son's wife would do the same, and her grandson's. Tidy away that past, and what is left?"

"Perhaps a present that does not blow out the candles as fast as they are lit! Hanford, the past may make a charming story, but one cannot live there. This is 1819, not some French fairy-tale." She turned back to her dressing-table and began to tidy the discarded bills onto her breakfast-tray.

"I see. And so you would sweep away everything our ancestors held dear?"

"Your ancestors, Hanford—not mine." His ancestors had owned Laceby and all its beautiful things. Hers had merely built it.

"You are, as always my dear, incisively correct.

I shall take my leave of you, then. In the unlikely event there is anything that you need—No, never mind. You can tend to your own requirements far better than I possibly could."

The house was very empty after Hanford had gone. Everything that could be done quickly to refurbish Laceby had been done: servants had been hired, stores replenished, and bills settled. Rugs and drapes and wall coverings had been ordered and must be awaited from London. The Laceby staff was as ample as money could make it; time hung heavy on Susannah's hands.

She occupied herself with a set of crewel-work chair covers and walked in the dilapidated gardens every day, and wondered how long it would be before sheer boredom drove her to attempt to drive Jupiter again.

When Lord Hanford had been gone for seven days (and could be expected, at the most conservative estimate, to be gone for seven more) a carriage drove up to the front door of Laceby Place.

It was drawn by six horses—job-horses, true, but good ones. It had yellow wheels and blue side-panels and out-riders and postillions and coachmen and footmen in powdered wigs and bright pink livery. Susannah would have recognized it instantly, but Susannah was in the stillroom trying to find the proper proportion of chamomile oil and sulfur to honey to produce "a soothing sirop for the catahrr."

In a drawer of the desk that stood in the corner of her sitting room she'd found a leather stillbook bound with a scrap of crumpled coquillot ribbon and an unsigned note on faded blue paper addressed to her and hoping she would find the recipes contained within of use. Puzzled, she'd shown it to the housekeeper. In the country one made instead of bought, Mrs. Danvers triumphantly explained, and identified the stillbook as belonging to Ancilla Hanford.

Ancilla again. The cousin her husband should have married, who would have found charm instead of inconvenience in Laceby's quaintness.

"Oh, bother this—as if you can't buy it from the apothecary at one-tenth the trouble!" Susannah muttered crossly. Her fingers were sticky with honey and powdery with sulfur, and the scent of chamomile was stifling.

"If my lady will excuse my mentioning it, the family has always preferred to use its own recipes," Mrs. Danvers said as she entered. Susannah ground her teeth shut on a reply that would make trouble and solve nothing.

"Yes, Mrs. Danvers; I'm sure they do." She wiped her hands on her apron. "Were you looking for me?"

"Yes, my lady. Your sister has arrived."

Susannah went first to the Blue Parlor but found there only a haphazard pile of string-tied bundles and a small white puppy industriously engaged in ruining the rug Susannah had spent so many weeks cleaning. The puppy was deposited with Mrs. Collins; Susannah eventually found Dinah in the first-floor gallery, gazing up at a portrait-line of dead Barons Hanford.

Miss Dinah Mary Potter would be nineteen years of age next January 9th. Her thick black hair had a suggestion of curl and her eyes were guilelessly blue. While she was not, perhaps, as beautiful as her sister, she was so charming and free from temper that it was a stony spirit indeed that could hold her in dislike. Where Susannah's tenure at Miss Farthingale's had been one of unmitigated anguish, Dinah had actually enjoyed a certain vogue—

ascribed not incorrectly by her sister to her habit of telling the unvarnished truth in an audible voice.

Dinah wore a deep-green pelisse trimmed with swansdown, and her traveling bonnet hung down her back from matching wide green ribbands. The tip of one buff-colored kid glove was between her sharp white teeth and she was industriously engaged in worrying at it.

"Dinah! Let me do that!" Susannah grabbed her sister's hand and began to peel the glove from it. "Why you are not in tatters with the way you treat your clothes—"

"Oh, Sukey—I have missed you!" cried her irrepressible sister, and threw her arms around Susannah's neck.

"And but wait till you see what I have brought you!" Dinah continued, bouncing back. "Laces, and the most darling ribbands, real French scent, and some confits, and—oh, I hope General Blücher mayn't have gotten into them! I left him in the parlor, and—"

"General Blücher, I collect, is the dog?" Susannah took her sister's arm and began to lead Dinah down the hall to her room.

"Oh, you found him! Fancia Bindleshanks gave him to me as I was leaving. I could not bear to part with him, and I thought that he would like the country."

"Well, we will hope that he likes the kitchen, at any rate; I have left him with Mrs. Collins."

"Is she your cook? You must have a great many servants now! Laceby is such a large house, isn't it?"

"Laceby has one hundred and twenty-seven rooms, and that has nothing to say to the question of what you are doing here." Susannah flung open the door to her room and rang for Ruby. Dinah followed more slowly, looking about her with considering eyes and talking all the while.

"Well, it was very nearly the end of the school year, and this is my last year at Miss Farthingale's, so—"

"Why, Miss Dinah! Whatever are you doing here?"

"Hello, Ruby! I have come home!"

"If you would, Ruby, bring up a can of hot water for washing, and tell Mrs. Danvers to prepare a room for Dinah and bring her trunks to it. There are trunks, of course?" This last was addressed to her unregenerate sister, who was seated on Susannah's bed regarding her sister's room with wide-eyed interest.

"Oh, of course! I brought everything, Sukey—at least, everything at Bath! I sent for the rest, but of course I haven't the least idea when they'll get here! It is rather like being gipsies, don't you think?"

Others might be fooled by the limpid gaze of those wide blue eyes, but Susannah had been acquainted with Dinah all her life. While at Miss Farthingale's, girls prepared to dislike her as Susannah's sister and a tradesman's daughter had been confounded by the matter-of-fact fashion in which Dinah acknowledged her birth and station. Confronting the chief of her tormentors, Dinah said that at least she was assured of the highest-quality gloves and laces, something that neither money nor birth apparently could command.

"That will be all, Ruby," said Susannah, to all appearances ignoring her sister completely. "And please tell Mrs. Collins to send up some tea and bread-and-butter."

"Now," said Susannah, bouncing down beside her sister, "if you'll kindly tell me just what is going on?"

"You look tired, Sukey," said Dinah judiciously. "And Laceby isn't half so grand as Papa's house, is it?"

"It is a great deal older, so it must be better," said Susannah with a faint trace of bitterness. "And it will soon be grand, Dinah."

"When Lord Hanford spends all of your money on it." Dinah stood and began to unhook her pelisse.

"Dinah!" Susannah gasped in automatic outrage. In fact, she was so glad to see her little sister again that she couldn't summon up much indignation at all. "Really, it's not like that. I thought it would be, but"—she hesitated—"he does not seem to wish to spend any money on Laceby at all—only to let it molder on into antiquity. So I have been spending the money on Laceby, while Hanford—" She stopped again.

"One must admit, he does not seem handsome enough to be a Baron," said Dinah meditatively, removing her hat and shaking out her long black curls.

The girls were used to conducting their conversations around the invasions of the servants, reverting to harmless topics when there was any likelihood of their being overheard. In this larger house Dinah's timing was off; Ruby did not appear, and she went off on a tangent. "Are all those pictures in the gallery of his family?"

"Oh, yes; at least, the ones that are imposing enough. Some of them are copies, since Laceby has burned down three times and been blown up once."

Dinah preened herself in Susannah's mirror and reached for her hairbrush. "And when will I—" But now Ruby was back, and they could not gossip in front of servants.

"Now you just set down right here, Miss Dinah, and let me brush you out." Expertly Ruby whisked the ribbon from Dinah Potter's hair and brushed it until the rippling mass shone like swoops and whorls of gleaming black glass.

"I am sorry you can't meet Lord Hanford just yet, as I know he will be as delighted to see you as I, dear sister, but he has gone to bring his family home from Dover, and we are not expecting him these seven days," said Susannah over the rhythmic sound of brushing. Dinah made a face at her in the glass.

Then the can left steaming by the grate was poured out, and Dinah was removed from her dress to stand in shift and stockings splashing water on herself while Ruby took the dress away to replace it with a fresh one—a little trunk-crumpled, but immaculate. Freshly habilimented in sprigged muslin and cherry ribbons, Dinah sat demurely as Susannah poured tea in her sitting room and awaited the departure of the last of the goggle-eyed, curious maids.

"Now." Susannah set down her cup. "The truth, Dinah. Why did you run away from Miss Farthingale's?"

"I didn't. I told Miss Farthingale that you wanted me to come, now that you were home from your wedding trip—and I am eighteen, you know, and school is out in only a few weeks." She studied her sister's face. "Don't you want me here, Sukey?"

"Wretch!" said her sister, laughing despite herself. "As if I would throw you out into the snow—even if there were snow to throw you out into. And if you think you've given me a right-tight-and-Bristol-fashion answer to why you're here, think again."

Dinah abandoned her bread-and-butter and all trace of duplicity. "But Sukey, I had to come. For three months you have been writing me that you are happy, until it would make a cat sick! And you are never pleased with anything, you know—remember how you used to write about the black crepe in Aunt Mary's parlor, and Cousin Ethan's clothes?—so I knew you must be in dreadful trouble!"

Susannah put down her cup, looked at her sister, and began to cry. "What a goose you must think me, Dinah!" she said after a moment. "Weeping in corners over nothing!"

"Are you in the straw, Sukey?" asked her sister with vulgar interest, and for a moment Susannah was tempted to take that easy excuse. But it was one that wouldn't hold up, and Dinah might blither it anywhere.

"No-o . . . And at Miss Farthingale's they would beat you for saying such a thing! It is just that . . . there is so much to be done; you see—" Despite her good intentions, Susannah found herself telling over the tale of the state she had found Laceby in and of all she had done to reclaim it. Of Hanford she did not speak at all.

"Well," said Dinah when she paused for breath. "It is plain that you do need me, so you are pleased after all that I have come," she stated decisively.

Susannah thought of Dinah's determined commonality on a collision course with Hanford's aristocratic snobbishness and winced.

"Perhaps. I shall at any rate write Miss Farthingale and say how glad I am she let you come to me. And tell her how glad I am that you will be returning there this fall."

"We'll see," said Dinah meaningfully, and added more cream to her tea.

Chapter VIII

MARCH 1819

HANFORD ARRIVED IN Dover a week after he had left Laceby. He traveled by easy stages and stayed two days in London attending to a number of matters, including the transfer of funds to cover Susannah's expenditures. As per his mother's instructions, he proceeded to the Bell and Anchor, a tavern near enough to the docks to be convenient but far enough from them to indicate that it catered to true Quality. The letter with his mother's arrangements had arrived before him; he was invited to inspect a vast suite of rooms that included a private parlor.

Privately he thought it was over-grand for what would surely be only a night's stay, but Rakestraw assured him it was just what he liked. Hanford was used to being told what he liked. He kept his true opinions to himself.

On the day the rest of his family were to arrive, he was waiting on the docks. The stiff Channel breeze undid all Rakestraw's careful work and thundered at the capes of Hanford's driving coat.

Our revels now are ended,/ another poet's words paced through his mind. */These our actors, as I foretold you, were all spirits, and are melted into air, into thin air./*

The trouble was that these actors were about to

appear, not vanish, and try as he might, he could not imagine a happy world that held both Mama and Susannah on the same stage. He would be forced to take sides; he would make one of them unhappy. . . .

A cry went up from the upper rigging of one of the docked ships, and a moment later Hanford could see the Channel packet as a dark speck on the horizon. Time seemed telescoped as he watched it grow larger; the signal for the opening curtain of a horrible play that he must nonetheless sit through.

Susannah wouldn't. For a moment he allowed the certainty to warm him; the memory of the vitality that allowed her to sweep through brandishing dustrags and bank drafts and remake the world nearer to her heart's desire. It was not in his nature. He was a Hanford of Laceby, born to conserve the past and hand it down unchanged.

There was bustle and shouting on the docks as the Channel packet berthed and passengers rushed to come ashore. Hanford waited patiently. He had never accompanied his parents upon their peripatetic revels, but he had heard about them enough times to realize that Mama's party would be the last to disembark.

He was right. When the last trunk and bundle had been portered away a delicate figure in challis and veils appeared on deck and peered about.

"Hanford!" this vision cried upon beholding him. "Oh, come quickly—your brother is dying!"

Below decks was another world. Peacock the butler and Meridew, Lady Hanford's dresser—and other servants Hanford didn't recognize—hovered anxiously around the narrow bed in the first-class cabin.

"Han!" said Peveril Hanford explosively. "Finally!"

Four years younger than the twenty-ninth Baron, at twenty-one Peveril Florian Gilchrist Hanford was the very pattern-card of the portraits on the

Laceby walls. He had the auburn curls and florid English complexion of all his Saxon ancestors, and loomed over his elder brother by a good four inches. Only his grey eyes betrayed their kinship, but where Hanford's were cool and watchful, Peveril's were merry. Or, at the moment, harried.

"Oh, Peveril, darling, how can you be so insensitive while my child writhes on a bed of pain?" the Baroness demanded with a theatrical gesture.

"Come to that, Mama, I'm your child too—so you oughtn't cut up rough with me." Peveril grinned conspiratorially at Hanford.

"It's his own fault. I say the little beast deserves it. And don't you go saying that I should have known better, Peveril Hanford, because I didn't see you offering to help!" Orinda Hanford drew her shawl more firmly around her shoulders and glared at her brother.

"Deserves it? How can you be so heartless?" wailed Lady Hanford. "Orinda, my pet, it is plain your nerves are sadly shattered, or you would never speak so of poor dear Athelstane! Oh, will no one succor a helpless widow?"

"Mama, what is going on?" Hanford pushed through the audience. "Peacock, we are at the Bell and Anchor. Go and make sure the trunks are there—and take these others with you!"

"Oh, but Lunsford must stay! She is Athelstane's nurse—"

"Or she was until she got sick," cut in Orinda.

"—and she can nurse him at the inn," said Hanford ruthlessly. Peacock, sensing the way the wind was blowing, gathered up nurse, dresser, and two others that Hanford automatically dismissed as his brother and sister's new servants, and went out.

Hanford advanced on the bed.

"Hullo, monster," he said, peering down. "How goes it with you?"

"Sick," said Athelstane woefully, and proceeded

117

to be. Hanford held his brother's head over the half-full basin on the floor. When the spasms subsided, a towel was thrust into his hands.

"Here," a new voice said. "You'll want this, I think."

Hanford looked up into his cousin's eyes. "Ancilla. It lacked only this. Welcome home, I suppose."

"Courtly as always," Ancilla Hanford said, and bent to stroke Athelstane's hair.

It was established that Athelstane was not seasick. In fact, he had been quite well until his nurse had succumbed to that malady. When Mrs. Lunsford had retired to her bed of anguish, Athelstane had been thrust into his sister's care. Since Lady Hanford had specifically directed that Athelstane be kept below decks—in order, put in Peveril, that they not have to turn back to fish him out of the middle of the Channel—his sister Orinda had kept him quiet with generous bribes from a box of sugarplums, with eventual disastrous results.

"I don't suppose you would like to tell me what you're doing here?" Hanford said to his cousin.

"Instead of residing conformably with Lady Daggonnet in Firenze?" responded Ancilla promptly. "Having been bundled out of England like King Charles, without benefit of either oak trees or spaniels, I felt I should return and say a proper good-bye to Laceby and all that adjoins it. Besides, you know I would wish to be here for Orinda's Season."

"And what has Dr. Elphenstone to say to that?" demanded Hanford, at the same time Lady Hanford said:

"A Season for Orinda this year? Ridiculous!"

"But, Mama, you promised!" wailed Orinda.

"That's quite right, Mama, you did," put in Peveril. "And what's more, I don't see why now that Han's got the blunt we shouldn't puff it off. Best thing to do's find Orinda some puffed-up noddycock who won't cut up rough at her—"

"Noddycock! Peveril Hanford, as if it wasn't you pining every day you were gone at the thought that Letitia Goodchild had forgotten your existence; begging my advice on—"

It seemed patent that Orinda was about to embark on a recitation that her brother was too well acquainted with to wish to hear. Instead of attending, Hanford took the blanket Ancilla handed him and wrapped it around Athelstane. The boy snuggled wanly into his older brother's embrace.

"I shall not allow you to risk your health, Ancilla, whatever delusions you may cherish."

"Oh, Dr. Elphenstone thinks I shall do quite well enough, Hanford. He has given me a tonic to take and a regimen to follow and extracted a promise that I stay away no longer than two months. I had hoped, you know, that I was welcome," she said.

"Well, you know you are always that," said Hanford in surrender. "Welcome home, then, everyone. Welcome home, Mama."

"Sick," said Athelstane.

The Bell and Anchor had seen many a drama in its days—including the clandestine departure for France of the wicked Lord Warltawk and his child-bride—and the descent upon that quayside hostelry of a gaggle of bating Hanfords perturbed it not one whit.

Peacock was as efficient as ever, and within moments of their arrival he had taken the family in hand. Athelstane was bathed and bundled into a bed with a hot brick at his toes and Lunsford to feed him hot milk posset. Orinda and Ancilla were taken off to be refurbished by Orinda's maid Nellie, and Lady Hanford was shown to her room where she conducted a full-scale assault upon the vapors (it being far too well executed to be a mere attack) before the slightly bored gaze of her remaining children until they were banished by the ferocious Meridew.

Exiled from the presence, Hanford and Peveril repaired to the coffee room, where a stronger potable than coffee was called for.

"Phaugh!" said Peveril, leaning back on the settle with a sigh while his brother worked with hot water, lemons, and sugar to make the rum punch. "I half wish *I'd* married the girl—then you'd have been banging about all over Europe and I'd have been here!" He ran a finger around his neck beneath his dark neckcloth—favored by those of the Quality for whom convenience rather than fashion was the goal when traveling.

"You haven't a title and you don't inherit; she wouldn't want you," his brother pointed out rather callously. He scooped up a cup of steaming punch and handed it to Peveril. "Here, try this."

Peveril accepted the cup with an alacrity that rather surprised his brother. He held the cup beneath his nose and inhaled deeply. "Ah, the perfume of England! It seems that every time I've taken a drink these last four months Mama has been right there to read me a lecture on the iniquitous disposition of distilled potables toward chills upon the liver!" Peveril made a face and drank. "She thinks I'm still in leading strings; and when I point out to her that you came to the title when you were four years younger than I am now *and* had to keep the whole family out of debtor's prison the while, she simply goes on about the line! Now I ask you, Han, ain't I your brother?"

"I had always thought so, Pev," said Hanford with a smile.

Peveril held his cup out for a refill. "So it stands to reason we've both got the same blood flowing in our veins, and Mama wasn't saying you were too young to know your own mind at seventeen, let alone twenty-one! And I do!" He flung himself into an even more exaggerated slouch on the settle and the fobs and seals adorning his waistcoat bounced in sympathy with his plight.

"Know your own mind, you mean?" said Hanford encouragingly. All the fashionable fantods newly adorning his younger brother could not disguise Peveril's essential nature: open, trusting, and lovable. The same genetic quirk that had made Hanford·so strongly resemble his Masham ancestors stamped the Hanford lineaments vividly on Peveril's features. It was as if the first Baron Hanford had stepped from his portrait in the picture gallery, but Peveril lacked any tincture of his Hanford ancestors' sharp self-interested wit.

"Of course! I met some grand fellows in Zurich and they put me in the way of it. You won't want me cluttering up the place now, Han, and I've got a plan that'll let me make my own way in the world."

"And so you've waited to tell me about it instead of Mama?"

Peveril looked sulky for a moment and then laughed ruefully. "Well, I knew Mama wouldn't like it—and besides, I daresay I'll need your help if I'm to go for a soldier!"

Hanford stared at his brother. Peveril had many flaws, but until this moment Hanford had not suspected feeble-mindedness lay among them.

"Pev, it's 1819, not 1812. Boney's been on St. Helena for four years and looks like being there forever; we haven't been at war with the Americas for—"

"You never know!" Peveril interrupted eagerly.

"There's no advancement in a peacetime army, and damn few berths. Where would you go? Ireland? India?"

"There's work for a man in the Indian Army, come to that—and I daresay we won't be at peace with France and America forever," Peveril said optimistically. "Han, it's what I want to do. You're lucky; you've always known Laceby was there for you. But I'm not smart enough for the law, and we don't have any vast estates to manage—and anyway, books and figures make my head ache—and if you're asking me to dangle out for an heiress—"

"Pity the poor heiress," said Hanford, and Peveril beamed.

"You do understand, Han! Oh, I knew you would! Just buy me a set of colors—a coronetcy in a crack cavalry regiment will do me nicely, don't you think?—and you've seen the last of me. Captain the Honorable Peveril Florian Gilchrist Hanford will ride into the sunset, a figure in fierce moustachios, gold buttons, and wolfskin, and you—"

"—will box your ears, my young scapegrace, if you make any such attempt to cut the family dead," said Hanford. "Very well, if that's what you want, I'll see what I can do. Maybe Uncle Brab's old regiment will have a place for you. But it won't be overnight, Pev, even if you are willing to sink so low as a commission in the Indian Army."

" 'Younger than he are happy nabobs made,' " misquoted Peveril giddily, "and speaking of the course of true love, I'd forgotten to ask: How is your wife? Don't eat me, but I've forgotten her name. Sarah?"

"Susannah. And, look, Peveril—"

But at that moment two ladies of the Hanford party chose to join them.

"Look, Cilla; I told you they'd be here. Drinking," added Orinda, wrinkling her nose at the smell. "What is it, Han? Can I have some?"

"You won't like it. And Mama won't like it either," said Hanford, offering her his cup. Orinda took it as warily as if it might contain snakes.

"Aunt Clementina is lying down before dinner. Meridew has been persuaded to brew her a soothing *tisane* and to see if any of her gowns has survived the rigors of the journey," Ancilla said from behind Orinda.

Next to Miss Orinda Hanford her cousin Ancilla

looked pale and wrenlike indeed; it was to both ladies' credit that they never appeared to notice. Orinda Lovelady Hanford was vainer than the vainest cat (so her older brothers told her frequently) but she was never heard to puff off the hair of guinea-gold, eyes of sky-blue, and skin like moonlit rose petals with which one smitten young mooncalf had endowed her—at least, not to Ancilla.

Orinda took a generous mouthful of the rum concoction and then looked wildly about for a way to dispose of it. Finding none, she perforce swallowed it.

"Oooh, Han, that is nasty! How can you possibly bear to drink it?" she cried with a shudder.

"Oh, men think it has its compensations—and then they will be disgracefully foxed at the dinner table and ride with aching heads on the morrow." Ancilla's words were for Orinda, but she shot a teasing glance at Peveril, who smiled sourly. "What are you telling, Hanford? Secrets?"

"Han's about to tell us all about his wife. I only saw her once—at the wedding—Lord, what a circus that was!—and, come to think of it, you never saw her at all, Ancilla. But I dare to swear you'll get your chance, living in each other's pockets for the Season!"

"Oh, Han, don't let Mama bring you 'round her finger! I'm nearly on the shelf—"

"Nineteen," Peveril commented in an aside.

"—and you know I should have come out years ago! Mama herself said I should have made my bow last year, and if I must wait another year I shall be quite twenty and I know I shall die of the mortification of it!"

"I cannot think there is the least need for that," said Hanford, thinking of his volatile family mewed up in Laceby with his equally volatile wife. At least if they were in London for the Season they need see little of one another. This would be the first Season since his marriage; the logical time and place to introduce his wife to the Polite World—and perhaps even to find a spouse for Orinda. There was no getting around it. The London Season must be done.

"Oh, Han, I knew you'd understand!" cried Orinda, flinging her arms around his neck and planting a fervent kiss upon his cheek. Moving quickly, Peveril rescued his punch cup and drained it. "And you will make Mama understand too—I know it!"

"Will he, by heaven?" asked Peveril of no one in particular.

"Oh, yes," answered Ancilla. "Though in general he is better at persuading Aunt Clementina to do things she wished to do in the first place."

The return of the Hanfords to Laceby was indeed prodigal, though not perhaps in the fashion intended by the originator of the expression. The single coach that Hanford had brought proved to be entirely inadequate; two more coaches needs must be found, in order that the servants and the family's numerous purchases (chiefly Lady Hanford's) could be accommodated. Only Hanford's repeated pleas of business at Laceby caused the Dowager to abandon London before everything purchasable in the town had been bought, and once on the road the party took on more the nature of a royal progress than a journey for the purpose of arriving anywhere. A day upon which the various coaches, carts, and outriders managed more than twenty-five miles was a day for celebration.

But at last they arrived.

Chapter IX

APRIL 1819

SUSANNAH HAD REASON to be glad of her sister's un-announced appearance, because in the ten days that followed it Hanford did not arrive. But others did.

"Dinah!" Susannah called, over the sound of pounding.

The workmen Susannah had so blithely bespoken in her first weeks at Laceby had descended upon her from London—carpenters and paperhangers, glaziers and masons and craftsmen of all description whose talents were not to be found in Lewesby-town. The careful orderliness of Laceby dissolved immediately in a welter of boards and scaffolding, and a strong scent of glue and sawdust hung over all.

On this particular April morning, if the report delivered in laconic Birmingham vowels was to be believed, the fountain in the front drive would once more bring forth water. And Susannah had been wakened from her slumbers not by Ruby with her morning tea and hot water, but by the fugitive sound of pagan drums.

Or something.

"Dinah!" Susannah called again. This time she was rewarded by the appearance of her sister, lacy mob-cap askew over disheveled curls, and a pegnoir far too *soigné* to meet with her sister's approval draped over her practical flannel nightdress.

"I heard the pounding. It must be those pioneers you told me about, Sukey," she said, yawning. She sat down on the end of her sister's bed and blinked at her like a sleepy dormouse. "The ones that tunnel in under the walls to leave bombs."

"Wretch! That was in Cromwell's time, not now! I think this is the men hanging the paper—they beat it with mallets, you know, so it will lie flat. At least that is what they told me."

"Do they?" said Dinah, with vague interest.

"But I have been ringing and ringing for Ruby—and since she did not come, I thought she might be with you."

"Perhaps they have beaten her with mallets," suggested Dinah with slightly more interest.

Susannah regarded her with only slightly exasperated fondness. If Dinah had not been there to charm the servants, jolly the workmen, and insist that if Lord Hanford did not laud Susannah's efforts he was a right clunch, she would have quickly succumbed to just the sort of hysterical vapors she had always professed to despise.

"Until, you know, she would—" continued Dinah.

"Dinah!" said Susannah warningly, but it was too late.

"—lie flat," finished Dinah with sleepy solemnity.

"You know perfectly well that you haven't the slightest idea what you mean, Dinah Potter, and that furthermore you don't believe it!"

A new storm of pounding shook the walls. Susannah threw back the covers and slid out of bed. A Turkey carpet, still grand but too threadbare to provide much protection from the chill, met her feet. "Help me get dressed—I must go see what has happened to Ruby."

"P'raps she fell down through the stairs," said Dinah, with the hopeful bloodthirstiness of the young. Since the servants' stairs had long since succumbed to the worm and were currently in the throes of replacement, this was not as impossible as Susannah might wish.

"Nonsense! They have told me that they would keep the stairs roped off whenever there was the least danger of falling through! It must be something else."

"P'raps—"

"Oh, Dinah, do be an angel and find me something to wear!"

Dinah obediently abandoned her entertaining speculations and went to Susannah's wardrobe, but instead of drawing forth a gown she gazed into its cedar depths.

"You haven't any new gowns, Sukey," she said meditatively.

"What?" said Susannah. "Oh, bother new gowns! I can't get any made here anyway—the pattern books are all out of date." She did not add that she had been both too busy and too ashamed to go into Lewesby in weeks. What must they think of her, when they had to come begging to the door in order to be paid money they were lawfully owed?

"Are you ever going to get any new gowns?"

"Dinah!" Susannah reached past her sister to snatch the first thing that came to hand—a hasty contribution to her trousseau; plum-colored (being just out of mourning, Susannah was leery of the brighter colors of matronhood), but with a skirt too narrow and trim too modest to be in quite the first stare of fashion.

"This will do—come on!"

Obediently Dinah turned her hand to the task of maiding her sister. But her mind was elsewhere.

"Won't Lord Hanford let you buy any new gowns,

127

Sukey? You said when you married that your gowns were all scrape and scramble—and it has been four months, Susannah, and they're still the same ones."

"Oh, for heaven's sake, Dinah! When I go to London I shall buy all the gowns I choose, and Hanford has nothing to say to the matter! Now button me up!"

"I should like to go to London with you," observed Dinah cunningly.

"Undoubtedly," Susannah said blightingly. "But for the present, stay right here while I go see whatever is keeping Ruby."

Pinning up her hair in hasty jabs, Susannah wrapped her shoulders in a thick cashmere shawl and ventured forth. It was not as if she were alone in the house, after all. Mrs. Danvers would have been the one to let in whoever was here, and there were two strapping young footmen to provide stout Warwick muscle in defense of their mistress, if needed.

But where could Ruby be?

The long gallery smelled strongly of sawdust and the new carpet was soft beneath Susannah's kid slippers. The best Belgian wool, and the color was all that she had hoped. She hoped Hanford would be pleased. She had ordered the refurbishing of the private rooms done first, in order that Hanford would have someplace quiet to withdraw from the bustle in the rest of the house, and only now did it occur to her that perhaps he would have preferred to put up with chaos in his rooms in order that his family should see Laceby serene and untouched.

Her stomach knotted at the thought of meeting Hanford's family again. She'd met them briefly at her wedding and remembered them chiefly for what she imagined Papa would have said about them. "Quality stock, Sukey-girl; you can always tell fine cloth by a fine hand." And she had replied, in her mind: "But, Papa, you don't make sails out of silk, however fine. Nor fine ladies' gowns out of canvas." The Dowager Lady Hanford, a frail woman in a beautiful blue gown, had stared silently at her and wept throughout the ceremony.

No, Susannah did not look forward to meeting them again. Perhaps their boat has sunk, she thought hopefully, before returning her mind militantly to the present and Ruby's mysterious disappearance.

None of the Laceby maids was on the main staircase—and since Susannah had given them permission to use it while the servants' stairs were being rebuilt, she thought it odd. She glanced at the light streaming in through the sparkling-clean windows at the head of the gallery. It was quite past nine o'clock. She should surely have seen someone by now.

The mystery was solved when she reached the dining room. From there a door led into the kitchen, through which the servants' rustica could be reached.

At least usually. On this particular morning she pushed upon the door and it did not move. She pounded upon it and was rewarded with unintelligible shouts and thumpings. The door was too thick for her to understand the answers to her shouted questions—if indeed the questions themselves had been understood.

She turned away and walked back into the main hall. Susannah had made it her business to be conversant with the architecture of Laceby Place, and cudgeled her brain for another way in to the underground servants' quarters.

She flung open the front door and stepped out. The April air was chill, with only a hint of softer days to come. Piles of gravel lay on the ground waiting to be spread, and a narrow trench gleaming with new lead and copper pipe led to the ornamental fountain in the drive.

At the outside entrance to the rustica Susannah was confronted by Mrs. Danvers and Mrs. Collins, allies at last, with Buckthorn the groom gazing about in a fashion that indicated this matter was no concern of the Laceby stables.

"Oh, Lady Hanford, thank the stars above you've come! Those dreadful men a-worriting of my kitchen, and the good Lord knows what's happened to Ruby and the rest!"

"I am quite certain that her ladyship does not wish to be bothered with our little domestic troubles, Mrs. Collins," interposed Mrs. Danvers.

"Oh, well might you say—when it's not your kitchen they're troubling! I do wonder though, Mrs. Danvers, what you'd have to say if they was to be among your silver, now!"

"Mrs. Collins, please!" began Susannah desperately.

"Tis Jacobites, is what," pronounced Buckthorn.

Partisans of the late Charles Stuart in Mrs. Collins' kitchen were almost less likely than Roundhead engineers tunneling beneath Laceby's walls. Susannah marched down the steps and rapped at the door.

"Oh, Lady Hanford, be careful, do!" cried Mrs. Collins.

Glancing around, Susannah saw that quite a number of the newly recruited Laceby servants were standing about—including both the new footmen and the three new grooms. But of Ruby and the maids there was no sign.

"There's no need to stand about gawking! Go on about your business!" The shamefaced servants vanished—except for the housekeeper and the cook, intent upon the defense of their territory—and Su-

130

sannah raised her hand to knock at the door. It was opened in her face.

"Lady Hanford," said the workman, looking pleased. "Have you come to see how we're getting on, then?" He opened the door wider to let her pass.

From Susannah's vantage point just inside the back door, she could see that the kitchen table had been moved to make room for the pipes and drains and engines the plumbers had brought and was currently barring the door into the dining room.

The kitchen pump had been removed from its block and teetered precariously against one wall. In the distance she could hear the sound of a servants' bell that jangled forlornly and in vain.

"You see, your ladyship, the closest source of water being the cistern for the Laceby kitchens, we thought we could just run a pipe through here. It's a gravity fall from a spring a few miles away—good solid pipes, those; clay and copper—so there's no fear of it running dry. Why, I daresay with a good windmill you might even put in baths upstairs, if you were a mind to! And furnaces to heat them!" The man beamed, obviously pleased with his ingenuity.

"Yes," said Susannah at random, looking about for any sign of Ruby or the others. "That sounds perfectly lovely, Mr. Peters. But have you seen—"

"Math!" Peters called over his shoulder. "Are you ready yet? Beg pardon, your ladyship, but Math's nearly got the thing ready and—"

"But where is my abigail?" Susannah demanded desperately. "She must be here somewhere!"

Mr. Peters shook his head slowly, a puzzled expression plain on his face. "Lady Hanford, I've been here since eight o' the church clock, and I haven't seen head nor hind of—"

"Ah, there you are, you villain! And what have you done with my girls, eh?" Reassured by her mistress's safety, Mrs. Collins advanced in defense of her kitchen.

"Now, Missus," Peters began.

"Mrs. Collins, Mr. Peters says he hasn't seen your girls, and I'm sure he would not wish to mislead you," Susannah interjected quickly.

"Well then, your ladyship, if he hasn't seen them what's he done with them, eh?"

As there was no conceivable answer to this, Susannah was perforce silent, and slowly she became aware of a faint, desperate pounding.

Holding up her hand to Mrs. Collins for silence, she advanced down the narrow hallway in the direction from which it seemed to come—the servants' dining hall, she remembered vaguely, from her studies of Laceby.

She winced at the marks left against the stout oak door by the shoring-timber the masons had brought in and, conscious of Mrs. Collins' inquisitive presence at her back, pushed it open.

The servants' table was still laid for breakfast, with tankards of ale and nubs of bread and cheese strewn around in a fashion suggesting hasty abandonment. She stood for a moment, gaining her bearings. Yes, the pounding was louder. Susannah stalked it to a small door in the wall, whose whittled wooden latch shuddered with every blow from within. Certainty growing in her, she flipped it back and swung the door open.

Ruby, along with six other grubby self-terrified village maidens, boiled out of the niche that had once been priest hole or root cellar and flung herself perforce into Susannah's arms.

"Oh, miss!" she wailed, bursting into fresh tears. "Tis Luddites come to kill us all—they locked us in here, and—"

"Don't be silly, Ruby," reproved Susannah, meanwhile giving her maid full marks for coming up with a villain slightly more plausible than Roundheads or Jacobites. "It's only the stonemasons, come to fix the fountain—and I dare swear you locked your own selves in—as you slammed the door the latch must have dropped." Susannah tried a coaxing smile on the flustered abigail.

Ruby drew breath to defend her position as Luddite victim, but just then Mr. Peters shouted down the hall.

"We're ready to divert the water, Lady Hanford!"

Gratefully seizing this escape, Susannah paused only to see that Mrs. Collins had her staff in hand and went forth to view the wonder. Ruby trailed her as she went back into the kitchen where Mr. Peters stood wiping his hands on a bit of oil-soaked rag.

"There now, your ladyship. In just one moment you'll see a marvel of Gothic craftsmanship restored to all her former glory—and without the slightest inconvenience to your ladyship! Just as soon as we've got her going we can connect her up at the springhouse, and there she'll be!"

He looked so innocently pleased, and so completely oblivious to the havoc he had wreaked among the maids, that Susannah had neither the heart nor the courage to upbraid him.

"Thank you, Mr. Peters; I shall like to see that," Susannah said cravenly. She stepped outside and around the angle of the house to the drive. In that moment she became aware that a coach was making its splendid way toward Laceby's door—drawn by six showy greys with liveried postillions and outriders.

"Coach a-coming!" shouted one of the stableboys with belated glee.

It was Hanford's mother, Susannah thought in despair. And she was in her oldest clothes. With panic-stricken determination Susannah scampered for her own front door. If she could just gain the safety of the house before the coach stopped she could pretend she'd never been here.

At that moment the fountain exploded into aqueous life.

The Hanford ménage had made an early start from the Rat and Dragon just south of Market Arden. Mist still hung over the newly plowed fields (which, as the Dowager lost no opportunity to remind them, had once been Hanford land), and with luck they would reach Laceby by eight of the clock.

Nothing occurred to contradict that happy hope for nearly two miles, when suddenly one of the horses drawing the baggage cart went dead lame.

Peveril's London-purchased mount, a high-mettled chestnut named Crusader, minced up to the stalled wagon to inspect it. The off-wheeler signified displeasure in no uncertain terms, whereupon Crusader bore his startled young master off over the hedge and into the field at a rapid clip.

"Well," said Hanford to no one in particular, "we know he has the makings of a fine hunter, at any rate." He opened the door and swung Athelstane down out of the carriage. "There you go, young monster. Try not to be too much of a nuisance."

His small brother regarded him with acute disdain for a moment and then ran to see if he could get under the feet of the skittish wagon horses.

By the time Peveril had brought his mount under control and removed (at least in his own mind) any suspicion that his horse had bolted with him, it was obvious that the baggage cart could not proceed with its present horses. There was nothing to be done but to send one of the servants back to the inn at which they had breakfasted for a replacement, leaving the servants and the baggage to follow. As a result, the carriage, alone and unaccompanied, drew through the Laceby gates a little after nine.

For the previous half hour the Dowager Lady Hanford had been craning out of the carriage giving little half-stifled gasps at what she saw—though what this was, beyond the Warwickshire countryside in spring, no one in the carriage could imagine. When the house first appeared she said, "*Dear* Laceby!" in faltering accents and lapsed into silence again.

The equipage thundered through the rusted-open gates to the Park and up the drive. From his backward-facing position next to Athelstane, Hanford could see nothing and wondered what sort of greeting they could expect.

As the horses began to slow, the fountain burst into life. The water exploded from the nozzles of the fountain like cannon-shot and sent violent muddy whips of liquid lashing far beyond the confines of its catch basin. There was a ripping sound as water hammered like meteors from heaven on the pocked gravel of the drive and an ominous stuttering came from the fountain's bowels.

The six carriage horses were good beasts and true, but they could not, by any stretch of the imagination, be expected to countenance this. They exploded in much the same fashion as the fountain, and tried to go six directions at once. Peveril's Crusader and the other outriders simply scattered.

The coachman plied his whip in vain. The carriage was hauled this way and that by the wild-eyed sweating horses, springs singing protest as it teetered—rocking now this way, now that—on the verge of overturning.

Susannah watched in horror, riveted to the spot beyond any thought of flight. She had been soaked to the skin in the first instant of the fountain's outburst and her disheveled hair streamed down her back, but she was oblivious to the picture she presented.

Laceby grooms rushed forward to grab the leaders' headstalls, and at last the horses stood still—after a fashion—blowing and shuddering and cocking, rolling panic-stricken eyes at the now gently spouting fountain.

"There you are, your ladyship! Just a little obstruction in the pipes for a moment, but it's blown free, and I'm bound to say—" Mr. Peters, strolling gaily around the house corner, stopped, and no one ever did find out what it was that he was bound to say. Seeing what he had wrought, he turned and strode hastily away. A new groom came running up to the carriage with a set of steps. He deposited it at the side of the swaying carriage and dragged open the door.

There was a pause. Hanford appeared in the doorway, holding the remains of a high-crowned beaver in one hand. He stepped shakily down the carriage steps, holding to the doorframe for support and gazing about at the assembled gaggle of grooms and gawkers.

"I say, Han—this is a fine homecoming!" Peveril cried cheerily. He tossed the reins of his skittish mount to a hovering groom and slid from the saddle. "Damned fountain hasn't worked since ever so! Are you all right?"

Hanford ignored him, looking abstractedly about as if in search of something. His eye lit upon the bedraggled figure standing beside the fountain, but the discovery did not seem to please him.

"Han?" said Peveril.

At that moment the Dowager Lady Hanford chose to make her appearance.

Her bonnet had been hastily restored to her rumpled coiffure and her travel pelisse showed hardly any sign that its wearer had been rudely cast to the floor of the carriage and rolled upon by various of her progeny.

"Oh, Hanford, dearest," she murmured, sinking gracefully onto her eldest's shoulder. "I was so afraid for you! I thought we might be killed at any instant," she added in trembling accents. "*How* could that fountain have chosen to work at such an inconvenient moment?"

Trembling her voice might be, but it carried. Susannah stepped forward, gritting her teeth.

"I am afraid the fault is mine, Lady Hanford. I never dreamed you would be arriving today, or I should certainly have given orders that—"

"Mama!" came a querulous inquiry from within the carriage. As all eyes turned toward her, Orinda Hanford surveyed the scene below her. Her eyes grew round as they settled on Susannah. "Hanford, is this—" she blurted, and then flushed a deep crimson.

"Yes, my dearest," said the Dowager in die-away tones. "This is dear Hanford's dearest little bride. We must all be grateful to her for working so hard ..." Her last resources of strength apparently expended by this graciousness, Lady Hanford leaned heavily on her son's shoulder. "Oh, darling, my head is aching—"

"Yes, Mama," said her dutiful son.

Hanford looks tired, Susannah thought in instant sympathy. "You will find everything in readiness, Lady Hanford," she said to her mother-in-law. "If you will come inside, I shall have Mrs. Collins make you a nice cup of tea." Susannah was suddenly conscious of her wet clothes, and shivered.

"Tea!" said the Dowager in weak tones of loathing, and turned her head away. Hanford looked at Susannah unreadably and then conveyed his mother to Mrs. Danvers' waiting sympathies.

137

"Don't mind Mama, La— Devil take it, what am I to call you?" Peveril Hanford turned his engaging grin on his new sister-in-law. "Can't call you Lady Hanford. Mama's Lady Hanford. That is to say—"

"—that Lady Hanford is now the Dowager Lady Hanford. And I am Susannah, if you like."

"Oh, by heaven, yes! Peveril Hanford—you can call me Pev," he said, taking her hand and bowing as if they had never met. As he bent over her hand his gaze focused at a point beyond her and he frowned. "It is going, though," he said of the fountain, as if daring anyone to contradict him. No one did.

Hanford returned and put a hand lightly on Susannah's shoulder. Quickly he stripped off his coat and draped it around her. She darted a guilty glance at him.

"My brother is the kindest of creatures, but no one has ever accused him of common sense," Hanford said in tones that might mean anything at all. "Come, Susannah, we must get you inside before you are quite frozen."

At that moment a small dusty boy burst free from Orinda's not-overzealous restraints and skidded to a halt before his eldest brother.

"Is she going to live here?" he demanded of Hanford.

"She lives here already. She is your new sister. This is Athelstane," he added.

"I already have a sister," said Athelstane in dark tones.

Hanford shook him gently. "Manners, brat."

"Do you?" said Susannah to Athelstane. "I have never had a brother."

Athelstane's expression was composed of equal parts dubiety and the better part of valor, but the answer he was about to make was lost to Susannah with Hanford's next words.

"Orinda and Peveril you know," said Hanford, turning a little away, "and I should like to introduce to you my cousin Ancilla Hanford. Ancilla, this is Susannah, my wife."

No, thought Susannah numbly, looking at the slender grey-eyed woman in the severely sensible travel clothes.

"Whom no person of sense or sensibility would be happy to meet under these circumstances," Ancilla finished for him. She regarded Susannah with ready sympathy. "How lovely to meet you, Lady Hanford, and if you are not carried away by the pneumonia I am certain we will be great friends. Hanford, it is no day to be standing about soaking wet," she said firmly, and took Susannah by the arm, effectively cutting off all conversation.

Ancilla swiftly detached Susannah from her husband, sent Orinda after her mother, commended Athelstane to Peveril's care and Peveril to view the stables. Then she swept Susannah upstairs, leaving Hanford standing.

Dinah had followed all these events from her bedroom window, and was waiting to pounce upon Susannah when she returned.

"Sukey! You're all wet!" Dinah flicked a measuring glance at the newcomer.

"She has had a fountain rain on her; not-at-all a nice experience, as you would know had it ever happened to you. Are you Susannah's sister Dinah? You had better ring for her maid."

"There are no maids," said Dinah sadly. "We looked all morning."

Susannah used both hands to sweep hair out of her face and tried to take charge of the situation.

"That has been taken care of now, Dinah. Ring for Ruby, and—"

"And you must change your gown, Lady Hanford, and take a cup of tea. If you will permit, I will give orders for Aunt Clementina's comfort—I am used to doing so, and I know just what she likes. It is a great pity that the fountain startled the horses, but it is nothing more than that."

The calm matter-of-factness of Hanford's cousin mortified Susannah. She had always been the one who was calm and decisive—now she was dithering like a wet goose before the people she most wished to impress.

"Yes. I am sorry for not showing you a better welcome, Miss Hanford—"

"Oh, do please call me Ancilla; we have enough Hanfords beneath this roof to stock a play! As for the welcome, how could you? You did not know we were coming, and the servants, who would have come before, are with the baggage some ten miles from here, and I hope we may see them before nightfall!" she said merrily. Susannah smiled tentatively back. Whatever Hanford's feelings might be, she found it impossible not to like his cousin.

"And you must call me Susannah, as I have already told Peveril he may. Whether it was my fault or not, I am truly sorry for the greeting you received. Please ask Mrs. Danvers for anything you need, and I will send my maid to Lady Hanford at once."

"Now that you must on no account do," said Ancilla firmly. "Leave Aunt Clementina to me and all may yet run smooth."

Hanford watched his wife and cousin ascend the stairs, and wished he could call Susannah back and somehow begin the morning anew. He knew how much she had dreaded meeting his family, and now. . . .

The beginning of a headache throbbed behind his eyes, and all the longing he had felt for Susannah's company was mystically transmuted to pure irritation.

It was almost funny—Lord Hanford, Master of Laceby, had fallen in love at last; and with that most unsuitable of objects—his very own wife.

All around him was furniture in Holland covers and oddiments of fabric and wallcover. The air was perfumed, not by roses, but with the reek of glue and sawdust. In the distance could be heard a faint pounding, and through the open door came the plashing of that damned fountain.

He'd all but told her to leave the fountain alone, but she'd done just as she wished—in that as in everything. Everything at Laceby had been set on its ear; the place looked like a draper's pattern-card instead of his home.

And Mother—! He closed his eyes tightly in anticipation of the scenes to come. Everything Susannah had done to "improve" Laceby would prove out everything the Dowager Lady Hanford had ever said about her.

An unsuitable bride for a Hanford. And he didn't care. No matter what she'd done to the fountain, it was *not* her fault that it had exploded in the horses' faces.

As always in times of trial, Hanford sought his sanctuary, pausing only on the very doorstep to consider that Susannah might have despoiled that too with her improving mania.

But his study was untouched. A silver bowl on the desk was filled with country flowers—iris and crocus and daffodil and hyacinth—the bright spring flowers in their strong-scented blues and yellows. It was the only change or addition to the room. He sat down at his desk and tried to think, but the layered shocks of the past few weeks were simply too much for him. It was hard, now, to remember why he had thought it so important that Laceby be left untouched. He could no longer remember what he had once thought of Susannah, or a time before she had been here. He only knew that he had not acted as befit a Hanford of Laceby and that Susannah would suffer for it.

His bleak reverie was interrupted by a tapping at the door.

"What is it?" he demanded. The door opened, and Susannah stood there.

He might have leapt to his feet and let the joy he felt on seeing her show in his face. He might have crossed the distance between them and taken her in his arms, and kissed her with a husband's right and a lover's passion. But a Hanford of Laceby did not do such things, however much he might wish to. Especially if he did not think he would be welcome.

"Susannah," he said instead, getting slowly to his feet.

"I know that you are not pleased at your welcome," she said candidly, leaving the door open behind her as she entered, "although if you had sent word I might have known when to expect you—"

Hanford could not know that she cursed the fatal instinct that led her to attack before she could be hurt even as the words left her mouth. "But talking pays no toll; you are here now. And so is Dinah. She came to bear me company while you were away. It is only till fall term . . ."

"Dinah?" asked Hanford.

"My sister."

Hanford remembered, as if from another lifetime, Peveril's careless gibes about La Cit's impossible relations whom he would be forced to push upon the *ton*, and shook his head to banish the unwanted memory.

"I believe I have a right to my sister's company,

142

Lord Hanford, or—" said Susannah, misunderstanding.

"I have missed you."

Susannah stared at him, and at last he did go to where she stood.

"I have missed you," Hanford repeated, trying the words for rightness. "I am sorry about the fountain, for your sake."

She came into his arms as if she had only waited to be invited. He held her pressed against him, suddenly certain he could find the right words to say.

"Susannah, I—"

"Hanford, dearest—" But it was not Susannah who had spoken.

"Oh, silly me! I did not mean to intrude upon you—and here is Susannah, who must have a thousand things to tell about all the quite extraordinary changes that have been made here at our dear Laceby! I was not intruding, was I? My little love, you must tell me I am not *de trop*, or I vow I shall be shattered upon the very instant!"

Lady Hanford stood in the doorway and regarded her son and daughter-in-law with a bright birdlike gaze as they slowly stepped away from one another.

Chapter X

APRIL 1819

ATHELSTANE HANFORD, EIGHT years of age and freed
from the bonds of mother, sister, cousin, and nurse,
ran helter-skelter across the courtyard in the direction of the Laceby stables. The stables had not been
fully occupied in his lifetime, but they remained a
favorite resort on those occasions when he could escape the entanglement of his womenfolk.

His elder brother Peveril followed at the stately
pace proper to a man of mature years and glorious
prospects. In all his years Peveril had not worried
overmuch about the means by which the family fortunes were to be mended, and now, it developed, he
would not have to. He had been barely thirteen
when his father's death put an end to the lavish
Hanford household, and the privations Peveril had
only lately learned to resent were now at an end,
so obviously there had never been a need to fret
over them. A dazzling military career beckoned, full
of glory and uniforms and—beyond doubt!—the
swooning approbation of Letitia Goodchild, who
would certainly cry when he departed and kiss him
when he came home on leave. In addition, there
were a number of horses in the district he now had
hopes of acquiring—none the equal of his Crusader,

but a cavalry man had need of a string of mounts to make a fine show.

Beyond that, he had no ambitions. Peveril Hanford regarded the universe with the serenity of a man whose every need is provided for, and at the moment he attained it that serenity was shattered.

There was a girl seated demurely on an oatsack just inside the stable door. She was dressed in a sprigged muslin frock and a straw bonnet trimmed with French blue ribbands. Lace mitts covered her hands, and when she looked up from the book she was reading, he saw that her hair was quite black and her eyes exactly matched the blue of the ribbands.

"Ah . . . hullo," ventured Peveril. He was at a loss to imagine how this elegant incognita had come to appear in the Laceby stables.

The girl regarded him with a fixed, catlike composure. The handful of Laceby horses were housed in the other wing and Athelstane appeared to have vanished. Peveril and the mysterious stranger were quite alone.

"I, ah, suppose you live around here?" he suggested hopefully.

The girl closed her book. "I suppose *you* live around here?" she echoed coolly.

Peveril was slightly too young to recognize the Grand Mannerisms of the Romantic Theater. He flushed angrily.

"I daresay I do, if it comes to that! I am Peveril Hanford, and my brother's Hanford of Laceby! This is Laceby."

"Pity," said the fair unknown, making the word into two bored, languid, yet brittle syllables.

"Pity? What the da—dev—*deuce* d'you mean, 'pity'?" sputtered Peveril, beginning to suspect himself the butt of some perverse joke.

"I was hoping you were someone nice," his antagonist said simply. She struggled to maintain her countenance and failed; unable to stifle her giggles, she leapt to her feet and fled into the stable.

Peveril followed, but as he would no more have laid hands on a gently-bred young woman of Quality than he would have flapped his arms and flown to the moon, he followed slowly. He saw the girl vanish into an empty box-stall and cautiously approached the door.

Peveril looked in. She was sitting balanced precariously in the manger, tilting her book so that the sunlight from the high barred window fell across the page, apparently oblivious to his approach. Peveril regarded her as if she might explode. He was beginning to suspect her identity.

"Don't you know it is very bad *ton* to pursue females with clandestine intentions—even unescorted ones?" she said without looking up.

"I say!" Peveril protested weakly, recoiling. He had no idea what clandestine intentions were, but supposed they must be a very bad thing to have.

"In fact," continued Dinah, in that same tone of merciless severity, "if you were not very nearly my brother-in-law, I do not know what people might not say."

"*You're* Susannah's sister! Why, you—"

"Hanford will not like you to call her a 'teasing baggage,'" the haypile beneath Dinah's dangling slippers announced. It rose up, shedding straw.

Dinah squeaked in alarm and pulled her legs up under her, at which the manger groaned dismayingly.

"He says you could get spliced that way. What's 'spliced' mean, Pev?"

"Athelstane!" said his brother.

Athelstane scuddered on hands and knees to his brother's feet. "Is it like when Davy Goodchild tipped you a settler because you said—"

"Stopper it, brat," said Peveril, recognizing at-

146

tempted blackmail with the ease of long association, "and say hello to your new sister."

Dinah leaned forward. "And what did Peveril say to Davy Goodchild?" she asked with interest. "Was it something unconscionable?"

Since Athelstane was not quite certain what "unconscionable" was, he fell back upon his manners and told her gravely that Hanford said that gentlemen did not repeat tattle. He then announced that he was very busy, and made his escape.

Peveril and Dinah stared at each other. "And have—" she began, but the much-tried manger, having been put to a purpose its makers never intended, responded by pulling free of the wall and depositing Dinah in the hay in a flurry of sprigged muslin skirts.

Dinah looked up at Peveril from her seat on the floor. "—you any other brothers, Mr. Hanford?" she finished a little breathlessly.

"No, thank God," said Peveril with feeling. "Shall we start again, then?" he asked, reaching down to help her up. "Allow me to introduce myself; I'm a Hanford of Laceby, soon to be a hussar in the King's service. My name's Peveril; what may I call you?"

The enchantress laughed. "You already know my name is Dinah," she said, "but you may call me Miss Potter," she finished grandly. Her lace-mittened hand rested lightly on Peveril's superfine-clad arm, and she was of a height that made it a pleasure to look down to regard her.

"Very well, Miss Potter," said Peveril. "May I show you about your new home?"

"Very well, sir," she said, with a gracious inclination of her head. She did not feel it in the least needful to remind this tall, handsome, and amusing stranger that she had been in residence at Laceby a month already. Her eyes danced with impish refutation of her imperious gestures, and she was delighted to see that he smiled in return. Athelstane was completely forgotten as Susannah's sister and Hanford's brother walked slowly from the stable.

"I am not certain I should like you at all," said Dinah Potter meditatively some fifteen minutes later. Peveril had insisted on showing her the Laceby gardens, and then was more surprised than she was at the sight of them. Danvers had taken his new mistress's open-handedness to heart, and decades of neglect were being ferociously obliterated by his small fiefdom of gardeners.

"And why is that?" Peveril said indulgently.

"Well, to begin with, you are, after all, the brother of the man who married Susannah just because she had lashings of money and gave her nothing at all in return," Dinah said, half serious. The matter of the dresses still preyed on her mind, and she was prospecting for allies.

"Nothing!" exploded Peveril. "I suppose Laceby's nothing?"

"Laceby Place is a tumble-down ruin in the middle of nowhere—or was before Sukey paid out to have it repaired. More mortgage than mortar, Uncle Abner says. And as for giving it to her, that's pure moonshine! Lord Hanford married her to keep it, and—"

It would have been far better for Dinah Potter had she waited longer before taking this novel tack with Peveril Hanford, as she would then have thought better of it. An older man, with a good thick coating of town bronze, would have let her rattle on without paying the least attention to what she said, but Peveril was neither subtle or sophisticated. He did not look for hidden meanings in any speech, nor did it occur to him to excuse her on account of her sex and age. Peveril's was a simple world, and Dinah was attacking his brother.

"Fine words, Miss! And I suppose you'll tell me your 'Sukey' didn't jump at the chance to be Lady Hanford and queen it over her betters—"

Dinah slapped him. Her gloved hand made a powder-puff sound as it hit his cheek, and she sprang away from Peveril and spoke with breathless haste.

"I suppose you think you're clever, Mr. Hanford, but I am telling the truth, and you're not. And I don't imagine I like you at all, no matter who you are related to. Good day!"

Dinah tucked up her skirts and ran off, and Peveril gazed after her, bewildered by the turn events had taken. She had no right to say those things about his brother—and after all, Susannah *had* married Han for his title.

Hadn't she?

Susannah wandered about Laceby's familiar rooms, feeling useless and shuffled aside. The moment the Dowager had stepped over the threshold, the governance of Laceby had slipped through Susannah's fingers, despite all she could do to prevent it. Only Mrs. Collins had remained loyal, but having her come to Susannah for her orders only pointed up sharply the dereliction of the others. Hanford's mother was closeted with him in his library—very robust despite her spasm, Susannah thought uncharitably—and Susannah did not need to hear her to know what was being said. The refurbishings to Laceby that had seemed so vital now only looked rude and intrusive, and everything she had done stood out glaringly.

Hanford was right. Hanford had always been right. She should never have meddled. Shoulders slumped, Susannah trudged up the stairs. All she wanted now was to hide someplace where no one would ever find her.

"Someplace" was tucked into a crumb of space between the old wing of Laceby and the "new" wing—i.e., the addition only a century old. Once it had been larger, but half its space had been taken for the new chimney-shaft, and now the effect was rather like standing at the bottom of a well. The room still retained the height of its long-ago gallery incarnation, and from the spacious window remaining you could look out over the tatter-demalian garden and down the golden sweep of almost-lawn to the oaks and hedges and hills beyond, but the rest was a freakish jumble of misproportion.

Susannah felt a certain kinship with it—neither of them was a part of Laceby that the Lords Hanford might be proud of. But on this occasion her refuge turned out to be disastrously tenanted.

"Oh!" said the occupant of the chair by the window. "I beg your pardon—I did not think that anyone would look to find me here."

Susannah stared down at Ancilla Hanford. "I am so sorry," she said at length. "I did not know you would be here. I'll go."

"No, wait," said Ancilla quickly. "You needn't do that. I know I am trespassing, and I do beg your forgiveness, but if I were in my room I should surely be read a resounding scold by everyone from Hanford to Jenny Collins, so I am hiding." She smiled entreatingly as she set aside her embroidery hoop. "I beg you will not betray me."

"Of course not!" said Susannah. "But why should Hanford wish to scold you?" She seated herself on the hassock at Ancilla's feet.

"For coming back to England. I am supposed to be in Italy, you know, but neither Dr. Elphenstone nor I could see the harm in a few weeks of English summer."

"Is it ... Are you ..." Susannah began hesitantly. Ancilla chose to misunderstand her.

"Is this your favorite room too, then? It has always been mine. I only have to think of how furious Hanford's great-grandfather must have been when he saw it, and what excuses the architect must have made for it. I do not believe he was ever paid, either," she finished musingly.

"Not paying their tradesmen seems to be a family trait!" snapped Susannah. Instantly she remembered whom she was speaking to, and groaned in dismay. "Oh, my wretched tongue!"

Ancilla laughed, unoffended. "Oh, no! I daresay most of the Hanfords did have the most shocking manners—and when Hanford had to settle his father's bills he was quite distracted by their quantity. He still talks about it sometimes, if you can tease him to it. But you have been settling the Laceby accounts yourself since you came, have you not?"

"I ... Yes."

"And doing quite a few more things that have long needed doing as well."

Susannah faced her stormily. "No. If you mean my improvements, there's no need to be kind. I know that I have ruined everything! Oh, Ancilla, I was so proud of what I could do for Laceby that I would not listen to a word Hanford said—how could I have been so blind? Now I have ruined his home trying to make it new again, and Hanford will never forgive that, never!" Susannah rose to her feet to go.

"What? Ruined Laceby, and in only three months? Odd; it still seems to me to be standing—and none the worse for new carpets and curtains and a fountain that runs."

Susannah stared at her.

"Susannah, please, come back and sit down. I know we do not know one another well enough for me to say what I am about to—but I must. There is no one else to warn you against the Legend."

"Legend?" said Susannah, still defensive.

"The Laceby Legend. Or curse. You have fallen prey to it, just as I feared—just as any Hanford bride might. It shows in everything you've done to put the house back the way it was—as if Laceby were something important."

Susannah was thunderstruck at the blasphemy. "But—it's Laceby Place! When King Charles Stuart—"

"Oh, Susannah—that's Hanford talking, not you." Ancilla got to her feet and faced her new cousin. "What do you think of Laceby? Really?"

"It's Lord Hanford's home. It's very important to him," said Susannah tightly.

"More important than his own wife? It was of you he spoke while he was away, not of Laceby. But now that he is home again ... I very much fear that Laceby will possess him once more. You can not know, Susannah, what it has been like to watch while this hideous vampire of a house forced Hanford to sacrifice all that he could be to The Duty Owed The Blood. He is the best of us, you know, and it has all gone for nothing."

"He should have married you," Susannah said bitterly. "You understand him, and—"

"But Hanford doesn't need someone to understand him. He understands himself well enough for any two people. He needs someone whose love is stronger than Laceby. Not I; we are too much alike. I hope it is you, Susannah."

Susannah hung her head and did not answer. Ancilla put a hand on her arm.

"And now I have spoken out of turn and been vilely rude besides—but if you love Hanford enough, Susannah, you won't let Laceby have him. It will

take his last drop of blood—everything he can be—
and give back nothing."

"But how can I stop it?" Tears of pure frustration
stood in Susannah's eyes. "I'm not important to
him, and Laceby is! He married me for Laceby—"
She stopped, unable to force the words past the
tightness in her throat.

"Ah, there you are wrong. He married you for
me. And there is your hope; because Hanford still
loves people a little more than stone and timber
and the Sacred Blood. He loves you, Susannah—you
must make him realize it before it is too late." With
a sigh Ancilla sank back into the chair, her cheeks
flushed with the effort she had made.

"And if I can't? Ancilla, how can I?—He doesn't
love me—he despises me!" cried Susannah franti-
cally.

"But he does love you, Susannah—it is only that
you are not-at-all what a Hanford of Laceby should
want, and so he despises himself for it. Make him
see that he has a right to more of a life than as a
link in the never-ending chain of Lords Hanford; it
is his only hope. If you can't . . . You will have the
most beautiful establishment in all Warwick, and
it will have no heart to it."

At six of the clock the family gathered for dinner.
They came from far-flung distances: Orinda from
the writing of letters and meticulous cataloguing of
her newest possessions; Peveril from a bitter ram-
ble through the nearby woods that left his Hessians
(in his valet's words) a scandalous disgrace; Athelstane from beneath the kitchen stove (to be banished to his nursery supper); and the others—Dinah,
Ancilla, Hanford, Susannah, and the Dowager Lady
Hanford—from their isolate and independent rev-
eries.

Nor had they much to say when they came together. Susannah was too preoccupied to notice that Dinah was uncharacteristically silent, Lord Hanford was brooding upon the tale of wrongs and slights and purchases to make that his mother had wearied him with all afternoon, and each of the others, in his or her own way, had found something in the day's events to commend silence.

Except Orinda.

"I shall be so glad to leave Laceby you can hardly credit it! Summers are so dull here—and besides, the place positively reeks of varnish!" Unconcerned with the reception afforded her artless confidence, Orinda helped herself generously to the salmon in cream sauce.

The Dowager held her peace until the footman had left the room. "Oh, but my darling, you must not be selfish—I am certain that Hanford's wife will wish to keep you by her side! Dear Susannah can hardly have had time to discover anything at all about Laceby and all our dear friends here—she will wish you to bear her up!"

"But Han is going to Town for the Season, Mama!" said Orinda, too startled to be indignant.

"Oh, certainly, darling, but never this year! In a few years, perhaps—"

"What, and leave his blushing bride unpresented to the *ton*?"

Peveril had already been several whiskies the worse for wear when he sat down to table, but his current bellicosity stemmed more from a certain incident in the garden earlier than from any deep potation. "The new Lady Hanford must take her so-well-earned place in society, Mama. After all—"

"More wine, Pev?" interrupted Hanford sharply. The meaningful undertone in his voice was impossible to ignore; Peveril's glass was still, after all, full.

"Oh, indeed, Mr. Hanford," Dinah sang out, "you

154

are so right! Why, if Sukey were not to be presented immediately to the *ton* in her guise as the highly-ennobled Lady Hanford I vow I could not pledge myself for her composure!" Dinah could pledge herself for the pears poached in wine and the quail savouries, however, and did.

Susannah gritted her teeth and wished Dinah were close enough to kick.

"I'm certain, Miss Potter, that—" Completely irritated now, Peveril Hanford waved away all offers to supply him with victuals and moved ponderously to give battle.

"Peveril, darling, how sad I would be if I thought these were the manners you would display before guests! One learns such bad manners by association; but how fortunate that we are dining *intime!*" The Dowager beamed upon the company.

"Oh, yes, Mama—but you oughtn't blame poor Pev, you know—who can he meet at Laceby? I just *know* that when he is on the Town his manners will improve." Orinda looked soulfully at Peveril, who glared at her and drained his wineglass.

Susannah saw Hanford's eyes glint with mockery at the thought of London improving anyone's manners. He saw her watching, and smiled for her alone. Flushing, she lowered her eyes to her plate.

"I should not wish to imperil anyone's composure, Miss Potter; so I will tell you that Lady Hanford is to be presented at Court and have her Season. You may be quite at ease on that head," Hanford said mildly.

"Oh, Han! I knew you would not be a beast! And I am to come too? You would not leave me all alone here in the middle of nowhere!" This passionate declaration was truncated somewhat by footmen returning with an array of glistening jellies and *cremes*, an imposing roast, and a platter of pork cutlets. Mrs. Collins had clearly outdone herself to welcome her family home.

"Laceby Place is hardly the middle of nowhere, Orinda. The lower left-hand corner, perhaps, but . . ." said Ancilla teasingly.

"Oh, pooh! When you are living in the middle of a howling wilderness, Cilla, who cares where it is! I shall go to London for the Season and be presented! Oh, and I shall have all the most beautiful dresses, and a match trio, and a phaeton, and—"

"—and a silver moon-carriage with horses that fly—" interjected Peveril.

Orinda rounded on him. "Oh, and I suppose you want for nothing, Peveril Hanford? As if I couldn't buy a whole wardrobe of dresses for what that one stupid horse of yours cost you!"

"And you will, I don't doubt. Look here, my girl, just because we are done with make-and-mend doesn't mean you're wanted to go and buy out the shops." A footman filled Peveril's wineglass again and he raised it to punctuate his point.

"Why not?" said Dinah sweetly. "You can afford to—now. Can't you?" Their gazes locked across the table, and Peveril flushed and set his teeth. He lowered his glass to the tablecloth with particular gentleness.

Susannah was on the verge of saying she had no intention of partaking of the *haut ton*'s precious Season this year or any other when the afternoon's conversation with Ancilla came back to her. This house was the cause of the trouble between her and her husband. Perhaps in London things would be better.

"I am so glad you brought the matter up, Hanford. I shall be delighted to see London again, and I know Dinah will be too," Susannah said firmly.

"Then it's settled," said Hanford firmly. "The Hanfords are going to London for the Season. Orinda shall make her come-out—and Dinah too if that is what you wish for her. I will engage a house and make any other arrangements required." His tone indicated that no further comment from his family was required.

"Almack's," breathed Orinda.

The Dowager Lady Hanford laughed merrily and beamed upon her eldest. "Oh, how much you sound like dear Jocelyn, my little love! 'We shall do this' you say and—pho!—it is done. I only hope that you are not attempting too much too soon. . . . But do not worry about me in the least; I shall be perfectly content right here."

The footmen, having served, had departed. Susannah saw the careful trap an instant before Peveril spoke, but it was already too late.

"But, Mama, you must come to London! Who'll sponsor Orinda—or be Han's hostess?"

"Oh, Peveril; are you quite sure you are not drinking too much? I do worry so . . . Can you have forgotten that your brother is married now? Surely Susannah will wish to . . . take my place."

Peveril darted a glance at his new sister-in-law. He had learned his manners in an unforgiving school, and thus he did not snort with disbelief. But Susannah felt the force of his incredulity as if he had shouted aloud.

And Hanford, who had married her to give his brothers and sister the chance of their rightful positions in society—would he stand by and chance losing all by having their bow to the *ton* conducted under the aegis of his rich City bride? Or would he say what he must think? That she wasn't good enough to associate with the Hanfords of Laceby?

"I am certain I could never supplant you, Lady Hanford," said Susannah, before she could find out. "And surely Orinda will wish her mother beside her to witness her triumphs?" Susannah concentrated on reducing her cutlet to mincemeat uneaten.

"Oh, if only I could! But even if I could bear to return to the scene of so many happy golden days, we must remember that Ancilla must start for Italy no later than June—and she will need me by her side. I must not think of myself, you know."

This gentle rebuke was delivered in such a way as to make Susannah's teeth ache with the effort of keeping her tongue between them.

"I do hope you will come with me, Aunt Clementina—but this is barely April, and you must admit that nearly anything could happen before June! Why, I could marry, or enter a convent, or be kidnapped by an Italian nobleman on a black horse, or—"

Orinda giggled. "If you were kidnapped by an Italian nobleman, Cilla, surely he would just take you back to Italy, and that would be very dull!"

"Russian, then," said Peveril helpfully. "Or—no! I have it!—a Prussian count, all brick and bluster. He'd swoop you up in his leaf-sprung chaise—"

"—with the red-lacquer panels and the crest picked out in gilded porcelain and gems—" added Orinda.

"—and then, accompanied by his enormous wolfhounds—" said Peveril.

Susannah watched in bewilderment. The conversation seemed to have veered rather madly away from the Season in Town.

Ancilla threw up her hands and laughed. "Oh, Peveril, no! *Not* the enormous wolfhounds! Not even for you will I be murred in a damp antique Rhineland castle!"

"A sultan would be warm," said Dinah, in tones that indicated she was on intimate terms with dozens of them. Susannah attempted to sink lower in her chair.

"A sultan!" exclaimed Orinda. "You mean from Turkey? With a turban and aigrette?"

Dinah nodded, unable to bear being left out of any game even if it meant giving up her pose of icy hauteur. "He would be tall, and regally fair, with burning eyes—"

"—and neither Orinda nor Ancilla can meet him in

Warwickshire, beguiling though the prospect is of disposing of both of them at once." Hanford looked imperturbably down the table to where his mother sat, and the main topic of conversation was brought back into play. "It would look very odd, Mama, if you were not there to make your new daughter known to the *ton*, and I cannot see waiting yet another year to bring Orinda out when you and she have talked of nothing else these three years past. And I know that you will wish to make Susannah known to all of your acquaintance," he finished.

Plainly the Dowager could not believe her ears, and Susannah, who had had little opportunity to observe mother and son together, did not realize that she was watching an act of open rebellion.

But others did. "Of course you will, Aunt Clementina. Only imagine the parties you may give to present her—and make the rest look all no-how, I know. I do so hope to see all those places you have told me of visiting with Uncle Jocelyn—and you know how pleased all your old friends will be to see you on the Town again."

The Dowager, who could well imagine with what spiteful envy her friends would greet her new prosperity, was visibly moved.

"I suppose you are right, my love . . . I really do owe it to my darlings not to bury myself in the country any longer. And perhaps," she added, brightening, "we shall have a betrothal to end the Season with!"

The doors had barely closed on Peveril and Hanford, relegated in solitary splendor to the port, when the Dowager began cataloguing every one of Susannah's renovations and lamenting the passing of its ancestor.

"Mama, shall I have as many ball dresses as you did when you were a girl? And parties—and a masked ball?"

The Dowager laughed indulgently. "Oh, dearest,

bal masques are utterly *de trop*! And if only it were within my power, my little love, you should have a new dress for each day of the Season. . . ." She sighed.

"But why can I not, Mama?" pouted Orinda, plumping down on the couch beside her mother. "We are rich now—everyone says so."

The Dowager put a fond arm about her daughter's shoulders and lowered her voice conspiratorially. "But reflect, dearest, that it is Hanford's money—and his wife will have her sister to launch into Society."

It was marvelous to behold, Susannah thought bleakly, how Lady Hanford could imply so much while saying nothing at all.

"But, Mama, I can't share a Season—not with her. I won't! You promised me!"

"Oh, my darling—my heart aches to see you so desolated, when I am helpless!"

"It is quite all right, Lady Hanford—I don't want a Season." Dinah spoke from the high-backed chair to which she had retreated with her latest novel. "After all, I don't have to hurry," she said condescendingly to Orinda.

It was hard to remember, thought Susannah ruefully, that eight months—if that—separated Dinah's and Orinda's ages.

"You—!" Orinda turned quite pink with indignation.

"Perhaps Dinah will play for us," suggested Ancilla. "It has been months since Hanford had time for it."

"And Orinda shall sing—just as she did with him!" added the Dowager.

With only a little more prodding the two young ladies took up their positions at the pianoforte, and Dinah thumped the poor instrument with tolerable skill while Orinda sang of her love for a heartbroken shepherd. The Dowager sat, watching raptly, the picture of only slightly martyred mother love. Susannah realized with painful clarity that there were greater obstacles in her path to Hanford's love than his cousin or his house. She was refining on this bleak observation when Hanford and Peveril entered from the dining room.

As if that were a signal Dinah bounced to her feet in a jangle of notes and announced loudly that she was very tired and intended to retire to her chamber at once. Susannah wondered how it was that Peveril Hanford had managed to get himself so thoroughly disliked in the space of a few hours, but wished her sister a good-night.

"I shall go up too, Mama; may I? I have some letters I must write."

The Dowager graciously inclined her head and received a kiss upon her cheek from Orinda. With another round-eyed, wondering glance at Susannah, Orinda vanished.

"Forgive me, Aunt Clementina, Lady Hanford; but I am afraid I must desert you too. I simply cannot keep my eyes open another moment. It has been rather a long day." Ancilla got to her feet and headed for the door.

"Town looks decidedly thin of company," Peveril commented, looking around the suddenly-empty room. "We might as well have stayed over the port. Care for a hand of cards, Han? If Mama will play, we can make up a table of whist." It was not clear from Peveril's tone whether he was pleased or disgusted by the possibility.

But Lady Hanford announced herself exhausted by the shocks of the day—and was quite certain that Susannah did not play.

"—in which case, my darlings, it would be much too tedious for her simply to sit and watch the three of us. Perhaps Hanford will teach her sometime, and then we may be comfortable."

"I shall look forward to that, of course," said Susannah, "but meanwhile you are quite right; it *has* been a long day, and I am no longer used to keeping Town hours. Do please excuse me; I shall see Ancilla to her room."

Susannah found Ancilla standing in the hall, where half-a-dozen chambersticks crowned with creamy beeswax candles stood ready. Susannah took a taper and lit one from the wall sconce.

"Ah, I see you have had dealings with Gammage's in Lewesby," said Ancilla. Susannah's ill-humor vanished and she suppressed a gurgle of mirth.

"Oh, yes—Mr. Gammage is the most comical man! It is just as well that Hanford never paid him, Ancilla, as I am certain he would not have gone over the accounts. Mr. Gammage had been over-charging Laceby on every order for years—you may be sure that I made him correct the bill before I paid it," she added severely as she lifted the candle to light them upstairs.

In Ancilla's room there was a small coal fire burning on the hearth. Susannah's spirits lifted further as she saw the bed turned back, the night-dress laid out, the can of hot water and the long-handled bedwarmer all waiting and ready. There was nothing in her way of holding house for anyone to find fault with here.

"The comforts of life, if not the elegancies," commented Ancilla, stretching, "which to my mind is far superior than the reverse. I will apologize to Hanford tomorrow for stealing you away—he would not like to think that you are not upon easy terms with his mother."

Susannah looked at her cousin-by-marriage, wondering how much Ancilla already knew, or guessed. What had been left at Laceby for her to find after her wedding trip was nothing less than outright sabotage. And if she knew, then surely Hanford knew the extent of the Dowager's resentment as well.

"You must try not to mind Aunt Clementina," said Ancilla as if she had read Susannah's mind. She rang for her maid. "She has idolized Hanford from the moment he was born, I think, and has quite an inflated opinion of his consequence. Why, if poor Princess Charlotte had lived she might have married him instead of Prince Leopold—and faced much the same welcome, I do assure you!"

Susannah went slowly down the hall to her room, wondering whether she could follow Ancilla's advice, whether the Dowager would ever be reconciled to her existence, and whether the most irrevocable choice of her life had been the most disastrous. Ought she to ever have married Lord Hanford of Laceby at all?

But he had missed her while he had been gone. He'd said so. And Ancilla had said that he loved her.

"Oh, what does love have to say to anything?" muttered Susannah crossly. "It's just a lot of nonsense for books!" She reached her room and shoved open the heavy oak door.

All the candles were lit, and the heavy brocade bedcurtains—now replenished bright and new—were drawn closely around the bed as no maid would dare to leave them.

"Dinah," said Susannah. The bedcurtains quivered electrically. Susannah crossed the room and thrust them open.

Dinah lay curled on her side, propped up upon pillows, a book before her. She was still dressed in the flowered muslin she had worn at dinner, and the candle she had taken into bed with her to provide light was canted crazily, spilling wax upon the pillows.

"Dinah! Mrs. Danvers will never be able to get this out!" Susannah scolded, seizing the candle. She

163

deposited the flaming relict safely on the bedside table and turned back to her sister, but the peal she had prepared to ring died unuttered on her lips.

"I want to go home," said Dinah, her eyes tragic. "I want my own house, my own room, my own things—I want Papa!" She threw herself on her sister's neck and clung tightly.

"Oh, Dinah," said Susannah inadequately. It was Dinah who had always been a rock in the depths of their bereavement, staunchly insisting that things would get better even when they looked blackest; Dinah who had refused to give house-room to grief. Had this only been another of Dinah's many performances? She hugged her sister tightly.

"I want to go home!" Dinah repeated, as if she were eight instead of eighteen. Susannah felt her own eyes sting with tears for the loss of the comfort and love that had ended when Jacob Potter died. It was barely a year, and suddenly the loss seemed as fresh and bewildering as ever.

"Hush, my darling. You shall go home. We shall open our own house on Lower Chapman Street for the Season, and you shall go back to your own room again and have your own servants around you. Don't cry, Dinah!"

"And everyone will say that you married Lord Hanford for his title," sobbed Dinah, burrowing more fiercely into Susannah's shoulder. "And say that you jumped at the chance of a handle to your name and so you could queen it over your betters!"

"Oh, Dinah," said Susannah again, feeling even more helpless. She could pretty well guess who "everyone" was and where Dinah had heard these things since this morning. "Say as well that Lord Hanford auctioned himself off to the highest bidder and sold his name and his family for round gold coin—there's as much truth in that, you know."

"But he did! And you didn't, Sukey—you never

wanted to marry one of Them!" Dinah struggled upright and stared earnestly into her sister's face with all the indignant fire of adolescence. Susannah suddenly felt old and lonely, as if an unimaginable gulf yawned between eighteen and twenty. She sighed and collected Dinah back into her arms and chose her next words with care.

"Dinah, I married Hanford and he married me for much the same reason. We both had . . . people who depended on us, and to marry was the only way either of us could take care of them. Lord Hanford's papa left his family deeply in debt, and our papa left us both very well off, but you know I needed to marry. And there was no one better."

Even as she said it, Susannah's sense of the words changed. There *was* no one better. Hanford was not the best of a bad bargain, he was the best choice—for her. "When you are older you will understand," she finished lamely.

There was a knock on the connecting door.

"Then you don't love him?" Dinah demanded eagerly. "I knew you couldn't. He's just what you said he was—a bloodsucking, Garter-decked maw-worm, and I wish you had never married him!"

The door opened and Hanford stood in the doorway. He had exchanged his dark-grey coat for a rather splendid dressing-gown with gilt tassels and bullion fringe and removed his cravat. "I'm sorry," he said. "I didn't realize you were engaged, Susannah."

"Dinah, run along off to bed," Susannah said hurriedly. She gave her sister a little shake and pulled her to her feet. "Now."

"I don't want to interrupt you. It's not important," said Hanford, turning to go.

"No, wait," said Susannah. Dinah scrambled off the bed and slipped out the hall door, pausing only to glare venomously at Hanford. He did not look so much surprised as resigned.

Susannah went over and closed the door firmly behind her. She turned around and leaned against it.

"May I sit down? I'll apologize now for Peveril. Mama is right; he is drinking more than he ought, but he's young and getting his first taste of freedom. I'll speak to him. It won't happen again."

"Hanford, you are . . . very kind." She gestured for him to sit.

He sat down on a high-backed bench near the fire and stretched out his legs. "Am I? I daresay you hold a unique view of my character."

Susannah colored, ever-so-slightly. "I am glad you came. I . . . wanted to talk to you."

"About the Season? I don't know what sort of maggot Mama's taken into her head, dragging her heels now about bringing Orrie out when she's talked of nothing else for the last three years. Actually I do know, but we shan't speak of that, if you please. But Peveril was right about one thing—it is time you were made known to Society, and partook of all the delights of the Season. I'd like to say you'll hardly notice it, but you will. You're lucky not to be a stranger to London, at least."

"I thought you wanted to go." Susannah drew up a stool and sat at his feet. Hanford took her hand in both of his.

"There's no point to wanting or not wanting to do something you must do, Susannah. I made a number of promises to your uncle before our marriage lines were signed. Presentation at Court, a Season in London, the entree to all fashionable houses, acknowledged as Lady Hanford before the *ton*."

"Oh, Hanford! I don't care about any of that!"

"Perhaps not. But I should look very shabby indeed to marry you and give you not even that much

166

in return. Which reminds me; in all of the, ah, excitement today, I forgot to give you this." He turned her palm up and placed a small object into it.

It was a flat black leather box from Rundell & Bridges, lined in white satin and containing the most dazzling pair of earrings Susannah had ever seen.

Blue sapphire teardrops set in plaques of scrolled yellow gold dangled from flashing rose-cut diamonds. The earrings were quite shockingly beautiful, and even Susannah could tell that they were stones of price.

"I'd say I thought of your eyes when I saw them, but that would be trite. So I'll say instead that it's always desirable to have negotiable gifts in hand. They'll buy them back, too, if the need ever arises. And it might."

"Do you really think so? In case you happened to overhear my earlier conversation, my lord husband, I have never considered you to be a bloodsucking, Garter-decked maw-worm," Susannah said dryly.

Hanford smiled. "I am delighted to hear it, since I confess I entertained the liveliest dread of being unhouseled and dispossessed for making up to you on false pretenses when you discovered the truth. I'm not a member of the Order of the Garter, you see."

It took Susannah a moment to untangle this, and when she did she laughed, weak with relief. "Oh, Hanford! Everything will be all right, won't it? I knew you must have heard her—how not, when she was saying such hideous things?"

"I suppose she has every right to think it. It is only what others will say, after all—and who can blame them?"

"I can! Dinah is just a little blue-deviled. She is homesick, poor darling; she has barely set foot in her own home since Papa died. But I have promised her that we may go home for the Season. I know she will be happier there."

"Do you miss Town, Susannah?" Hanford asked neutrally.

She took the earrings from the box and held them up before she answered. The glow of the coals reflected through the stones kindled sparks of pure blue fire.

"I thought I would, of course. I had never lived in the country before. But now . . . It seems rather hard to have to leave it just as the flowers are starting to bloom. The earrings are beautiful, Hanford. Thank you!"

For some reason her praise seemed to make him uncomfortable. "Practical, actually. You'll need something to wear for the Season, and I'm afraid the family doesn't run to heirloom jewels anymore."

Susannah tilted her head back to look at him.

"We will be home again by August; you will still find flowers enough to suit you then. The roses will be in bloom, too—and we will find you something better than Jupiter to drive." He raised his hand and let it drop, hesitantly, on the cushions just behind her head. Susannah leaned her head back on his knee, the eardrops cradled in her hand.

"I think there are some diamonds of Papa's, if I really do need them. I mean, they were meant to be my diamonds, but I have never yet worn them. They are in a vault, I think, at the bank."

"Take them out as soon as we reach London and send them to be cleaned—you'll need them for your presentation at Court, plus every bangle Mama can borrow. But we'll go up at once, even if it means perching in a hotel for a fortnight or so while Soberton finds us a suitable house. I've already written to him to watch out for a property to lease—or you might prefer to buy, instead, if there is anything to be had."

"But, Hanford; I told you—we don't need to rent or buy. We have a house already. Papa's house on Chapman Street is still standing vacant, and most of the furniture is there. It is quite big enough for

all of us for the Season, and I have already promised Dinah we can live there. With all her own
things around her I'm sure she'll soon be all right."
She closed her fingers over the glittering stones in
her hand and felt them, sharp and hard and heavy.

"You told your sister that we would live in your
father's house for the Season?"

Something about the tone of his voice made the
skin on her neck prickle. Susannah straightened up
and turned to look at him. "Yes, I did," she said
slowly. "It's our home—Dinah's and mine. I know
it does not have a fashionable situation, but it is
comfortable, and—"

"It won't do," Hanford said abruptly. "I'm afraid
you will have to break your promise to your sister,
Susannah. I am sorry you were foolish enough to
make it."

"I beg your pardon, my lord?" Susannah said, but
she was afraid she had heard him all too clearly.

"Chapman Street is quite impossible. We cannot
possibly carry off the Season from—"

"—from a Cit's hovel on the docks? Oh, for heaven's
sake, Hanford! You've seen it—it's one of the grandest
houses in East London—Papa paid out hundreds of
pounds to have it furnished—and it's ours freehold. It
even has a ballroom! And it's just sitting there empty.
After what Laceby has cost, and the way your brother
and sister have been spending, we shall have to economize somewhere, and—"

"—and pioneering the City is not the way to do
it! My God, don't you have a brain in your head
that isn't occupied with accounting?'

Susannah leapt to her feet, but Hanford stood too
and grabbed her before she could fling herself away.

"Or is it that you think you are the only one
who can keep bargains? I promised your uncle I
would bring you into my world. I can't manage it
if you insist on dragging about Town smelling of

169

the shop! You must live where I tell you and do as I tell you—"

"Let me go! Let me go!" Now she did pull herself free, and stood staring at him, panting. "Dinah was right! I was right! You don't care about anyone or anything but keeping your stupid promises—and you'll spend us into the ground trying to do it! If we do not plan for the future the money will be gone, Hanford—we cannot afford to simply throw it away on your foolish pleasures!"

"And that's what a Season is to you—foolish pleasure? I am thinking of your consequence, Susannah—your place in Society."

"You are talking about yours—that everything should be done as befits a Hanford of Laceby! You will not compromise—you won't even listen!"

"Have you? You knew from the moment you accepted my suit that I needed to establish my family—yet the moment I brought you here you began throwing your money about, as if anyone would thank you for it. Nothing I could say would stop you—and now you are telling me that my family must suffer the consequences of your extravagance? Think again! The Hanfords are going to London, my wife—and not as a raggle-taggle band of gipsies either."

"Then you'll need these!"

She flung what was in her hand at him and ran from the room. He heard her sob just as the door slammed.

The sapphires struck and glittered on the hearth. Slowly Hanford knelt to retrieve them. The delicate gold was bent and one of the stones was cracked.

"Susannah," said Hanford to the empty room. He pressed the earrings to his lips and closed his eyes.

PART III

An Inconvenient Marriage

Chapter XI

APRIL 1819

SUSANNAH PICKED UP a little porcelain figurine. She remembered the day Papa had brought it home with him, grumbling fiercely about adding another fantod to a home that already resembled a curiosity shop. Dinah had been six then and had broken its predecessor. Her father had entrusted the replacement to her, and eight-year-old Susannah had been very careful to keep the pretty new china lady out of her sister's hands. As careful now, she set it back on its table.

Susannah closed her eyes tightly, refusing to give vent to tears. Only let the servants see her weeping and there would be no end to the gossip—and servant's-hall chatter always found its way to the wrong ears. No one would be allowed to say that the new Lady Hanford regretted her marriage of convenience.

After a moment, she straightened and went on with her inspection tour of the London town house. The green-and-coquillot striped couches glowed in the afternoon light, and seemed a little cowed by the flamboyance of the massive sopha covered in red Chinese silk. The little sphinx-footed wine table that Jacob Potter had bought when Nelson's Nile victories made Egyptoiserie the crack of fashion sat beside it as it had always done, and all around Susannah lay the opulent and joyful gleanings of a merchant in a nation made imperial by trade.

She wanted to go home.

Susannah groped for the door handle and then slid the door quietly shut behind her. She wiped her eyes on her handkerchief and took a deep breath, and only then realized that, still confused by the unfamiliar house, she had not gone to the morning room as she'd intended, but into Hanford's library.

The library was a drum-shaped room lined with bookcases that stretched from the floor to the silk-covered ceiling. The edges of the shelves were gilded, and the narrow expanses of wall that were visible were not paneled, but enameled in deep green. Bullion-fringed curtains of the same color as the walls insulated the room from the noise of Audley Square outside, and a wholly-unnecessary fire was laid in the grate of the carved serpentine fireplace. The study was furnished expensively, exquisitely, and in the very latest style.

The only reassuring note in the jewelbox elegance was the presence of several large wooden crates—one half unpacked and spilling straw—that stood stacked neatly by the window. Susannah felt as if she were an unwelcome intruder here, but instead of leaving, she walked over to the curved satinwood desk. It was not among the things that had been brought from Chapman Street when the house had been sold. Who had furnished this room for her husband and chosen the delicate modern furniture? She looked around the room. The bookshelves were filled with volumes bound in green morocco, each identical to the next and uniformly new.

She looked to where the crates of books shipped from Laceby stood, brought to bear Hanford company through the rigors of the Season.

She sat down heavily in the chair behind the desk. She knew who had designed the room and chosen the furnishings.

After that disastrous interview two weeks ago, Susannah had waited for Hanford to reproach her for her behavior, to thunder that he would be master in his own house, to coax her with compromises—in short, to do anything but what he did. He pretended the entire interview had not taken place, and for a while Susannah was craven enough to hope it truly had been forgotten and the plans for the Season abandoned. Then the letter had come.

It was from her Uncle Abner, full of gossip— Cousin Ethan was being sent to the Americas with a last chance to mend his fortunes; Egyptian cotton was still frightfully dear and the price of American cotton was rising as well; Uncle Abner had met a Mrs. Andrews at Aunt Doolittle's last month and would be very well pleased to meet her again—and equally full of bracing admonishments on the necessity of burning bridges and looking forward to the future. (It would be very hard to look forward to the past, as Dinah had said when she'd read it.) It had taken him several paragraphs to come to the point, and Susannah several re-readings to understand what he was trying to tell her.

Hanford had given orders to sell the Chapman Street house.

It was his right, of course; he was her husband, and her property was his to dispose of. But he had done it without a word to her—and had bought the town house in Audley Square equally silently.

In public her husband was courteous and deferential. But in private she was shut out. Lord and Lady Hanford had nothing to say to each other when they were alone.

Hanford, it seemed, had made his choice. He had married for his family's sake and had found noth-

ing in his bride to render her of equal importance.
And the love that had sparked between them at
their first meeting, that had grown in her even
through all the misunderstandings of the past
weeks, was a gift that Hanford did not want.

Susannah struck the desktop with her fist, and a
door in the desk swung lazily open. Papers slid from
the shelves of the inside and spilled out onto the
floor.

More bills, Susannah thought automatically, and
bent to gather them. But these were not bills. The
pages were inscribed in an elegant sloping hand,
and on each one was a poem.

Susannah glanced through the sheaf of unsigned
manuscript quickly, trying to see if these were by
anyone she knew. Then she stopped, and read more
slowly.

'Could I but reach an hour's respite grace . . .'

Her eyes prickled with tears again, and this time
she let them spill over. Someone else felt as she
did—lonely and forced to lead a life that held no
possibility of happiness. After a moment or so she
blew her nose and wiped her eyes and felt, unac-
countably, better. She retrieved the rest of the
pages from the floor and the cabinet in the desk and
made a tidy pile of them on the top of the desk.
They were written on plain foolscap such as anyone
might have in his writing-desk, and the writing was
the highly-impersonal script of any educated man.
Whose were they, and why were they in Hanford's
desk?

"Susannah, dear—I confess I was hoping to find
you." The door opened again, and the Dowager
Lady Hanford entered the room.

The Hanfords were just arrived in London, and a
wait of at least a month could normally be expected
before they shed out their dowdy country plumage
for the dazzling feathers of Town, but Clementina

Hanford had decided to bloom at once. In deference to her status and the Season, the Dowager Lady Hanford was wearing a cornette of aerophane crepe trimmed with blond lace upon her short fashionable chestnut ringlets. Her jaconet petticoat was lavishly trimmed with several rows more of the lace, and the embroidered overrobe of amber *gros de Naples* that completed her toilette was dashing-yet-matronly and the very latest thing. Susannah, quite automatically, priced the Dowager's clothes and blinked at the figure she arrived at.

"I—I beg your pardon, Lady Hanford?" She hoped she didn't look very much as if she had been crying.

The Dowager settled her shawl more comfortably about her elbows. "I have been searching all over for you, Susannah—I just knew I would find you here. I'm sure the servants have been all that is diligent, but I confess I would rather be back at that dreadful hotel than living in a house in such a state of confusion, and you, of course, must feel just the same. It is a peaceful room, it is not?"

Susannah looked around. Peaceful was not a word she would have chosen to describe the library.

"Jocelyn and I spent so many happy hours here! I could not believe that Hanford meant to buy back my dear home, but when he did I gave orders that the library was to be put exactly as I remembered it! Oh, not the furniture, and of course it is a different carpet—and the walls, I believe, were not precisely that shade of green—but it is just the same."

"I am sure you are happy to have your home back, Lady Hanford," Susannah said automatically.

"If you could only conceive my astonishment when he told me! With all our other expenses, I said to him, can we possibly afford it?—and he said, 'Mama, while I am alive you shall lack for nothing!' Only imagine!"

Susannah tried very hard, but could not imagine Hanford saying any such thing. The memory of their last conversation was still vivid, and she fiddled with the stack of papers under her hands.

"But I did not come to boast of my happiness, Susannah, but to share it," the Dowager continued, settling into a chair. "I know that we have had little time to become acquainted—I can hardly believe that scarce a fortnight ago we returned to England!—but may I speak to you as your own dear mother might? After all, we are in some sense connected, my great-aunt Clarendon was Amelia Clarendon's second cousin, you know, so we are quite family."

Susannah had not known of the relationship until this moment, and wondered why Hanford had not told her. "Did you know my mother, Lady Hanford?"

"Oh, good heavens—how could I, when she'd married your father?" the Dowager exclaimed artlessly. "But I beg you will allow me to presume upon the relationship nonetheless; you see, my darling is all my life, and a mother's intuition tells me that you and Hanford are not happy."

"I . . . It is only that he has been working so hard, Lady Hanford. I'm sure that . . ."

"Oh, my dear! You must not subject me to these polite evasions when I know that what I deserve from you is a resounding scold! Susannah, can you forgive me? You must know what I have done."

"I'm sure I don't know what you're talking about, your ladyship," Susannah said doggedly.

"Oh, I know it was wicked—but when Hanford told me that he had made an offer of marriage to a girl I had never seen simply to save the family from ruin, I was certain it would be much better for us all to be utterly ruined than for him to subject himself to an existence of utter misery—and so I told him!"

"What did he say?" asked Susannah, with commendable composure.

"He said the wedding was in ten days and I might attend or not as I chose," said the Dowager. She sighed. "When Jocelyn was alive he was never so cross with me. I'm afraid I ran quite mad—closing Laceby in such a rush and sending Ancilla and the servants on to Dover. And then when I saw what you had done for Laceby, and realized that you loved my darling just as I do, I was jealous that you could do so much for him that I could not." The Dowager lifted an exquisite lace handkerchief and dabbed at her eyes. "And now you despise me—and that is your right, for what am I but a meddling old Mama-in-law?"

"I am sure you are not that, Lady Hanford," Susannah began.

"If I am not, then perhaps I ought to be! I did nothing but tell him how unsuitable a mésalliance this would be—but my love, I never saw him look so happy as when we were turning home toward Laceby. I know you have had some silly quarrel—but I will do anything for my child's happiness, anything!"

"There is nothing anyone can do," Susannah said in a low voice. "We have quarreled about money, and I'm afraid it is past mending."

"No! I will not believe it! You will tell me the whole on the instant, and you and I shall contrive something."

Under the force of the Dowager's kindly determination Susannah told her the whole: her exasperation at the shocking state Laceby Place had fallen into, her fear that the hidden mass of unpaid bills would bankrupt them, her realization that they must economize or face ruin and Hanford's flat-out refusal to do so.

"And of course he was right to sell Papa's house,

Lady Hanford, if he did not wish to live in it—but I cannot help worrying that he will find himself in debt again," Susannah finished inadequately.

"Oh, I am sure he does not mean to go into debt, Susannah; you must not fret yourself on that head. Hanford has always managed all of my affairs beautifully, and I am sure he means to manage yours as well." The Dowager dismissed Susannah's nagging fear with such airy unconcern that the new Lady Hanford wondered if she had been wrong to worry at all.

"I do not care how well he manages them if only he will talk to me. I have wanted to tell him that I do not care what he spends—but, Lady Hanford, he will not listen to me!" The miserable truth was out, but the Dowager only smiled understandingly.

"He thinks you will only nag him to further economies—and I assure you, anything that smacks of such a course would be fatal. You must show him that you trust him to manage your affairs—leave all to him. There is a plan I have had in mind for quite some time—perhaps you will like it as a gesture of rapprochement. But what's this? Can it be that you have hit on the same notion?" The Dowager peered intently at the pile of papers Susannah held.

"These . . . These are some poems I found in Hanford's desk. I did not mean to pry; I was sitting here, and they . . . fell out."

The Dowager swooped to her feet and pounced on the manuscript.

"But this is the very notion I had—to publish Hanford's poems!"

That her husband was the poet whose work she had admired was a shock quickly smothered by the magnificence of the Dowager's plan.

Susannah was familiar with the slim pocket-book

editions of poetry—credited to "A Man Of Fashion" and known at a glance to be the work of Lord So-And-So—in which gentlemen of *bon ton* displayed their literary yearnings. What better way to make a peace offering than to publish a handsome edition of her husband's poems, paid for out of her own allowance?

"I have always looked to see my darling take his rightful place in Society, and how better than as a great poet? But each time I suggested it he told me that there were far more important things to spend our money on than empty frivolity—"

Empty frivolity and foolish pleasure. But both looked the same to Susannah—except that she would far rather see something done that made Hanford happy than please the *ton* by living at the correct address.

"But if I were to do it he could not object, could he? And then he would know—" Susannah broke off, eyes shining.

"He will know that it is no longer necessary to practice these awful economies—and that you have not the least interest in forcing him to do so," said the Dowager firmly. "And then you can be happy together."

Impulsively Susannah leapt up and embraced her mother-in-law, her mind already dwelling in the future in which her husband told her that everything she had done was perfectly justified.

Dinah Potter was a woman wronged. Hadn't she given up any number of agreeable plans for the summer to rush to the aid of her Only Surviving Relative who had been married in a fashion little better than a Slave Auction to a clutch-fisted, improvident libertine? And hadn't Susannah, rather than reposing every confidence in her Only Sister as was proper, chosen to tell her instead that everything was fine as fivepence when Dinah could plainly see Sukey's new relations were fiends from the most stygian of pits? And hadn't she, Dinah, to cap matters, been denied a Season and relegated to the schoolroom?

Dinah kicked at a pebble. The fact that none of these things was the case did nothing to calm her ferocious mood. There was, after all, the overriding matter of Mr. Peveril Hanford.

Dinah was not absolutely certain what there was in Mr. Hanford's character that made her so long to drown him, but whatever mysterious ingredient that was, she had realized its presence from the moment she had first laid eyes on him. Of late, however, he did not seem to be quite the same odious tattlemonger she had once known. Her outrageous remarks were not returned in kind; he seemed to have forgotten her.

Only let him try! Dinah snarled to herself. If he thought he could say that Sukey had married to elevate herself and get away with it, when it was well known that it was actually Lord Hanford who had married for money, then . . .

Dinah kicked at another pebble. Nothing was going as it ought, even their arrival at their new home. She knew the Audley Square house should please her. The address was as shatteringly fashionable as any top-of-the-trees could wish. She had her own room, her own furniture, her own dresses and the promise of more, the chance to be as much a belle of the *ton* as any of her classmates at Miss Farthingale's might envy, and all that she could think of was that Mr. Peveril Hanford had been very little among them since they arrived in London, and soon would go away altogether.

"Odious beast!" She tugged her shawl more tightly around her and continued seeing what there was to see in the mews, lanes, and gardens, that surrounded the town house. It was that or go back inside, and if she did that, her sister might force her to be useful in the matter of the unpacking.

Perhaps, she thought, she could hide out in the stables. But the carriage-house here was nothing at all like the untenanted stables at Laceby. Here the eight stalls were filled with high-bred cattle fresh from Tattersall's and a showy set of match greys for the Dowager to drive out with her new landaulet—all recent acquisitions. The chief groom sauntered out for a breath of air as Dinah approached; seeing her, he touched his forelock and went quickly back inside.

Balked of her refuge, Dinah turned back to the house. There was nowhere else to go but there. But before she could gain the front steps, the bright clatter of approaching hooves made her press herself back against the wall of the building.

Peveril Hanford turned Crusader down the little alley leading to the stables at a spanking trot, with precious little concern for anyone who might be in the way. He saw the muslin-draped figure pressed against the house too late to slow his mount safely—Crusader was an animal of dash and verve, and had a tendency to swerve when checked—but the alley was wide enough, just, to allow him safe passage to the stables, or so he thought.

Then Dinah's shawl fluttered, and Crusader attempted to remove all four feet from the ground at one and the same time. Peveril spurred his mount sharply, translating vertical motion into a horizontal bound that carried horse and rider past the traitorous bit of challis.

Once in the courtyard there were a brisk few moments before the stableboys could grab Crusader's bridle and drag the affronted creature to a halt, but once they had it was a simple enough matter for

Peveril to slide from the saddle and advance upon the architect of his misfortune.

"Oh, it's you, is it? Well, I daresay that's a fine how-d'ye-do? What the devil did you mean getting underfoot like that—you could have been killed and Han wouldn't have been half pleased!"

"I'm surprised you didn't try harder! I'm sure it would save him all manner of fuss and bother to have me conveniently out of the way—and you too!" Her relief that Peveril had not been hurt expressed itself in a fashion that Peveril could hardly be blamed for misunderstanding.

"Oh, Lord, don't you run mad too," he groaned. "Look here, are you all right?"

"Fine—no thanks to you!" Dinah lifted her chin and turned to go.

Peveril put a hand under her elbow and steered her toward the front of the house. "Well that's something, anyway. I can't think what Han would have said if I'd run you down. What with him biting a fellow's head off one minute and wishing he may be very happy the next—when I can tell dashed well he don't wish anything of the sort—it's enough to make any fellow take the King's shilling and go as far away as possible, I promise you!"

Dinah's heart gave a leap of pure terror at this announcement. "But surely Lord Hanford can't have been that disagreeable to you, Mr. Hanford? And when you had most specially assured me that he was the most amiable of men!" she said in a rush.

"I never did! And if you'd just stop ripping up crosswise at a fellow just for saying what's no more than everyone knows—! Well, anyway, it's a good job Cilla's settled and Orrie's to marry a fortune—and that I'm off for the Army as soon as a place can be found—"

"Then you haven't enlisted?" Dinah demanded sharply.

"Do I look quite as if I've got windmills in my

184

nob? Catch me going for a foot soldier; there's no advancement there! I'm for a cavalry regiment if Han can get me one; with a string of bang-up blood-and-bone under me and a prime pair of Mantons in my pockets!" Peveril said with the satisfied air of one who has considered the matter thoroughly.

"Then isn't it fortunate for your ambition that your brother has the money to stand the nonsense, even with all he's been spending? It's two thousand pounds to buy in, I hear, plus horses and guns. And horses and guns take money too, Mr. Hanford."

But Peveril was too well-pleased to take offense. "What doesn't? But at least you're getting something for your blunt this way—not like the tables. I was just down at Roantree's—Han got me in—and Bobs Gressingham told me he'd seen one fellow plunge thirty thousand pounds on no more than a turn of the cards at White's not four days ago—Han'll never do that, I'll be bound! I think if I'd ever taken the plunge he'd have had the skin off my back with a horsewhip—gaming pretty well ruined Papa."

"But Lord Hanford recouped the family's fortunes," Dinah said cuttingly. "How convenient."

They had reached the street, and Dinah turned to go up the walk. She was not prepared for Peveril to grab her by the arm and yank her back into the byway.

"Look here—I'm sick of listening to you rip up at Han just because he had the sense to marry money when we hadn't got any. Do you think it's easy for him to know he can't keep a wife, and she has to keep him instead? I don't see why we should all live like churchmice just to please you. Or maybe you don't know how it is, having to dodge the tradesmen and have them call you high-and-mighty for it; seeing your sister cry because she hasn't a dress fit to be seen in church in; being pretty well frozen in winter with no coal to light and going out with the guns every day into the bargain just so your

185

cook can have meat to put on the table. D'you think Han's fool enough to take a chance of going back to that? It's true he married your sister because she could sport the ready—but Susannah won't ever lack for a thing, so you might allow she's better married to my brother than to someone who doesn't know what it's like to be without a penny to bless himself with!" Peveril stopped, rather bewildered by his own eloquence. "I'm sorry."

Dinah stared at him, her eyes huge dark pools.

"I didn't mean to shout at you; it's just that you . . . Always deviling a fellow and . . . Han hates Town anyway; he hasn't been fit to talk to since we came back from Dover. If he hadn't promised Mama . . . Look, are you going to cry?" Peveril demanded at last.

"No," said Dinah in a small voice.

"Want my handkerchief?"

"No."

"Look, you know I didn't mean . . ."

"Peveril, have I been really awful?" Dinah interrupted.

Peveril smiled down at her. "Pretty awful," he said softly.

Dinah sighed lugubriously and smiled up at him in turn. "But Sukey was so unhappy, Peveril, I just couldn't bear it. And you were so mean! You did say that she married Lord Hanford to have a title. You did."

Peveril took her hand and squeezed. "I did, and I'm sorry now. But dashed if I can figure out why she did marry him, Miss Potter. If she wanted a title, there's lots higher for sale than plain Lady Hanford—and Han says she accepted him on ten minutes' acquaintance to boot! You don't believe in love at first sight, do you?" he asked suspiciously.

"Sometimes," said Dinah—and blushed.

Chapter XII

APRIL 1819

LORD HANFORD OF Laceby, neat to a shade in high-crowned beaver felt, Limerick gloves, and neat-toed Turkish pumps, ascended the three steps to 39 Audley Square and rapped at the door. He spun his gold-knobbed cane absently, waiting for Peacock to appear.

Hanford had spent an appalling and exhausting afternoon making the rounds of his clubs—at which the arrears in membership fees had been settled discreetly some time before—and the matter of Peveril's commission was well in hand. But as the shadows lengthened the elite turned homeward to dress before an evening's pleasure, and so Lord Hanford too sought his own hearth.

Odd to think of Audley Square as home once more; but when Soberton had told him the lease had come on the market he had not stopped to think. His mother had always been happiest in London; if he could present her with the home his father had taken her to as a bride perhaps she would be content there, and leave Laceby to Susannah—if it wasn't sheerest air-dreaming to imagine that Susannah wanted Laceby at all.

The door opened, and Hanford gave all the

ephemera of a man of fashion into the hands of the waiting butler.

"Good afternoon, Peacock; please tell my mother that I have returned and shall be in my study if she wishes to see me."

The house looked the same and not the same—he had left the decoration of it in his mother's hands, as a further eventual inducement to her to take up residence here. She would not want Susannah's furniture, of course, but it would be a simple matter to send it to Laceby once the need for it in Town had ended. But that was a matter to broach after the Season was over. He opened the door to his study.

A tide of subaqueous light washed over him. "It's like living in the bottom of a well," Hanford muttered crossly. He strode to the heavy velvet curtains and yanked them open.

He hadn't remembered the library as being this dark—but he had only been here once or twice, and undoubtedly his father had never seen it in daylight at all. This unfilial reflection pleased him, and he returned to his desk.

The stark modern inkwells and their accompanying sander were full; the penknife was sharp; and the supply of quills was adequate—but a hasty ransacking of the drawers of his desk failed to produce the writing paper he sought. Peacock, when applied to, said that the expected order from Crane's had not yet materialized. A further reconnaissance through the jumble of the half-unpacked library disclosed writing paper and sealing wafers at the bottom of one of the crates, and so after only a slight additional delay Hanford sat down to write.

"Dear Lord This, Dear Major That, The Honorable Peveril Florian Gilchrist Hanford, younger brother of the present Lord Hanford and nephew of the late Major Brabazon Roderick Hanford, an officer in the King's Own Hussars, being desirous of a military career, begs the favor and honor of a position in his late uncle's regiment. I hope and trust in your generosity, as if he isn't out of the house by Thursday week, I may throttle him. Yours sincerely . . ."

That wouldn't do at all. Hanford chewed on the end of his pen and thought about Susannah.

Squandering money for spite, she had said, the shopkeeper's daughter who felt that given and received should balance on some hypothetical scales. And if she trusted him so little, how could he expect her to believe him when he told her that sometimes it was necessary to pay hard gold coin for . . . nothing?

He couldn't. She wouldn't. And what was love without trust but an infatuation of the senses?

Hanford picked up his pen again. The prospect was quite as bleak as he had warned Peveril, though there were glimmers of hope—as well as the awful threat that he might actually be forced to take up his seat in Parliament in order to make use of them.

And what sort of welcome would the returning Lord Hanford of Laceby have received, with an address down by the East End docks engraved on his calling cards?

Money cannot buy happiness, my love—we are living proof of that—but it can buy so many other intangibles. It made no sense, and so it was a case that could not be argued. But it was nonetheless true. Why wouldn't she understand that?

Hanford flung his pen across the room.

"Hanford dearest, Peacock told me you—Whatever in the world is this?" The Dowager Lady Hanford picked up the object her delicate kid slipper had trod upon.

"It is a pen, Mother."

"Well! There is no need to go into the miffs with me! But my poor darling, I am sure that it is only that you are worn to a thread with all this planning and furnishing—you must not tire yourself so."

"A full-dress Season is hardly likely to rest me, Mother."

The Dowager frowned uncertainly and Hanford relented.

"But we did not come to Town to rest, did we, Mama? You look ravishing; is that a new dress? You must take Susannah with you the next time you go to Madame Francine's; I know she will enjoy it. But tell me, how did your calls go? Are we to be received?" He smiled at her encouragingly.

The Dowager laughed and patted his cheek. "Silly boy! I am not quite nobody, you know—and you are a Hanford of Laceby! Orinda and I left cards on a number of our acquaintance, and we may expect cards of invitation in due course—you did say I was to have a free hand in the matter of entertainment?"

Hanford hesitated. He knew that his mother did not have the slightest idea of how many shillings went into a pound and no notion of economy; on the other hand, she had a fine sense of style and no desire to be a laughing-stock before the *ton*.

"Of course, Mama. I could ask for no better hostess to usher my wife into Society."

The Dowager fidgeted with the fringe of her shawl. "It is about that which I particularly wished to speak to you, my dearest love."

Hanford set down the penknife with which he had been shaping another quill.

"You know that I have always supported every decision you have made regarding the welfare of the Family, Hanford, and of course Susannah is a charming girl—why, to see her one would never suspect . . . but never mind that! I know that you have sworn to bring her into fashion, no matter what your own feelings might be, and of course . . ."

"If Caro Lamb could be received, Mama, I do not see why my wife will not be."

"Oh, but dearest—Lady Caroline was not attempting to obtain vouchers for Almack's!"

Almack's Social Club, where a mere ten guineas could purchase an entire Season's worth of boring Wednesday evenings—boring, that was, if you had the entree.

"I am nearly certain that Emily will oblige me for Orinda's sake; but Susannah—how can I ask it of her, when you know how Princess Esterhazy can be? It would be better, I think, not to raise the subject at all."

"I am sure you are right, Mama—if they have refused the Duke of Wellington they will hardly scruple to snub a mere Baroness. I think it is better that we avoid Almack's altogether."

"But . . . altogether, my love? Surely you do not mean that Orinda mayn't go? I have already—"

"Whatever plans you have made, Mama, will include Susannah. It would look very odd, you must agree, if my sister had the entree to places my wife did not. But if you wish to go for your own enjoyment, there can be nothing in that to excite gossip. And who knows, perhaps the Princess will relent."

"I only hope you may be right," the Dowager said ominously.

The very next morning, Susannah rose early, dressed, and went, accompanied by her maid, to interview the firm of Lovell and Challoner regarding the private publication of a book of poems.

Her reticule bulged with the roll of banknotes Hanford had given her for pin money, and if that were not enough, she was sure the Dowager could help her obtain more.

Susannah alighted from the hackney carriage in the noise and bustle of a busy commercial London street. She gazed about her at the scene of chaos with the practiced indifference of the Londoner, then hurried across the street dodging draymen and hawkers and carriages of all descriptions.

The scene greeting her within the building could not be more divorced from the world outside. She might have stepped into an ancient Greek temple dedicated to the Muses, or some other gallant goddess of the written word.

The foyer was completely surfaced in white marble, with tasteful Corinthian half-columns ornamenting the corners. Through an archway decorated with severe marble ladies in draperies, Susannah could see a masculine-looking oak-paneled room, with a counter behind which sat a thin stooped man in gold-rimmed glasses. It looked much like the other shops of Susannah's experience, only far more elegant, and with no wares displayed. Conscious of Ruby's disapproving presence behind her, Susannah moved forward.

"May I help you?" The reedy young man behind the desk looked up from his labors—he was writing, with hasty grace, across a pile of yellow foolscap—and regarded Susannah with resignation.

"Is this Lovell and Challoner, the publishers?"

"Yes'm. 'Purveyors and publishers of volumes of refinement.' It says so on the sign."

"I should like to submit a book for publication. I am Lady Hanford. The Dowager Lady Hanford recommended you to me."

"I see. And what sort of book might this be?"

Susannah resisted the urge to tell him that it might be any sort of book at all, but what it was, in fact, was a book of poetry. When she had explained, the young man looked even more dyspeptic and said:

"Begging your pardon, your ladyship, but we're up to here with poetry. Every man fancies himself the new Corsair—and every woman his Medora, and the fact is, we've bought so many poems that if we published till Doomsday we couldn't get rid of them all. I'm afraid you'd be best advised to take your poetry elsewhere."

"But my mother-in-law—the Dowager—told me I could pay to have my book printed here!"

At the word "pay" the very enervated young man's interest sharpened visibly.

"Oh, you want to buy an edition, do you? You ought to have said so at once! You'll have to talk to Uncle Nathaniel for that."

Uncle Nathaniel was to be found at the end of a long dark hall leading even further into the building, and proved to be Mr. Nathaniel Lovell, one of the partners of the firm. The price he quoted Susannah for an edition of one hundred copies made her blink.

"But my dear Lady Hanford, you must consider. Since the end of the Continental Tyranny prices have risen alarmingly—and naturally, the figure I quoted you is for an article making use of only the finest materials. French kid leather, pure gold edging and embossing, Chinese silk endpapers, and naturally, it would be printed on the very finest paper obtainable. On the other hand, if you wished to consider something cheaper . . . in cardboard covers, perhaps?"

"Of course not!" Susannah said quickly. Hanford, she knew, would never count the cost of something like this, and so she wouldn't either.

"Excellent. I am certain you will feel that the end product rewards all the care you have taken with it. Perhaps your ladyship would be so good as to choose your design from our pattern-cards so that the contracts may be drawn up . . . and then, perhaps, a small deposit on account . . . ?"

The "small deposit" proved to be nearly the whole of Susannah's bankroll—but for her pains she had secured the creation of a book of poetry bound in primrose leather stamped in gold, with red silk endpapers, a title page in three colors of ink, and printed on paper of the finest—"straight from our Edinburgh mills, my lady, and I can say without fear of contradiction that you will find no better paper anywhere in the land!" It would be hers six weeks after she brought the manuscript to Lovell & Challoner.

"Six weeks! But—I had hoped—" Six weeks would be nearly the end of June—far too late for the Dowager to view the fruit of her suggestion.

"Well, I don't like to make promises, but, seeing as you're a lady of Quality, I shall do all that is within my power to get them to you sooner. Now, regarding delivery; where shall I have them sent?"

"I shall send someone for them. They are to be a surprise for my husband, you see, and . . ."

"I understand perfectly, Lady Hanford. Discretion!—that is the watchword of Lovell and Challoner. You may repose your entire confidence in me."

Susannah was not quite certain of that, but she was desperate—and honest enough to know that she had no way of determining whether Mr. Lovell was honest or not.

"Thank you very much, Mr. Lovell. I am quite certain that your services will prove satisfactory." And after all, the Dowager *had* recommended him.

The Dowager Lady Hanford's sitting room was a small third-floor chamber decorated à la Russe. Numerous black lacquerwork screens depicting Russian wildflowers had been erected to cover the walls, and everything from curtains to tablecovers was said to be authentic. Authentic it might be, but the delicate desk at which she sat with her daughter had come from no further east than Paris.

"—oh, Orinda, I do not see how you can say that books are dull! Why, nothing scandalous can be dull, and it is rumored that Lord Byron is to give the world a new poem this fall. You'll see some fun then!" Dinah said happily.

"Orinda, my love, you are not attending. If you wish Madame Francine to have ready for you all the gowns you will need, you must choose them now." The Dowager turned the pages of the *Ladies' Repository of Fashion* and tried to summon Orinda's attention back to her assault upon the *ton*.

"Oh, Dinah, how can you bear to read the work of such a dreadful man? Why, he left his own wife to go and live among savages!"

"The Greeks will be glad to hear you say so," commented Ancilla. She shifted her chair closer to the fire and picked up her embroidery hoop again.

"But see here, Dinah-my-girl, you can't compare sitting in a stuffy old room reading about some Turkish fellow to actually doing something!" Peveril protested.

No one knew by what dread threats Lord Hanford had moderated his younger brother's conduct, but in the fortnight since the family had removed to Town Peveril's behavior had been exceptionally demure. He attended the clubs for which his brother had sponsored him but did not gamble, and his evenings, though spent in the main away from home, inclined to the relatively staid amusements of the theater. And as he could be counted on to attend the family breakfast the following morning with a clear eye and a detailed report of the previous evening's bill, there was no suspicion that he might be cloaking other activities with this show of virtue.

Dinah closed the book of poems she held and made a face at him. Peveril bowed without stirring himself. The Dowager tried another tack to summon Orinda's attention.

"It is such a pity Dinah will not also be making her bow, my love; the two of you would look charmingly together—and only think of the gowns you might have!"

Orinda looked speculatively at Dinah. She knew perfectly well that her guinea-gold coloring would show to great advantage paired with Dinah's raven-wing curls—and that fickle gentlemen who could be cold to one maiden or the other would be dazzled by the combination.

"I say," said Peveril. "Why isn't Dinah making her bow, Mama? She's as old as Orrie is! It'll be dashed inconvenient having one chit in the school-room and the other on the Town!"

"Anyone would think that you were still in the schoolroom yourself, with as much address as you display, Peveril," said Ancilla.

"Oh, but dearest Peveril, you know that Susannah felt that it was much too soon after her bereavement for dear Dinah to be subjected to a Season—it would hardly be fair to ask it of her, don't you think?"

"But, Mama! I know Dinah would wish to go to parties with me—and if she does not make her bow, I shan't either!"

"That is blackmail, you know," said Dinah appreciatively.

"I think it may only be blackmail, Dinah, if Orinda's threat were to cause you great mental anguish," said Ancilla. "Do you feel yourself to be experiencing anguish, Dinah dear?"

"But we could go around together, just like sisters!" said Orinda. "We'd have ever so much fun together, Dinah!"

"And I daresay I could be persuaded to stand up with you—if Mama was to throw a dancing party," added Peveril.

"What a treat that would be for me!" gibed Dinah cheerfully.

"Oh, but Dinah, I hardly like to force you against your inclination," said the Dowager. "And you

know that I do not stand in any sense your parent—
we must win Susannah's permission."

"You'd better do it soon, too, if you want to be
rigged-out in time for the Coldmeece Ball."

The Dowager Lady Hanford had tended her *ton-
nish* connections with scrupulous care and in due
course had secured her prize: an invitation to the
Hanfords to attend the ball that the Earl of Coldmeece was throwing for his two young cousins.

"It hardly sounds like fun at all," Dinah mused.
"Sitting for hours in a cold carriage, crammed chap-
by-cheek with people in other carriages all going to
the same place—whom you must pretend to ignore—and then when you have finally gotten to the
door you can't stay above half an hour before you
must call for your carriage again—assuming you
want to return home before noon the next day—and
then you must stand about in the hall for hours
waiting for it to come."

"My, what a dismal prospect! It hardly sounds
worth doing, does it?" Ancilla said, smiling.

"It will be lovely." Orinda looked up from the
pattern-book and sighed. "Thousands of candles,
and garlands of flowers, the musicians in their gold
coats and powdered wigs and everyone in diamonds
and pearls . . ." Her eyes shone with the splendid
visions that waited just out of reach.

"You needn't sigh over it as if you aren't going
to have it," Dinah pointed out ruthlessly. "I went
with you to order your ballgowns last week."

"Oh, Dinah, why do you always have to be so
mean? They are beautiful dresses, and—"

"—and if the Regent had had a son instead of a
daughter, and if he had lived, he would be of an age
to take one look at you and be instantly smitten,
and you would be the next Queen of England," Ancilla teased. "You must not mind Dinah, Orrie dear;

it is just that we are both so very jealous of your extreme beauty."

But even Orinda found this too difficult to believe. She gave up the unequal struggle, and laughed. "Oh, Cilla, what a bouncer! But Mama does think I am very well indeed and will show to advantage—don't you, Mama?—and then I shall become the Her Grace the Duchess of By-Your-Leave, with a house and servants and no Hanford forever telling me that I must save my pin money. I don't see why I shouldn't spend it when I have it, since I didn't spend it when I didn't."

Neither Dinah nor Lady Hanford could find any fault with this logic.

"I think it would be a very good thing if you were to be presented this Season, Dinah," said the Dowager decisively, "and I shall tell Susannah so at once. I am sure she will be agreeable." She rose from her chair and left the room.

"Should you like to be married, then, Orrie?" Dinah asked curiously. She darted a sidelong glance at Peveril, who attempted to fix her with his quizzing-glass. Unfortunately for his pretentions to dandyhood, Peveril was too large and solid for its peacock display. He found himself regarding her through his thumb, and dropped the glass sheepishly.

"Oh, yes! I would miss my family, of course, but I am missing most of them now, or will be soon. Peveril doesn't count, as I should be glad to miss him, but Cilla is to go back to Italy in June. I even miss Athelstane, the little monster; isn't that odd? I never thought to be sorry that he was not here to cut all the lace off my best dresses. But perhaps he has mended his ways, now that you have given him your puppy."

"And perhaps he has not," said Ancilla. "He is only eight, after all, and cannot be expected to understand the finer points of Fashion. But he can hardly commit any crimes upon your dresses from Laceby."

"Oh, Dinah, must you go back to school?" cried Orinda. "It would be sadly flat if you were to leave! Only think; Han is sure to have a houseparty in September—and then there is the Little Season, over Christmas ... Perhaps I shall be engaged by then, and we might both spend Christmas at my fiancé's house. He will be very rich, and so it would be very grand ..."

"And have you already culled this paragon from the herd?" asked Dinah.

"Of course." Orinda blinked in surprise. "Oh, I have not met him yet, but I know just the sort of man he must be, so why shouldn't I dream about him? Don't you? Surely, Dinah, you too have thought about the man you will marry? How else are you to know when you have found him?"

"I think ... I'd like ... to follow the drum," Dinah said slowly.

"Be a soldier's wife!" said Orinda. "How could you possibly? When you are to have thousands of pounds a year and might marry anyone."

"A soldier's wife would have an interesting life, don't you imagine, Peveril?" asked Dinah unblushingly.

To Ancilla's sinking dread, Peveril smiled, like a man who has discovered that there is more good fortune in the universe than he had hoped. "I imagine she might, Miss Dinah," he said. "If she wanted to."

"There!" said the Dowager, returning. "All is settled, and now, Orinda, you must help Dinah choose the dresses she will need, as well."

"Only think of it," said Orinda. "Perhaps twin brothers will fall in love with us, Dinah! They will both be Dukes, and rich as Golden Ball, and—"

But Ancilla, watching unregarded from her seat by the fire, thought that Dinah's mind ran to a very different sort of husband than a Duke.

Chapter XIII

MAY 1819

LIFE IN AUDLEY Square resolved itself into an unceasing round of preparation for this fête or that, until Susannah had no time at all to brood or, indeed, to do anything else. Despite the Dowager Lady Hanford's encouragement she was as far from a reconciliation with Hanford as before—when she had asked him to give her the housekeeping accounts so that she might go over them, he had told her curtly that he was quite accustomed to handling them and preferred to go on doing so. Pride kept her from making any more explicit appeal to his feelings—that, and the growing fear that there might not be any feelings for her to appeal to.

And so, Susannah thought sourly, Susannah was here—in front of her own dressing-table, on her own carpets, in a house that her house had paid for, on the first of May, 1819, preparing for her first Society ball. Perhaps she would go mad, Susannah thought with gloomy relish. Then Hanford would have to keep her locked away in an attic at Laceby, from which she would escape at intervals to terrorize his guests. This pleasant fantasy occupied her until Ruby arrived to begin the layering and lacing of her evening costume.

When Susannah had still been in pantalettes, the

fashionable lady wore seven ounces of gauze to dress her whole person. But Susannah was no longer in pantalettes, and the weighty modern fashions required ladies as well as gentlemen to corset their figures to create a fashionable line. Grimacing, Susannah adjusted the cylinder of flesh-colored buckram around her ribs and told Ruby to lace it up tight.

"Not so tight, Ruby!" she protested a moment later. A wave of nausea washed over her, and she clutched the back of her chair for balance.

"Are you all right, Miss? I thought you wanted yourself strapped up like always—there's a good span o' daylight showing yet."

Susannah gulped down sickness and took a deep breath. "Perhaps . . . not quite so tight as all that," she said weakly. Ruby, muttering, tied the laces off and stepped back.

Susannah looked at her corseted form in the mirror, and over her shoulder she saw Ruby regarding her with the natural suspicion of every interested lady's maid.

"Bring my underdress at once!" Susannah said quickly.

Was she breeding? Susannah wondered, gazing into the mirror. She was dressed and coiffed and jeweled for the ball and had sent Ruby away; but the question remained. Certainly she had done everything needful to place herself in that interesting condition, and Aunt Mariah Doolittle's lecture preparing her for the wedded state had been thorough if nothing else. But no lecture, however comprehensive, could create certainty where none was possible.

Susannah opened the drawer in her dressing table where lay a manuscript copy of Hanford's poems. It was a little like having a secret lover, she thought to herself. The man whose existence she had only suspected was revealed in these pages, and with these written words he courted her as his living self had never done. She lifted the page that lay at the top of the stack.

My love is fair, and chaste makes foul wanton me/ Ravisher of silks and sunlight; pillager of flowers—

But perhaps he didn't mean her to be the subject of these poems. Certainly Susannah could not imagine herself as the miracle of fire and music her poet-husband wrote of.

Engrossed in her dreams, Susannah did not at first realize that the image in the mirror had its basis in actual fact. Then she did, and slammed the drawer with a guilty groan.

Even at this early hour Hanford was already garbed for the ball. His knee breeches were grey, of a slightly-lighter shade than his severely-correct evening coat. He wore the carnelian signet ring as usual, and one chaste correct fob dangled from his silver brocade waistcoat. In his hand he carried a small leather notecase.

"My dear, you look charmingly. Willoughby will be around front with the coach in just a few minutes. I know it is hours yet before the ball, but if we were to start at a reasonable time we wouldn't get there till daybreak . . . and I wanted the chance to speak to you alone first. Privacy is not so easily come by in Town as it is in the country, is it?"

"Yes. No. What is it?" Susannah said shortly. A rising wave of nausea made her clench her teeth. Had he seen her shut the drawer? Would he demand that she open it? What could she possibly say when he did?

"I realize that you do not approve of this move to Town, or of the arrangements I have made—but I do not propose to discuss them with you now, if you please. You are certainly capable of managing your own money, and ordinarily I would not pursue this matter, but since all of Mama's bills come to me I have your bills from Madame Francine's as well, and I could not help noticing . . ."

Wouldn't he come to the point? She felt perspiration break out on her face and neck and wondered if she were going to faint. "If you please, Hanford," Susannah said sharply. She saw him draw back at the formality and could have wept. She snatched up her swansdown powder puff and began to dab fiercely at her neck and throat.

"The point, my lady wife, is the bills. You are spending far too little to be dressed as you should. You've ordered barely half-a-dozen dresses from the dressmaker—surely you cannot expect your trousseau to suffice you this entire Season?"

"Of course not." Her breathing was coming easier now and the spasm seemed to have passed, but this was the last topic on earth she wished to open with her husband. "I have ordered other dresses, Hanford—from my own dressmaker, in the City."

He had not sat down, but as she spoke he stiffened as if he had been jerked abruptly upright. "God in Heaven, am I to have you drag my family through the muck by appearing in public in rags bought from a pedlar in Edgewater Road? Despise me if you must, but think of your sister's chances!"

Susannah dropped her powderpuff and rounded on him. "I *am* thinking of her! I am thinking that I do not want her inheritance squandered as well as my own. You promised me, once, that we should have a fair bargain in our marriage, and perhaps by your lights you have kept it. But what I do not see is why nothing is any good unless it costs twice what it is worth!" Susannah blinked back tears. Ancilla and the Dowager had been wrong, each in her way, she suddenly realized. Hanford cared for nothing but his consequence.

"Oh, my little shopgirl," Hanford said unhappily. "I should have been brave enough to let you marry your hideous cousin. He would have had you in the Fleet for debt by now, but you would have understood him. Tell me, Susannah, when you are paying fair price for fair value and getting that which is necessary into the bargain, are you spending too much money?"

"Of course not. But—"

"No, let me finish. Our fair bargain was that you would come into my world—the glittering world of fashion, frivolity, and high degree." Hanford's tone was dryly ironic. He tossed the wallet of bills onto her dressing-table and sat down. "This you agreed to and this I am undertaking—hampered only slightly by a helpmeet who thinks I have instead run mad and am flinging gold sovereigns by the bushel into the street for the sheer novelty of it."

Susannah flushed and stared at the wallet as if it were a serpent. "Hanford, it is none of your business where I shop. It cannot possibly make any difference to the *ton* whether I spent thirty shillings or thirty guineas on a dress."

"Ah, but it can—and it does. My love, do you think I sold your home out of spite? It was precious to you, I know—but your home is Laceby now, and you must play the Fashionable World's games. If we keep the proper style now the Polite World will forget our impolite past. Sometimes who you are doesn't matter, providing you do that. Mama's family is in trade too, did you know?"

"*In trade?* Hanford, you are lying to me," Susannah said uncertainly.

He shook his head. "Have you never heard of Sir Phillip Masham? Or Robert Masham? I admit that Barbadian plantations are not on the same scale as selling sugar by the loaf at a confectioner's shop, but without doubt the Mashams are scandalous antecedents. Between that and Great-grandfather Christian having been hanged for treason, you can quite understand that we Hanfords must be exceedingly nice in the company we keep."

"But for heaven's sake! I never . . . Hanford, why didn't you tell me about your mother before?" He was cruel to rouse her hopes again, but surely he would not speak so to her if he did not care.

"Would there have been a point? Mama does not puff off the connection for obvious reasons, and her family has not wished to know us since Grandfather Masham died. But I wish you to know that I have reason to know the wisdom of what I am telling you. Oppose me in whatever else you choose; follow your whimsy and fling the consequences in my face, but in this one thing do as I tell you. Cut your connections with the City. Buy your dresses at Madame Francine's—or whatever other mantuamaker the Fashionable Pure see fit to patronize. Do as the *ton* does, and you may move through my world with impunity."

"But I don't want to! I never wanted to—and the more I learn about 'your world' the less I like it. I married for a husband who would not squander Papa's estate, Hanford—and there's no reason to pay so much when you can buy the thing for half the price, except because you can. It's foolish, and wicked, and I won't do it!"

"Bargains again." Hanford sighed, and rubbed his temples. Susannah realized with surprise that he was deathly weary. Yet they were going to a party tonight from which they could not expect to return before dawn.

"Tell me, my little Jacobite, if Dressmaker A charges twenty shillings for a dress and Dressmaker B charges thirty, isn't A a better bargain?"

"Of course she is—but you're about to tell me I should buy the more expensive dress just to spend the extra money. Well, I shan't!" And if she said they should stay home tonight, he would refuse, on the grounds that his precious Society expected them to go out.

"But you must," insisted Hanford gently, "because Dressmaker B is modiste to Quality, and for that extra ten shillings you not only receive any gossip she is willing to pass on, but you are entitled to gossip about her as well. Small-talk that does not ruin reputations is hard to find—and on some occasions it could be vital. Extra value for extra shillings—surely the better bargain, wife."

"The better bargain! As if I wanted to spend my time in overheated drawing-rooms talking to—"

"—blood-sucking, Garter-decked maw-worms. Yes, you have aired your feelings on that head before. Susannah, when we have established my family you may live in any style you choose, but until then, buy your pretty dresses by the dozen from Mama's dressmaker, and leave the rest to me. With your settlements you can at least command a *pensione* in France if I am hanged for debt."

"Oh, Hanford, I—"

There was a tapping at the door. "My lady, h'its the coachman waiting down front!"

Susannah got to her feet; Hanford offered his arm. And nothing had been solved at all.

The Dowager's at-home the following morning partook of every symptom of a rousing success. The Dowager, being a practical woman, did not even mind that its success owed nothing to her own machinations. The drawing room of the Audley Street town house was filled with the hum and clack of busy tongues because the Coldmeece Ball had been a scandal from first to last.

Had not the Earl himself proposed marriage to his niece and ward, a girl young enough to be his daughter? Had not his disinherited heir, the rich, handsome, and affable Augustus Templeton, announced that he would straightaway marry the next woman he saw? And had not the entire ball been marred by the grim shadow of the family's visiting American connection, Kennard Upshaw, known to have been a privateer, gun-runner, and slaver?

"Actually," Susannah said quietly to her sister under her breath, "I doubt very much that any of those things are the case—for do you know, Dinah, I did not see any events answering to such descriptions while I was there! I did see the American, though—and he was very dark!"

"I do hope he does turn out to be a pirate—but you may count on it, Sukey, that he will be something very dull, like a cloth importer!" Dinah sounded personally aggrieved by this, and looked around for Peveril, who had promised to attend.

"Hush, Dinah—or the Dowager may hear you!" Susannah bent her head low over her embroidery as she said this, but Clementina Hanford was hardly likely to take notice of the irreverent remarks of a schoolgirl when she was at last set in her rightful sphere once more.

The Dowager Lady Hanford looked all that was charming in a dress of spring-green challis trimmed with darker green velvet. Hanford had obviously never had the need to lecture her on the importance of buying additional dresses. In her own demure round taupe dress of Circassian cloth—one of the several bespoken from the despised Town dressmaker—Susannah felt underdressed and, worse, tawdry. Fortunately no one seemed to notice.

Though it should have been Susannah who seized the ribbons of conversation and drove the company where she would, she had resigned that task to her mother-in-law with real relief. The Dowager knew

207

each of her callers and could summon up some harmless bit of news about each for the amusement of all, and as Susannah watched the Dowager Lady Hanford shine at her chosen art, she knew that she herself could never hope to equal her.

Susannah looked around the room filled with fashionable ladies and elegant gentlemen, and thought of the ball the night before, with its squandered magnificence of hothouse garlands and beeswax tapers. The Dowager had been radiant—greeting old friends and enemies, gossiping wittily, and drawing about herself a small admiring court. And why not? Everything she valued and had worked so hard to regain had been gathered in that third-floor ballroom on Half Moon Street.

Those same things were worthless to Susannah—and being worthless, were nothing Susannah would ever be able to bring herself to strive for. The game played was not worth the cost of the candle to light it.

But Hanford seemed to think it was. Even as her husband mocked the "fashion, frivolity, and high degree" of Society, he was willing to make any sacrifice to gain it for himself and his family. If he loved her at all it was not quite as much as he loved the place of the Hanfords in Society.

And if Susannah loved him despite that, how could she ever think well of herself again?

She felt a headache coming on and thought, hopefully, that no one would notice her absence while Clementina Hanford shone so splendidly. But before she could discover some task that would take her from the room, the fast and fashionable Lady Pamela Lockridge entered.

Lady Lockridge had married her distant cousin Gerald almost before the ink was dry on his letters patent. Gerry Lockridge had a lineage of the most impeccable, and had—gossip ran—been ennobled for clandestine services to the Foreign Offices. But a brand-new baronetcy did little to render him a fit match for the daughter of an Earl, so Lady Pamela Withers took matters into her own hands.

Some gossips said it was a Gretna marriage, but others said that the indolent Lady Lockridge could on no account be prevailed upon to do anything so uncomfortable. Regardless of how she had entered the married state she was here now; her fine, light-brown hair escaping in disordered wisps from its confining cap and a froth of tiny Maltese dogs, each on a different-colored ribbon, foaming about her ankles like a canine ocean.

"Clementina! How wonderful to see you again. Isn't it lovely to have children to give one an excuse for doing what one wishes to anyway?" Lady Lockridge was childless. "And—oh, dear! Negus! Ratafia! Arrack! Stop that, you! I am sure he doesn't precisely mean to, but all the same, it does tangle!"

Having brought all conversation in the room to a complete and utter halt, Lady Lockridge looked about her with mild blue eyes. "Gerry says that it is just a stage," she offered hopefully.

The dog in question, having wound himself and his brethren into one immobile panting knot, regarded his mistress with a bright black gaze.

"If only they wouldn't look at me so. There is no point in telling me to discipline them when they look at me. It's quite hopeless, really."

"Let me help you, Lady Lockridge." Susannah rose from her seat and came forward.

"Why you must be Denzil's little bride! I'm sure he couldn't possibly be old enough to marry, but since he married you, he must be, mustn't he?"

Susannah, bending low among dogs, took a moment to remember that "Denzil" was one of her husband's numerous and hallowed Christian names.

"If you'll just give me the ribbons, Lady Lockridge, I'm sure I can sort them out." She could not imagine anyone addressing Hanford as "little Denzil."

Pamela Lockridge deposited the cluster of ribbons in Susannah's hands and, at her urging, stepped free of the wriggling mass.

"Thank you! I'm afraid Arrack has no sense of direction at all. I thought I might be here until Gerry came with a coachman to carry me home in a rug. You know, you are really quite tolerable, my dear. I know I oughtn't say so, but I do so wonder . . . what can Caro have been thinking of?" Lady Lockridge gazed at Susannah doubtfully.

As Susannah held her tongue and unknotted dogs, it was revealed to the company that Lady Lockridge had just come from the Dowager Countess of Coldmeece and could tell them absolutely that not only was Coldmeece to marry his ward, the Dowager Countess was to give a masked ball at Coldmeece House in a month. At this, half the company rose up to bear the news elsewhere, but as they were instantly replaced by new rivulets in the flood of callers the loss was not felt. Susannah was beginning to feel like a martyr on the gridiron and surreptitiously glanced at her brooch-watch. Another half hour at least before this would be over.

"Here they are, your ladyship."

There were only seven of Lady Lockridge's dogs after all. Keeping the maverick with the green ribbon—Arrack—well separated from the rest, Susannah led them over to Lady Lockridge.

"Thank you, Lady Hanford—you're ever so kind! I don't know what Gerry will say when I tell him how silly I have been, but you must bring your husband to call on us soon!"

Cautiously Susannah said that she supposed that would be delightful, divining somehow that the ab-

sent Gerry was not expected to call his wife silly
for extending the invitation to call to Lord and Lady
Hanford.

Susannah retreated to her seat. Despite Lady
Lockridge's friendliness, her head was pounding
now in good earnest, and the light in the drawing
room seemed far too bright. After a moment she
rose and slipped from the room.

The cool gloom of her bedroom was soothing, and
Susannah took a moment to soak a handkerchief
with Eau de Cologne and apply it to her temples.
Then she sat down at her dressing table. She had
available to her a better refuge than hartshorn. She
slid open the drawer of her dressing table.

But the manuscript of poems was gone.

She searched for it as best she could, halfheart-
edly turning out the other drawers of the table and
searching the corners of the room—but she already
knew she would not find the poems.

Susannah cupped her face in her hands. The book
was to have been a surprise, but suddenly it seemed
unutterably foolish. After going on to Hanford last
night about the value of frugality and thrift, how
could she explain the logic of spending several hundred pounds on something of no use whatsoever?
He would surely feel it was some arcane form of
sabotage of his plans for his family.

If only she could be sure about the baby! A child—
someone she could love, and who would love her
unreservedly—the heir to Laceby upon whom so
much depended. Not for nothing were children
termed "pledges of affection" between husband and
wife. The baby would settle everything between Susannah and Hanford; he could not be angry with
her if she had borne him a son.

A son. An heir for Laceby. A cold dread settled
over Susannah as she realized what that meant. A
son for *Laceby*. Another sacrificial offering to the

self-consequence of the Hanfords. And no way to save him from that, none at all, if she lost his father's love.

She fled to the refuge of the Dowager's sitting room and was there when Lady Hanford ascended to it a few minutes later.

"Why, Susannah—what are you doing here? I hope you are not ill. What a madcap crush—I vow I have not enjoyed myself so since dear Jocelyn . . . but, Susannah; you look ill."

"Oh, Lady Hanford—I went to look at Hanford's poems—and the manuscript is gone!" Even to Clementina Hanford she could not speak of her real worry. Ancilla was the only one who might understand, but there was nothing she could do.

"Oh, my dear! I sent it to the publisher this morning. I know it was very bad of me to sneak into your rooms like that, but I know you will wish to present it to Hanford as soon as may be, and you hardly have time to take them yourself—not with Orinda's come-out in scarcely a month!"

The Dowager Lady Hanford was, as Susannah by now had suspected she would be, perfectly right. Weeks passed: Lord and Lady Hanford went to the theater and the Opera and one or two dinners and had what the Dowager called a quiet Season and Susannah called a non-stop social whirl. Dinah's school-friends came to call, and even the haughty Adelaide Featherton was persuaded to cross the Hanford threshold—to be castigated, sighingly, by the Dowager as "not quite the thing."

Despite Susannah's every attempt to see her husband alone Hanford kept her at arm's length—and the hideous toll of bills kept mounting.

Susannah had never suspected the number of things there were to buy in the world—all, apparently, vital, and most overpriced. Apparently no one saw anything amiss in Hanford's conduct but she—even her Uncle Abner, as sharp as he could stare when it came to matters financial, supposed that Lord Hanford knew what he was doing.

Susannah supposed that he did not. And it would not matter to her—Hanford's relatives were as charming as they were irresponsible, and she had grown to love them—if only she did not feel herself set outside the charmed circle of her husband's love.

On this warm spring night in London entertainments were being mounted that filled the spectrum from freakish to tasteful and limned every degree of extravagance. In Audley Square the time had come when the Hanfords would see and be seen, drink, gossip, game, and be assessed from their wall-hangings to their kid slippers by interested observers. And afterward the *ton* would make up its collective mind, and the cards of invitation would follow—or not—in accordance with the verdict.

Only grim determination made Susannah able to take up her hostess role, and she was certain she did not sparkle in it. She stood a little to one side of the worst of the crush with Ancilla beside her, and as glad, for Hanford's sake, that tonight was a success—and that it was a success could be easily determined by the number of people who had managed to cram themselves into Hanford House's microscopic ballroom.

From where she stood Susannah could see the very tall, very elegant Mr. Bartholomew Rainford addressing a few words to a violently-blushing Orinda Hanford as the Dowager beamed approval. Orinda's success was assured, and oddly enough, it was Hanford who had done it. The friendship that was so unlikely between the arbiter of the *ton* and the bookish young baron was nonetheless a fact, and the Dowager had told her that Hanford had prevailed upon Rainford to come.

Sir Gerald and Lady Lockridge were here, and the Dowager Countess of Coldmeece had come with her ragtag and bobtail American—only to find some new awful thing to say, Susannah was sure, but nevertheless, she was there.

"Good heavens," said Susannah inadequately.

"Isn't it?" Ancilla agreed. "Tomorrow we shall doubtless open the *Gazette* and see this evening described as 'a madcap crush at the town house of Lord Blank on the occasion of his wife's presentation to Society.' I can't imagine why they don't print names, as everyone knows who is meant."

"Everyone east of Oxford Street, you should say. I must confess that when I look into the paper of a morning, I cannot tell one 'Certain Gentleman' from another, and only marvel that they can all lose such enormous sums at cards!" Susannah looked at her cousin-in-law. In the scant six weeks since they had come to London, the fever-roses had returned to Ancilla's cheeks and the pigeon's-breast grey of her *Soie de Londres* gown did nothing to give her an even color.

"I beg your pardon, Susannah. I am certain that in this case, ignorance truly is bliss, and soon I will share it. Soon I shall be bound for Italy, and I can hardly be expected to trouble myself with news of the Polite World if it is three weeks old before it reaches me."

Susannah felt a sharp pang of regret. When Ancilla was gone she would be even more alone. Dinah was younger and distracted by the social whirl, and Susannah had made no friends among the *ton*. Suddenly the thought was unbearable.

"Ancilla, may I—Shall I—Shall I go to Italy with you and Lady Hanford?" she burst out.

* * *

Miss Dinah Mary Potter, of Audley Square and the Farthingale School in Bath, eighteen years old and an heiress in her own right, quickly removed herself from the vicinity of everyone who wanted to pronounce her "a tolerable chit," speculate on the cost of her pearl brooch, compare her eyes to those sapphires she was not yet allowed to wear, or give her good advice on how to conduct herself in Town.

Since that pretty well took care of every person in the house tonight (saving the servants, some of whom might also wish to give her good advice), Dinah had evaded both Susannah, who would keep her by her side, and the Dowager, who would let her do as she liked but mention the fact later when it was most inconvenient, and made for the one bolt-hole where she was unlikely to be disturbed.

The night air was cool on her face and neck as she stepped out onto the balcony and pulled the curtains closed behind her. Before her London spread like an earthbound constellation: the torches of link-boys and the candles of coachlamps; the lights in the neighboring houses and the spill of light from her own; the lanterns of the parish watchmen and the cold moon above. She tried to imagine the same scene as it would look bleached to garish brightness by gaslights such as those on Regent's Street, but lost interest in the flight of fancy before it had fairly spread its wings.

She was usually more than willing to spend her time in Cloud Cuckoo Land, returning to earth only to criticize the follies of its mortal passengers. But at the moment it was Real Life that had the upper hand, and the fact made Dinah very cross.

She was a woman grown and knew precisely what she wanted of life. She wished to marry Peveril Hanford and follow him around the world, and they would live in any number of establishments, all of which would be either dreadfully exotic, mysterious, and strange, or slap up to the echo.

The only trouble with this plan was that she could see no way to achieve it. Peveril's commission papers would be delivered soon, and whether they were or not, Lord Hanford was returning to Laceby by the first of July and it was not certain whether his brother would wish to follow. That left barely time to call banns, which was rather previous as no declaration of love had been exchanged.

"Oh, hullo, Dinah."

Peveril Hanford was too young and inexperienced to scorn an entertainment as sadly flat simply because his brother was hosting it or to believe that adulthood consisted of denying his family's claims on his time. He was the pattern-card of dearly-bought luxury from the narrow toes of his gleaming Turkish slippers to the glistening pomaded curls of his chestnut hair, and he wore the expression of one who thus far had been pleased by everything that had come his way.

"Mama's wondering where you've got to, so I said I'd look. What're you doing out here—I said I'd dance with you, didn't I? And you're missing all the fun." He beamed upon his companion with untroubled cheer.

"Why should I care if I do?" said Dinah sulkily.

"Well, ah . . ."

"It's not as if you are any great inducement to pleasure," she went on waspishly. "A regular here-and-therian—and I certainly don't propose to waste my time and consequence on someone who is simply going to run off the moment I turn my back! Take yourself off, Peveril Hanford—you're of no interest to me."

Once again Dinah had misjudged her auditor. Peveril might find the passion with which these sentiments were delivered excessive, but he never doubted that they represented the unvarnished truth.

"Oh," said Peveril sadly. "I'd thought ... Well, talking pays no toll, as they say!" he added bravely. "I'll tell Mama I didn't see you, shall I?" He turned to go.

"Oh, *damn* you, Peveril Hanford!" Dinah burst out in sincere frustration. Artifice, planning, and intention good and bad were cast aside in the passion of the moment. Before she realized quite where she was Peveril seized her and was holding her on tiptoe.

"You keep a civil tongue in your head, cat!" he said, his face very close to hers. "Or the offers you get won't be of marriage, I promise you that!"

Dinah laughed and flung her arms around his neck. "Oh, Peveril, you do mean it? Will you marry me? If you don't I shall cut your heart out and feed it to the pigeons!"

"Wouldn't want it," said Peveril knowledgeably. "Bloody-minded little thing, aren't you?" He put an arm around her waist. "And what do you mean 'marry'? Nobody's made you an offer!"

"Oh, Peveril, please! I don't want to spend all that time on parties and lovemaking, trying to find someone convenable to marry when it's you I want! You would be very good for me, you know—and I don't mind at all about the Army! Oh, please, Pev! You'd like to marry me—you know you would."

"You know, chit, it's the man who's supposed to do the asking. Lords of creation, you know, master of all we survey. What if I don't want to marry you?"

"Then I shall fast, and pray, and throw myself from the highest cliff until Lord Hanford makes you marry me to shut me up—and you could love me, Peveril—you know you could!"

"Could," said Peveril, "and do—you're dashed

217

well sure of that, I imagine. But love ain't marriage, Dinah. Marriage's work."

"But I can cook, and clean; hold house, manage the servants; I know English and French and Italian; I can sew a straight seam—and I do have a very large portion, Peveril; the money does help."

"Oh, sweetheart, how do you know I'm what you'll want in ten years?" Peveril folded her into his arms and looked down at her in exasperation. "I'm older than you by a good two years, and I'm neither a fribble nor a farmer. You'd be a soldier's wife all your life."

"I want to be!"

"And what about your sister? She's responsible for you. How does she feel about me?"

Dinah bit her lip. "I could bring her around, Peveril. Sukey won't care a feather that you haven't a title!"

"You can tell her I'll be a Duke someday . . . but no. I'm not going to make up to you behind your sister's back, chit. Get her blessing, and we'll talk."

She knew that look, and that once Peveril had made up his mind there was not one weapon in her quicksilver armory that could make him change it. It was why she loved him, but at the moment it was maddening.

"At least, if you love me, Peveril, you have to kiss me!"

He laughed, and pulled her closer, and nothing in her experience had prepared her for his kiss. It made her heart ache and terrified her with the thought that Peveril might be taken away from her.

When he took his mouth away she leaned her head against his chest and sighed.

"You know, it's not at all as it is in the books, Peveril. The heroine always faints, you know—and your kisses weren't burning at all."

"Well, I did only kiss you once. P'raps I should

try it again," suggested Peveril in a spirit of scientific inquiry.

Dinah obediently tilted her head back and Peveril carefully put his arms around her. A few minutes later he was less careful, but Dinah apparently saw no cause for complaint.

"Italy?" said Ancilla. "Are you quite sure you are well, Susannah?"

Susannah smiled wanly. "I tried to follow all your advice, Ancilla—but I think you were wrong. All Hanford cares about is taking his place in Society, and I'll never want that. What else am I to do?"

"Anything else! Have you spoken to Aunt Clementina about this plan of yours yet?"

"No—I did not want to admit how bad things were. But, Ancilla, when you and she leave I shall be all alone—and he does not want me here."

"I know you are wrong, Susannah. If you will only be patient with him a little longer—he is counting on you to sponsor Orinda and Dinah to the *ton* when Aunt Clementina is gone."

"Oh, but how can I? I am not a Hanford, to command the *ton's* acclaim! I am more harm than help, and ought by rights to vanish away—but I need not vanish farther than Laceby if you don't want me."

"Why, you are shaking, Susannah. Come, it is not as bad as that. It is true, I have heard that there is some gossip—but nothing, surely, that anyone will say to your face. And you can hardly abandon Hanford."

Susannah smiled wanly. "I ought not mind what people say, I know . . . but I cannot bear being laughed at!"

Ancilla put a soothing arm around her shoulders. "I cannot think of anyone who enjoys it, and it is cold comfort to know that you share your situation with every other debutante upon the *ton*. I know you believe they hold you in dislike, but nothing could be more fatal than trying to make society's arbiters like you. The kind ones already do, and the bullies will despise you for weakness."

"And which is Hanford? Kind—or a bully?"

"Hanford is your husband, Susannah—and anything that touches on you affects him. I assure you, he despises the pettifogging rules of Society quite as much as you do."

"Oh, yes, Ancilla—but he follows them."

Ancilla looked at Susannah and sighed. "He does. But he might be happier rebelling. Come, Susannah—that is no face to show to Society. People will say you have the headache and are not properly enjoying this rare entertainment! Come out onto the balcony with me for a few minutes."

Hanford looked about the ballroom, but none of the members of his family was in sight, save for Orinda, dancing with a likely young man whom Hanford could not place just at this moment. It was amazing what "the ready" could do to repair a damaged reputation—or gild an impeccable one.

He tried to see the room as Orinda would, but it was no good. She saw the glitter of gallant ladies and the shine of fine gentlemen; Hanford saw only the waste.

What did Susannah see?

He had thought that only money separated him from the world he had been born to, but now that he had it, he saw he was wrong. The years of poverty had worked their sea-change. There was to be no easy assumption of privileged innocence for Lord Hanford; he was fated to see the cost.

And wonder if it was too high.

Susannah had her arm around Ancilla's waist and was attending more to her cousin-by-marriage than anything else, so she was upon Peveril and Dinah before she realized.

Susannah was nearly two years older than her sister, and from that lofty perch had watched Dinah grow up. It was understandable that she had stopped watching a year or two before and had neglected to note that Dinah continued to get older.

The evidence of the aging process that was presented now for her delectation took a moment or so to commend itself to her attention, but when it did, she became violently aware that her infant sister was reposing in the arms of the least suitable man in the entire world.

"What do you think you're doing?" demanded Susannah unnecessarily. Dinah jumped back.

"Oh, hullo, Susannah, Cilla," said Peveril uneasily. Dinah placed a possessive hand on his arm.

Dinah regarded her sister's flashing eyes. "It's all right, Sukey," she said conciliatingly. "I'm going to marry Peveril."

"You most certainly are not!" responded Susannah instantly. "I never heard of anything half so wicked!"

"See?" said Peveril to Dinah, with the air of one making a point. "I told her that was how it would be, Susannah, but—"

"Oh, Peveril!" said Susannah in despair.

"I know it looked deuced smoky," Peveril began unhappily.

"You can't stop us!" Dinah put in ringingly.

"Yes she can," said Peveril firmly.

"Susannah, I know this is a shock, but why not discuss it when we are all calmer? I am sure that Peveril meant nothing insulting toward Dinah; perhaps it would be better to save the matter for a better time."

"Oh, Sukey—you can't be angry! It's high time I

was married—and Peveril must be an agreeable suitor, when you have married his brother."

"Do you think I'm going to let you throw your life away too?" Susannah demanded.

There was a stricken silence. Peveril bowed without speaking and walked out, very stiff.

Dinah stared at her sister in shock, then burst into tears and ran after him.

Susannah leaned back against the railing and took a deep breath.

"I didn't mean to say that," she said rather inadequately. Susannah pressed her gloved fingertips to her eyes to ward off tears.

Ancilla put an arm around Susannah's shoulders.

"Then you will mend it tomorrow. I have known Peveril since I was a child. His understanding is perhaps not large, but his heart is good. And I do not think the attachment is at all one-sided. If you will only bring the matter to Hanford, I know he can help you decide what is best. Please, Susannah—for my sake?"

Susannah nodded reluctantly.

Chapter XIV

MAY 1819

BUT WITH THE best and most sensible of intentions
this promise proved difficult to keep. When Susannah finally dragged herself out of bed the next
morning, sick and heavy-eyed, Hanford was not in.
Nor were the servants able to give her any clue as
to his direction. She wondered, not for the first time,
what it was that her husband did all day. She really knew so very little about him. Ancilla said that
he did not game; he was not politically-minded (so
far as she knew) and there was only so much shopping one could do in a day. Perhaps he had a mistress? The thought was so unlikely that she didn't
even bother to entertain a spark of jealously.

What Hanford had done that morning was what
Hanford had done every morning since he had come
to Town, and Susannah would have been astonished had she known of it.

Following a breakfast only a very few hours separated from his bedtime, Lord Hanford rose and
took himself off to the City, where he spent an hour
each morning at Drummond's Bank followed by two
at his lawyers', attempting to shift the interlocking
burden of mortgages and bills enough to provide a
breathing space for Laceby.

Susannah had been right. But he had not seen the harm in his spending—just a few purchases to salve the years of privation. But between his presents to his family and Susannah's whole-scale renovation of his home, the comfortable cushion that was to have gone to purchase back the acres of land that had once belonged to the estate had vanished.

Now, as he looked, he could actually see the money dwindle. Three hundred pounds for a single presentation gown, and four had been bought. Twelve hundred pounds. Enough to keep a pink of the *ton* in whist and blue ruin for two years. Enough to buy the whole of a good young woods with a dependable stream running through the bottom of it, and the fertile field that lay beyond.

But the money was gone, and now as much and more again must go to secure Peveril a place. And though he grudged neither the dresses nor the commission, neither expenditure would bring a return.

He had talked so grandly of the purchase of intangibles to Susannah, when all along she must have known they could not afford them. Buy three-per-cents, and the Funds would always pay out. Buy land, and see your return in rents and crops.

But spend even what seemed like a trifling amount on "intangibles," and see that and all the rest go sliding after, with nothing to replace it.

Oh, they weren't in debt. Not yet. But how quickly, how easily, they could be poor.

The morning after Orinda's presentation he found it impossible to keep his mind on the rates and figures and investment schemes with which Coltharp deluged him. He had advertised for a manager for Laceby—small as it was, he did not possess the skills to run it—and now he must read through a mass of letters and references to find which candidate for the position he must engage. And soon he, in Mama's absence, must sort through an entirely different set of candidates, to find the man to whom he would give his sister, in the optimistic case that she received any offers even remotely suitable.

He sighed and rubbed his eyes, but nothing could dislodge the throbbing sick headache brought on by too many figures and too little sleep. At length Hanford rose from his seat.

"I'm sorry, Mr. Coltharp; I do not seem to be a very good student just now. Perhaps another day."

The sun of early afternoon was warm on the west side of St. James Street as Hanford walked toward home. The carriage ride back from the City had done much to restore his comfort, and on impulse he had told the driver to let him out here. The walk from here to Audley Street should be enough to banish the rest of the headache—and the mass of paperwork awaiting him there required his full concentration.

Society's wheels ran on rails of kinship and friendship, and the Hanfords had been forced to attenuate many of those ties. Little could be accomplished without them, but their repair was a tedious work of letters and promises, small gifts and invitations. Still, for the Family it must be done.

As he came abreast of the Roantree Club he saw two men descend the steps with more haste than grace—one short, slender, and dark-haired, and the other tall and broad-shouldered with a flaming crop of chestnut hair.

Peveril. With a second look at the situation, Hanford plunged off the curb and across the street.

He reached the men just as Peveril was attempting to pass through his companion and return to the club. Hanford recognized him as Mr. Robert Gressingham, a raconteur who lived on a combination of his wits and the generosity of an older unmarried sister; rather more flash than Hanford cared for—having earned the *nom-de-nocturne* Lightfoot Bobby for a certain notorious steeplejacking escapade—and actively unlikely to be a member of the mild and moderate Roantree Club.

"Let me go, blast you! I'll draw his cork for him!" Peveril said fiercely.

Hanford put a hand on his arm. "Peveril, what in—?"

"Ah, brother, ain't'cha?" Mr. Gressingham looked relieved at the arrival of reinforcements. "Take him home. Foxed."

Peveril spun around and glared at his brother before returning to the fray. "Damn you, you wall-climbing grub-worm, I'm not even the least bit well-to-live!"

"Peveril." Hanford caught his sleeve warningly. "Why don't you come along and tell me about it?"

"Tell you? I'll tell the world? He—" Peveril swung back again, looking like a maddened auburn bull, and Mr. Gressingham danced back out of the way.

"Not me! Common knowledge, old man—and a bit of harmless fun, eh?"

"Fun! I'll show you fun, Gressingham? When your sister—"

"Oh, come, Pev, let's leave sisters out of this, shall we?" Hanford said hastily. "Your servant, Mr. Gressingham. Come *on*, Pev."

"Now," said Hanford, pushing the library door shut behind them, "just what is all that in honor of? Brawling on the steps in front of Roantree's at one in the afternoon; you'll be boxing the watch next! And what in God's name convinced you to pick a quarrel with Robert Gressingham, of all people?" His headache was back in force, thundering behind his temples hard enough to dim Peveril's words.

"He started it! He and Viscount St. George—a bet, you know, that they could take a drink in every

226

club on the Street without being tossed out—came in, and— But I didn't have a quarrel with Bobs—not until he stopped me from calling out St. George!"

" 'Calling out St. George?' Does insanity run in this family, or is it just you?" Vainly Hanford attempted to hold his temper, and knew that he would not.

"D'you know what he said, Han? It's very amusing—the match of the Season! 'The Bartered Baron and his Ill-Bred Bride!' You and Susannah! I couldn't stand still for that—in any case, she's Dinah's sister, you know. You should have let me plant him a facer!"

"And be known as the 'Ill-Bred Baron and his Bartered Bride'?"

Peveril threw himself into a chair and glared at his brother in exasperation. "But it isn't fair! If they'll say that about Susannah, only think what they'll say about Dinah, and—"

The nausea that usually passed off by midmorning today only continued to worsen, and nothing Susannah did provided any relief at all. She was cravenly grateful that Dinah avoided her—she had no strength to sort out the tangle of her sister's violent espousal of her brother-in-law.

Peacock had orders to notify her the instant that Hanford returned home, and sent a footman to do so just as Susannah was considering the desirability of returning to her bed for the immediate future. She set her Commonplace Book quickly aside at the summons and hurried downstairs.

"How now, Peveril, kind words for 'La Cit' at this late date?" Susannah stood outside the half-shut library door, neither daring to enter nor to go away. "You once were pleased to call my wife a title-mongering mushroom—do you think the *ton*

227

will be kinder? But I forget; she has fed and clothed you, and rendered them no such service." Hanford was not alone, and he was not pleased.

"Dammit, Han, if you weren't my brother I'd draw your cork for that!"

"I'll say what I choose about my own wife—who has given up every familiar comfort for a social position that you seem determined to destroy! If your ill-considered hysterics have turned an *on-dit* to a scandal I promise you— That's enough. Get out."

"The Devil! You can't stand her yourself and you think everyone agrees with you! No one says a word when a man goes after an heiress and marries her. Why should—"

"There is no reason why!" Hanford's voice was raised as Susannah had never heard it. "I wish we had never come to this godforsaken place— I wish there were no Laceby and no Hanford! I wish—" There was a crash and Susannah swept through the library door.

Peveril was on his feet in front of the fireplace staring at his brother. A clutter of pens, papers, and inkwells that had lately covered the desk was strewn about the floor.

"Get out," said Hanford without looking up.

"Han! It's her!" Peveril said desperately.

"Thank you, Peveril—that will be all from you, I think." Susannah walked across the room and knelt down beside Hanford's chair, "Hanford? It's Susannah."

Hanford raised his head and looked at her. His hair was disordered, and his face was grey and drawn. "Susannah," he said blankly.

She did not stop to reflect on how matters stood between them. Without thinking, she opened her arms and gathered her husband to her breast.

"Peveril," Susannah said steadily, "you may certainly go away now. And please make sure the door is shut when you do."

Hanford clung to her like a drowning man. It was indecent of her to feel such happiness in the face of his torment, but she could not help herself. Whatever unimaginable battle he was engaged in, they were at last on the same side.

She heard the sound of the library door open and close. She stroked her husband's hair.

"Well, whatever it was, I am sure that Peveril will not do it again," she said encouragingly.

"There are times when I think I shall go quite mad." It was as if he were only continuing a conversation that they had had before. His tone was matter-of-fact, reasonable—everything the words were not. "Did you hear? I never meant to hurt you. It should have been Peveril who inherited. You are everything that is good, and brave, and beautiful, and what am I but a compendium of all the family failings; the worst in every generation."

"Hush, my darling," she said, soothing him as if he were a child. "I know that Peveril did not mean what he said."

His arms tightened around her. "Do you know, Susannah, I was away at school when I heard my father had died, doing all that I could to keep from assuming my proper place in Society. He left so many debts . . . I was sure we were ruined, but then I thought, 'at least I shall be spared this eternal bowing and scraping.' There was no money for it, you see, and I was selfish enough to be glad of that. But now I have no such excuse for not fulfilling my duty to the Family. I thought I could bear it . . ."

"Is it your duty to drive yourself until you drop? You would not use an animal the way you are using yourself. Your family could not ask that of you. No one could."

"No one asks, Susannah. England expects every man to do his duty. . . . God, I am tired. I can't sleep save in your arms . . . and you do not want me.

229

What a poor thing you have married, that can't even manage eight weeks' frivolity." He pushed away and sat back in his chair, eyes fever-bright in the drawn face.

All Susannah's illness was forgotten as she knelt before her husband, rinsed away in an unreasoning fury against whatever could hurt him so.

"How could I not want you? You are my husband, Hanford, and I— You have been working yourself to the bone just so Peveril can wear a uniform and Orinda a coronet of strawberry leaves—I don't call that frivoling!" She squeezed his hands, willing him to believe her.

He smiled down at her. "Do you think—my lady wife—that if I tried I might manage a duke for her?" The carnelian of his signet ring took fire as he reached out to stroke her hair.

"Oh, my love, I am sure you may manage anything you choose!" Susannah said desperately. "I swear I will do everything in my power to help you. It is idiocy but I do not care—only rest now."

But it was Susannah who needed to rest, as Hanford repeatedly told her, and at last he convinced her to retire to her rooms. She was tired; her eyes were fever-bright. She had not looked well since he'd brought her to London, and he cursed every coldness he'd ever displayed toward her.

He thought a moment, then took up his pen to write to Lord Childwall that the Hanfords would not be coming tonight to dine.

In his wild fancy London became a lamia queen, stalking the streets like a great grey cat and leaching the life from all those he loved best. Susannah. Ancilla. He must persuade Ancilla to leave England at once—even an English summer was too harsh for her to support. And he must mend fences with Peveril; God knew how.

He scribbled a few hasty lines and sealed the note with a wafer. Now one of the numerous footmen that Lord Hanford's consequence demanded could come and take it away, and then he would rest.

The door opened, but it was not in answer to his ring. The Dowager Lady Hanford, garden-bright in a morning dress with embroidered muslin overrobe, peeped around the edge and then stepped into the room.

"Dear one! Peacock told me I would find you here! It was naughty of you to scamper off so early this morning and keep me from sharing my triumphs! The cards! Orinda is very nearly a success—and may yet be a Toast with a very little effort. Almack's, of course, is a necessity—oh, I know what you have said, my love, but you can hardly mean it—and a baroche for driving in the Park would do no harm. And then you and Susannah must certainly begin to go about more in the world—"

"Mother." The Dowager blinked at him in surprise. "No."

"No? But my dearest—what have I said?" A tiny crease appeared between her perfect blue eyes.

"Nothing, I suppose—only that I must give lavish entertainments, and purchase a baroche . . . and vouchers. There is no money for that, Mama, and even if there were, I told you before: Orinda will not go where Susannah and her sister are not welcomed. I will try to make it up to her, somehow, but I do not think it will be at Almack's."

"But Hanford, dearest, only reflect a little on the folly of such a course! Now your sister is known and admired, but such renown lasts only for a moment—hesitate, and all will be lost." The Dowager fluttered like an agitated partridge, and settled into the chair Peveril had so recently left.

"Then, Mama, it must be lost. I will do many things for you, but I find I draw the line at self-immolation.

Susannah is my wife. Her happiness comes first. Orinda must content herself with modest success."

"Modest success!" The Dowager made an unconscious gesture to wield the accessories of her girlhood, but the fan was long outmoded. "What are you saying? Orinda is a Hanford, too, my love, and she is entitled to a certain style of life! Surely you cannot mean to—"

"To ask her to live within means that are merely comfortable—instead of *en prince* as befits a Hanford? She must, you know. You and I saw to that, Mama, with the marriages we made. Beggars can't have scruples, and honorable men must keep their promises."

"And what of your promises to your family? It is true that after dear Jocelyn died we were sadly flat, but you have made the ultimate sacrifice and mended all! Now there is no reason that you—"

"Cannot fling all my wife's money after my father's, chasing the same empty glory? I'm sorry, Mother. I would look a great fool riding breakneck that way after something I didn't even want. I don't want to cut a dash in Society, you know. I never did." Hanford stood, and clasped his hands behind him.

The Dowager looked up to him and reached out one perfect creamy hand to him in an affecting gesture he once could not have withstood. "Oh, that I should live to see the day that found my own dear one being so odiously selfish! Hanford, my love, you cannot think only of yourself."

"No, Mama. I must think of my wife as well."

She let the hand fall to her lap. "Oh, Hanford," she said sadly, and Hanford came forward to kneel by her side. After a moment he spoke.

"The year that I was born the mobile was guillotining aristocrats in France—I grew up wondering how it would be if some day Papa's tenant-farmers came to Laceby with their pitchforks and demanded he come out and be hanged. But Papa never wondered.

He was so certain of his place in the world he never conceived that it might change—when I asked him about it once he just laughed."

"And so he should have—dearest, you cannot compare Englishmen to French peasants! You are only blue-devilled over Susannah, that is what all this is in aid of, but my love, she is quite one of us, you know!"

"No, Mama. Susannah is not one of us, thank God. She is herself, and she—and I—are entitled to be happy. I am not my father—I don't think I could be so certain of anything if I tried—and I cannot want the things he wanted. There are no more grand courts. Let us dwindle into pleasant obscurity."

Hanford bowed his head, and after a moment the Dowager placed her hand upon it.

"Mama—" Hanford began.

"Hush, my dearest. I confess I do not understand, and I think you are a fool to throw over Society for some ridiculous point of honor, but if that is your wish I cannot bear to dispute you. I will not tease you anymore. Go home to your silly pile of stones and your 'pleasant obscurity' and leave London to me."

Susannah left the library and walked down the corridor to her sitting room. Hanford would not rest unless she did—and if he went on much longer as he was his nerves must inevitably fail him.

Her husband had been carrying a crushing burden alone for far too long, Susannah realized. But no matter what it took on her part, that time was past. As soon as possible the Hanfords would remove to Laceby, and there would be an end to the destructive nonsense of Hanford taking up his place in the *ton*. Ancilla had said he did not want it, and today Susannah had seen proof that it would be as fatal to him as an English winter would to his cousin. There was no choice but to leave.

But what, in that case, would become of Dinah and Orinda? Perhaps Ancilla would be able to offer a suggestion; Susannah had none. She opened the door to her sitting-room.

Peveril was standing over her desk, leafing through the Commonplace Book that she had left there when the footman had come. Of late she had added her favorite of Hanford's poems to the compendium.

"Is Han all right?" Peveril sounded subdued.

"He's resting. Peveril, how could you have been so cruel as to tease him like that?"

"I never thought— And it wasn't me anyway! It was Bobs Gressingham! He said—" Peveril stopped.

"Yes, I know," Susannah said steadily. "And I don't care—and I shall tell Hanford so until he believes me. But that is none of your concern. What we must settle now is what happened last night."

Peveril nodded glumly. "I've been trying to screw my courage to the sticking place, as they say. I daresay after what you heard you haven't got any good opinion of me, but I love your sister, Susannah. I ain't saying I'm what she ought to look for in a husband—told her so, in fact!—but she's fixed on it. And I told her I'm not going to stick about and be a charge on the family—Han says the coronetcy's as good as set. I want what's best for Dinah. In the Army I'll have prize money and my pay, and I daresay I can scrape by."

"But can you support a wife? And do you want to? I know my sister—and Peveril, you haven't said anything about your feelings."

Peveril blushed. "Look here—I told her she shouldn't be throwing her hat over the windmill until she'd spoken to you. And I came to promise that, well, nothing will happen under this roof that you don't like."

"I know it won't, Peveril."

Dinah peered around the bedroom door. "Then

may I marry him? If we call banns now we could be married at the end of the Season—and Orrie would be positively livid!"

Susannah slanted a glance at Peveril and was reassured to see that he thought as little as she did of that as a reason to marry.

"Whether you marry Peveril or not, you are certainly not marrying him this year," Susannah said firmly. "Nor are you announcing an engagement; so you may save your breath from asking."

"But, Susannah—"

"I say, this bit looks like Han's stick." Peveril, trying desperately to turn the conversation, seized on the closest thing he could find.

"Yes, I copied out some of his poems. I'm having an edition of them published—it's a surprise," she added firmly, fixing her gaze on Dinah.

"Good God, Susannah! I didn't even know he still wrote. And he won't want anyone else to either— what, after Papa read out a bunch of 'em out at the dinner table and then threw the copies into the fire? You should have heard the peal Papa rang over him—I was still in the nursery, then, and I heard it." Peveril stared at her. "Who put such a nonsensical maggot into your head?"

"Then," said Susannah in dawning horror, "he wouldn't want to see them published. But Lady Hanford said—"

"Mama never did have any sense—she always wanted to see him become a lit'ry lion like that Byron chap, and Han said he'd be damned—sorry!— if he would. Hanfords don't write, you see. Daresay Han got it from Mama's family."

"No," Susannah said quietly. The feverish nausea rose in her again until it threatened to choke her. The publication of Hanford's poetry was no girlish mis-step; it was the end. Of her, of her marriage, of her children . . .

"Susannah!" Dinah screamed, as Susannah fell to the floor.

Susannah had opened her eyes upon her familiar bedroom—but the looped-back curtains admitted the pallid grey light of dawn, and the guttering candle-stubs in their holders signified an all-night vigil.

Her only clear thought was that she must rise and dress and go to Lovell & Challoner at once to stop the publication of the fatal poems, but when she tried to fling back the covers Ancilla stopped her.

"But I must get up!" she protested.

"Not now, Susannah. Just lie quietly. The doctor will be in to see you soon."

"Doctor? But I'm not ill. Where is Ruby? I must get up."

"Hush, Susannah," said Ancilla. "You must not make things worse for yourself."

Susannah turned her head, and could see Hanford and the Dowager sitting beside the bed on the other side.

"Hanford? You should be resting. Is something wrong?"

"Not now." He took her hand and held it, hard.

"But why are you here?" Even so much effort exhausted her; she lay back against the pillows and closed her eyes.

"She is asleep again," she heard the Dowager say.

"Will you go to bed now, Cilla, or will I have the doctor here for you as well?" Hanford asked.

"I will not tell you I am perfectly well, as I am sure you would not believe me, but I am very far from being all in and it is nearly morning. Poor love—and Dinah certain she was the cause of it. Will Susannah have to be bled again, do you think?"

"If the fever does not break, they say she must be. I do not know what I will do, if—"

"Hush now, my dearest!" cut in the Dowager.

"There is no need at all to entertain such gothic fancies. Undoubtedly Susannah is merely breeding, just as the doctor says, and you may take her back to Laceby just as soon as she is fit to travel."

But that time, it seemed, would not be soon. Susannah was indeed going to present her husband with a pledge of her affection, but the fever was broken only after a battle that left her unable to rise from her bed, let alone travel home to Laceby. Uncle Abner and Aunt Doolittle, discomfited by the style in which they found themselves, had nonetheless come to sit with her. Aunt Doolittle had presented her with all the latest news of Ethan, and retailed in grim detail all the particulars of her own confinement, in which, she told Susannah, she had nearly died. Condolences were tendered by select members of the *ton*, and Lady Lockridge even paid her a fleeting butterfly visit, but the nagging threat of the poems would not let Susannah rest.

Who could help her stop their publication? The Dowager saw no harm in it in the first place, and Ancilla was too frail to entrust with such a commission. Even now, when she suspected she would be forgiven, she could not bear to tell Hanford, and Dinah's approach to any problem was nothing her sister could view with equanimity. There was really only one person she could ask.

"Peveril, will you help me?"

The summer sun spilled through the window of Susannah's sitting-room. She had recently graduated to lying on her chaise all day, and all the rooms of Hanford House had been plundered to heap Susannah's invalid chamber with riches. Peveril had been allowed in to present her with the joyful news that his commission papers had come; in a month he would be off for France.

"Goose! Of course I will; but whatever can you possibly want that you don't have here?"

"You must go to Lovell and Challoner for me. You must tell Mr. Lovell that I do not want Hanford to be famous!"

"Hold hard, Susannah. If you fret yourself Han will put an end to me, and I *do* want to be famous. Tell me what you want, and I'll do what I can."

Peveril was soon put in possession of all the particulars. No matter what it cost, the edition of poems that she had paid for was to be eradicated and rendered as if it had never been thought of.

"You must get them Peveril! If Hanford ever found out, oh, he would not think well of me, and—"

"Who wouldn't think well of you, darling? Whoever he is, let's throw him out, shall we? He can't be anyone important."

Hanford approached the chaise and leaned down to kiss her.

"I'll be toddling along now, Susannah. You may leave everything to me—not that there's anything, is there? I mean . . . Afternoon, Han."

" 'Whom the gods would destroy, they first make maddening.' I hope England will survive Peveril's sojourn in its Army." Hanford seated himself by her side and took Susannah's hand. "I have just come from the bankers'; matters are not so good as they might be, but with a little care we are far from ruined."

Susannah summoned up her courage. "It does not matter. Hanford, I do not wish to go about in Society. I never wanted to—and neither do you."

In one sense Susannah's collapse had been the best thing she might have done for her husband. It removed from Hanford the least need to shine in the Polite World, and with that grinding toil eliminated he had soon recovered his equilibrium.

Hanford squeezed her hand and smiled. "My secret revealed. My love, I told you once that all would be

238

just as you wished when my family had been established, but I find I owe you more than that. Mama has never cared for country life, so she intends to make her home in Town. If you like, she will take Orinda and Dinah with her when she travels to Italy so that they may take on a little more polish, and next year she may foist them upon the *ton*. You are my own dear wife, and if it pleases you, we may rusticate at Laceby until the end of time."

"I think it would please me more than anything." Despite herself, Susannah yawned. "Hanford, do you think Dinah ought to marry Peveril? That would settle her—and she seems so very fixed on it."

"Good lord, who am I to pronounce on the suitability of partners in matrimony? I hold to the thought that if I put off having any opinion for long enough, I shall not need to have one at all."

Several hours later Susannah had slept, and wakened, and taken a strengthening bowl of soup. The doctor had been to visit once more, and prescribed, before departing, a strenuous dietary regimen designed to produce the fittest possible heir for Laceby.

"And what shall we name him?" Hanford asked a while later.

"Him? Are you so certain, my lord? Well . . . Averil?"

"A libertine."

"Christian?"

"Worse yet—he was the one they hanged."

"Brabazon?"

Just then the door was thrust open, and Peveril Hanford stood framed in the doorway. "Oh, ah, Susannah! I didn't know anyone was still here." As a conspirator Peveril was no asset; guilty duplicity was writ large upon his honest open features.

"Oh, come now, Pev; a mere husband can hardly be regarded as anyone at all." Hanford beckoned his brother into the room.

A moment more of this and Han is bound to ask him what is wrong, Susannah thought anxiously.

"Susannah and I were just choosing names for the heir. Now I was always fond of Uncle, but it seems unfair to saddle the boy with a name that's longer than he is. What do you think of 'Brabazon,' Pev?"

"Oh, er, ah!" Peveril looked desperately at Susannah.

"Peveril wants to talk secrets, Hanford, and finds you in the way. You may go and think of girls' names if you like, for I am certain our daughter will not wish to be named 'Brabazon.'"

"Oh, very well, but he's not to tire you—and if it's about the Chinese jade snuff bottle that he bought in the Bazaar, I already know." Her husband kissed her cheek and went out.

"Peveril, anyone would think you'd just gotten back from stuffing the Woolsack with gunpowder instead of from a visit to Town! Was it too late to get the money I paid refunded? I don't mind about that very much."

"It's worse than that, Susannah—much worse!"

Peveril had gone promptly to the firm of Lovell & Challoner to demand that the book Susannah had paid for be stopped or handed over. Since Peveril was not himself bookish, nor possessed of even so much experience of the publishing world as Susannah had acquired, he was not certain whether this was to be best accomplished by force or violence, but the indolent young clerk of the firm had been perfectly willing to assist Peveril Hanford to the limit of his ability to do so.

Unfortunately, his assistance made the situation worse rather than better.

The edition had already been returned from the printer's, and was in the office awaiting Lady Hanford's direction. In addition, samples of the volume had been sent to Audley Street several days ago—

as well as to Hatchard's, Hookam's, Colburn's, and the other subscription libraries in town.

"Oh, Peveril—no!" Easy tears came to Susannah's eyes as she struggled up off the chaise. This was publicity beyond her wildest nightmares—for poetry that Hanford wished to remain completely secret.

"Here now! Dash it all, Susannah—there's nothing to be done now. The sneaking little mushroom said it was what you paid him for. I have the rest of them at any rate—they're downstairs." Peveril pushed her back against the plush velvet upholstery and tucked the blanket firmly about her once more.

"What am I going to do?" whispered Susannah in horror. "This is all my fault—Hanford will despise me."

"Devil he will. We'll tell him I did it," said Peveril decisively. "Safest thing all around—and there's nothing he can do about the coronetcy now."

"No, I won't have you taking the blame for what I have done. But I cannot bear . . . Peveril, where did you put the others?"

"Safest place for them. I put them in the library."

Hanford, being banished from his wife's bedside, wandered downstairs to his library. Doubtless Peveril was attempting once more to persuade Susannah to allow at least an engagement between himself and her sister before he sailed for France.

Having himself been fully briefed by Ancilla on the attachment and its history the morning after the party, Hanford was not minded to forbid it. But now was not the time to tease Susannah with a matter that concerned her so nearly. Dinah and Peveril might consider themselves pledged to their heart's delight for all of Hanford, but not so publicly that the discovery of mistaken emotions would be cause for embarrassment.

He opened the door and was enveloped in the

green darkness of the library. It would be a great relief to abandon this urban Dower House to its rightful inhabitant. At Laceby he and Susannah could start again, and concentrate on their commonalities instead of their differences.

Groping his way toward the desk, he tripped on an unexpected obstacle. On closer inspection the object was discovered to be a crate, its lid disarranged by the impact, with the legend "Lovell & Challoner" stenciled on the side.

Frowning with curiosity, Hanford lifted the lid.

"The library! Peveril, he is sure to be going there now!"

"What matter if he is? They're crated up—can't tell a thing about them—and where else was I supposed to put 'em, anyway? A hundred copies of anything takes up the very devil of a lot of room."

"Oh-h-h-h . . . Let me think," Susannah commanded, pressing her hands to her temples.

There was a tap at the door, and Peveril rose to answer it. "Susannah's thinking," he explained to Ancilla.

"I certainly hope so—let me in, Peveril, I must see her."

Ancilla Hanford entered the room, the object in her hands concealed by her shawl. "Susannah?" she said in a strained voice.

"I would not for worlds bother you when you are so ill, but this will not wait. I spoke to Aunt Clementina, and while I cannot precisely credit her tale—"

"You have been to Hatchard's," Susannah said emotionlessly.

Ancilla drew a slim volume bound in primrose leather out of the folds of her shawl.

At first Hanford thought he was the recipient of more of his mother's taste in library decoration.

This heartening fiction lasted exactly as long as it took for him to lift and open one of the books.

Quietly he replaced the lid of the crate and went upstairs, one copy still in hand.

"Oh, Peveril, do reflect!" Ancilla begged. "Not only will no one believe such a ridiculous story as that, but it will not solve anything!" Ancilla, having been made recipient of Peveril's hopeful explanation, gazed at him in loving exasperation.

"Well, it's better than having everyone say Susannah's done it—and after all, Cilla, she didn't know about Papa and the poems and all."

"But I should have known—if I had more interest in my husband and less in my own way!"

"My, what a quakerish sentiment. Am I to take it then that your wardrobe is now to reflect your rank and not your convictions?"

The three conspirators turned and stared in horror at the apparition. Hanford gazed mildly upon his family, the book of poems displayed like an award of battle against his chest.

"Peveril, I told you not to tire her. Prosecute your suit with Miss Potter on some other occasion. Now scat."

Reluctantly Peveril left the room.

"Hanford, Susannah does not deserve a scold from you."

"Nor do I intend to give her one. But as this is a denouement of a sort, I feel that I am at least entitled to communicate with my wife in solitude."

Try as she might, Ancilla could not mistake his meaning, and Hanford stood in waiting silence as she too left.

"Susannah, my love—" He gathered her quickly into his arms and tossed the book aside. "Forgive me, but I could not resist just a bit of Cheltenham! You all looked so absurdly stricken." She could feel his shoulders quiver—this time with suppressed laughter.

"Then you do not mind, Hanford?" A part of Susannah thought that this was very unfair, after all the work she had put in being afraid of this moment.

"I suppose I ought to—but I am done with 'ought,' sweetheart—and all the rest of the ritual deadwood. I don't suppose most of my ancestors were pattern-cards of virtue; why should I be?"

"But it is in all the lending libraries, Hanford, and everyone will know they're really yours!"

"Then I suppose I shall have to resign myself to fame, or to well-deserved obscurity. The saving grace of disaster, you know, is that it points up what we should hold important, and you are more to me than all the empty observances in the world."

"But—" Susannah was rather taken aback by this sudden volte-face. "But your poems— Your father—"

"Oh, it is true; my father would have shot himself rather than see his name linked with foolish scribblings, but I am not my father, my dear love. You were the only one who had faith in that, and I am very much afraid that your faith will be rewarded for a very long time."

Susannah nestled into the hollow of his shoulder. "Then you have no regrets, my Lord?"

"Oh, many. But none of them are you."

Epilogue

DECEMBER 1819

"HERE YOU ARE, my love. Roses in December." Hanford set down the silver bowl of forcing-house roses on the table beside his wife's bed.

Outside the Warwickshire winter slapped at the new double-glazed windows, but inside all was serene. Coals provided by Mr. Andrew Gammage radiated warmth from the black-leaded grate, and the heavy brocade draperies around the bed countervailed the last possibility of a chill.

"I know Mr. Danvers complained so when you had it put in, but it is so lovely to have fresh fruits and flowers through the winter—and I know that *she* enjoys it!"

The eyes of both Hanfords turned to the newest occupant of the room.

"She is too young to tell an apple from a quince," Hanford said, lifting his daughter out of her cradle.

The Honorable Miss Amelia Clementina Hanford was just six weeks old today, but already it could be seen that her eyes would be grey, just as her father's were.

"Oh, give her here!" Susannah said coaxingly. "Your opinions, my lord, are nothing to the point—when everyone can see that Ammie is the most intelligent, the most beautiful—"

"—the most thoroughly spoiled—"

"Oh, but Hanford, how can you say so? I haven't had time yet!" Susannah protested, and they both laughed. She settled her daughter more comfortably in the crook of her arm. "How is the poem going?"

"Nearly finished—though it has been nearly finished since before Ammie was born and does not seem to advance appreciably. Why I was ever mad enough to suppose I could write an epic is beyond me just at the moment." He settled himself on the chair by Susannah's bedside.

"Oh, Hanford—I am sure that you can! And everyone did like the last book."

"Ah, but I had very little to do with that one. This time Lovell & Challoner is clamoring daily for the manuscript—or will be, as soon as the coaches can get through the roads."

"I hope that will be soon. We have heard nothing from Peveril for months, and you know how impossible Dinah is when he does not write."

"Fortunately his affections remain fixed; since if they did not we should have to erect an additional establishment in order to house your sister and garner for ourselves some peace and quiet."

"Oh, Dinah is only high-spirited . . ."

". . . which of course manifests itself in fashions rich and strange. For a while I wondered if Mrs. Goodchild was ever going to forgive her for the matter of the goat at vespers, but having been married to Matthew all these years I suppose she has had practice."

Susannah pulled a face at him, but at that moment Miss Amelia ventured to make her desires known, and there was silence for some minutes while her mother satisfied them.

"We are very happy, aren't we, Hanford?" Susannah said at last, tucking the baby back into her basket.

"*I* think so, at any rate; but my opinion is the veriest trifle. It is fortunate indeed that we are not allowed to choose our own happiness."

"I never would have chosen you."

Hanford raised an eyebrow. "There were times, my dearest, when I wondered if you had. Hold out your hand."

Wonderingly, Susannah did.

"I know that Ammie is a mere female, and that gifts are only to be proffered at the birth of an heir, but I thought you might like to see these again." He reached into his pocket and dropped something onto her palm.

Blue sapphire teardrops dangled from flashing rose-cut diamonds. One of the stones had cracked across and was carefully mended with a leaf-thin wire of pure gold.

About the Author

Rosemary Edghill lives in the Hudson Valley area of New York. She is also the author of two other Regency Romances published by Fawcett Books, TURKISH DELIGHT and TWO OF A KIND.